GRAYSON DU

RECKLESS WOMAN

CATHERINE WILTCHER

ISBN: 978-1-8380448-7-9 (eBook)
ISBN: 978-1-8380448-8-6 (Paperback)

Cover design by: Steamy Designs
Photographer: CJC Photography
www.cjc-photography.com
Model: Alexandra St. Martin
Editing/Proof by: N. Isabelle Blanco
Editing/Proof by: Sarah DeLong
Formatting by: Midnight Designs

Sign up to my Newsletter:
https://catherinewiltcher.com/newsletter/

SINFULLY SEXY ROMANCE

The Santiago Trilogy
Hearts of Darkness
Hearts Divine
Hearts on Fire

Grayson Duet
Shadow Man
Reckless Woman

Standalones
Devils & Dust
Black Skies Riviera
Hot Nights in Morocco
Unwrapping the Billionaire

Anthologies
Men of Valor
Stalk-*ers*
Possessed By Passion

Blurb

Lose him. Break him.
Use him. *Love him.*

I don't dance with the devil.
I dance with his shadow, instead.
He found me.
He killed for me.
He took my broken past,
and he offered me a dangerous future.

But there's a new poison in our lives.
He's death by another name…
Now, everyone we've ever loved,
Everything we'd thought we believed in,
Will lie in ruins before the night is done.

A ruthless enemy brought this chaos down upon us.
Only a reckless woman can make it right.

To all the Santiago readers.
This one's for you...

A Note from the Author

Please note that Reckless Woman is **not** a standalone. The story incorporates characters from the Santiago Trilogy, Devils & Dust and Shadow Man. It follows directly on from Shadow Man and wraps itself around the events in Devils & Dust. **Major spoilers alert!** HEAs guaranteed.

Reckless Woman is a dark mafia/cartel romance that touches on subjects that some readers may find offensive or triggering. Those include kidnapping and captive scenarios, drink and drug abuse, hospital trauma, graphic violence, non-consensual situations and human trafficking.

This book is unlike anything I've ever written before. I never plotted a single scene, I just let the characters direct me through their pain, fears and heartache, all the way to their HEAs.

No one ever said it was going to be easy…

Chapter One

ANNA

The late afternoon heat is red and vicious, burning up the cloudless sky like God himself touched a match to the heavens.

"What is this place?" Shielding my eyes with the crook of my hand, I turn back to the car. The atmosphere feels heavy and intense. It's weighing down the corners of my smile.

"Hell."

Joseph's leaning against the side panel of the black Dodge with his arms crossed—a tall, Texan depiction of heaven, in denim jeans and a faded gray shirt rolled up at the sleeves. His face is expressionless, but that's nothing new. His truth is concealed behind a pair of dark sunglasses and a wall of history I've yet to dismantle.

"Why did you bring me here?"

"A compulsion."

"A compulsion to bring me to *hell*?"

Turning back to the burnt landscape, I squint at the carcass of an old farmhouse that's stinking up the horizon with ghosts and neglect. Sweat is trickling between my breasts. There's no breeze today. No let-up. There's barely any sway in the overgrown wheat fields bordering the dusty driveway we've parked next to—with its ugly, brown surface uneven and pockmarked.

Hell.

I knock the word around my head again, hearing his past in his measured drawl.

"Come here, Anna."

"Give me a moment…"

"Are you making me repeat it?"

Bloody caveman. "Hell, huh?" I turn back again, but I don't budge an inch. "I was expecting a few more chains to be lying about the place. Maybe a horned demon or two."

The sunlight catches on his Wayfarers, glinting wickedly. "Oh, there's a demon alright."

"Doubt it. He's back on an island in the Pacific."

Joseph's lips almost twitch. *Almost.* "Get the fuck over here, Anna. I won't ask again."

He crooks his finger to me and I acquiesce, my stomach muscles tensing as I turn away from the farmhouse. This feeling of dread worsens with every step. It's like the ruin is a gutless criminal who'd shoot me three times in the back at any moment.

What is this place?

Hell.

I never paid much attention to instinct until I met a man who lives his life by it, until I fell so hard I allowed every part of him to seep into my soul. Now I feel as much as I see, and there's an evil lurking here that's icing up my overheated skin.

A few feet out, he's grabbing me by the wrist and wrapping

his arms around me so tight I can scarcely breathe.

"This farmhouse means something to you," I mumble into his hard chest.

His ensuing silence stretches on and on like the empty highway we're standing on.

"Tell me, Joseph."

His hands drop to my ass, sliding underneath my khaki mini, his fingers straying dangerously close to the lace trim of my black panties. "Tell you what?" There's movement at the corners of his lips again before he's burrowing his face into the side of my neck, making my senses spin.

"You *know* what," I say, grasping the hem of his shirt and tugging.

"You want me to tell you how hot you look in this short skirt?" His fingers find the crease of my ass and trail downward— *slowly...tantalizingly*—rewarding me with a trickle of wetness between my thighs. "Or about all the filthy fucking things I want to do to you right now?"

My traitorous core starts to throb. "Stop with the distraction! You brought me here for a reason."

"Yes, to fuck some good into this place."

"I don't believe you."

His fingers brush against my slit and I bite out a moan.

"It wasn't the original plan, but I like corrupting shit."

"Damn you for being so good at it..." I trail off with another moan as he slides my panties to the side and drives a finger deep inside me.

"That, and other things." His hot breath is spicing up my jaw, trailing kisses toward my mouth.

"You're a manipulative bastard, Joseph Grayson," I rasp, clenching, sucking him deeper into the soft whirlpool of my pussy. I've fallen so far so fast these last couple of years, but his sin is the only place I want to land. "You have me right where you want me, so now what?"

His dark blond stubble grazes my skin in delicious torment. "First, I'm going to bend you over the hood of this Dodge and fuck you so hard you'll be tasting gas fumes for the rest of the day."

Holy shit.

"What else?" Still impaled on his finger, I reach up with a trembling hand and remove his sunglasses. I'm blasted with twin rays of hungry, gray-blue steel for the privilege. This bad man wants to do bad things to me. He wants to fuck me whole again. We're like a perfect symmetry of sexual attraction…

If it wasn't for that stupid instinct-thing again.

There may not be a breeze today, but I sense the changing winds in him, regardless. What he wants to make here isn't love, it's something harsher…Hungrier. When his finger starts pumping in and out of my body, it's to a brutal rhythm.

"You think you're such a shit-hot seducer," I whisper, tipping my head back.

He growls in response. "You didn't let me finish." One finger becomes two, and then three—stretching me wide open for him. "After we're done, I'll be keeping your legs spread to watch you mess the paintwork."

My breath catches. "What then?"

"I'll be pushing my cum back inside you to keep you wet and thinking about me for the rest of the day."

"I only ever think about you."

Our mouths crash together, demanding all the sex and all the violence. A beat later, he's making good on one half of his promise, and pushing me up against the hood of the Dodge. My skirt's already bunched up around my waist. My panties are lying torn and discarded in the dirt.

"Do it," I whisper as he lifts me up, giving him the permission he seeks from me every time.

In response, he wraps my legs around his waist and slams into me so hard I damn near ricochet off the side of the vehicle.

Locking my arms around his neck, I hold on tight as he pounds dents into the vehicle's bodywork and unspoken emotions into my pussy.

Rage.

Frustration.

Pain.

This is us. *All of us.* With no frills and sweet words—just this rule-breaking, mind-bending screwing that smashes our bruised and broken souls together with the force of a thousand wrecking balls.

"Oh god!"

"Fucking feel me, *Luna.*"

He's jackhammering into me now, splitting me in two. Taking me so damn hard, I'll be walking sore tomorrow.

He has me where he wants in no time—sliding me so fast toward the edge of that cliff, I imagine ripped and bloody fingernails in my head. Some men can play with you for hours, with a finish as tedious as the main event. Joseph creates voodoo magic in minutes, making me crave him harder, faster, dirtier…

I come with a scream.

He follows with a curse.

I open my eyes to find his fixed on the old farmhouse in the distance. When he lays my exhausted body down on the hood, he's still hard inside me, but the rest of him is lost to the past.

Talk to me, Joseph…I bled myself for you. I opened every

wound. Why can't you do the same for me?

The metal is burning hot against my bare skin. I push up on my elbows as he slips from my body, my legs tumbling from around his waist.

This time our silence is a never-ending question.

"Did you live here?" I blurt eventually.

His jaw clenches. "Not for long." He fixes his zipper and winches his belt back together. Darkness passes over his face, and I see the anarchy in his self-control. "But this is where I'll come to die."

Chapter Two

JOSEPH

Carlos Gomez Junior won't be making his dinner reservations tonight, or on any other night, for that matter.

The writing's been on the wall for over an hour now, and it's not just me who's itching to underline it in crimson. The guy won't stop fucking *talking,* and the more shit he spews, the bloodier and more protracted his death is going to be.

Give me the order, Dante, and let's get the hell out of here.

I drank too much last night. My head is pounding out beats like a drum and bass track on acid. From my position by the door, I catch the Colombian's eye—watching in frustration as it slides away with a measure of disinterest. *What the hell is he waiting for?* On any other given day, Gomez Junior would be gathering flies on the parquet flooring already. It's unnatural for a predator like Santiago to delay the killing blow, unless he's started playing with his prey again…

Since the birth of his daughter, he's been tamer in that

respect—shooting to kill, not wound and torture. But after what went down in Colombia recently, I've sensed a shift in him.

Sadism and carnage are back on the menu.

Dante Santiago is slipping back into old habits and enjoying the fall.

"Naturally, I'll be taking over all of my father's old processing plants, señor." Gomez Junior leans back in his chair to puff on his complacency and his cigar, but the smoke encircles his throat like a hangman's noose. Words delivered with a shit-eating grin carry no conviction around here. Add in the fact that his father held a gun to Anna's head a couple of months back, and he's a walking, talking death warrant as far as I'm concerned.

"Is that right?" Dante's fingers start drumming lightly on the table.

"Rest assured, señor, my loyalty is with you. *Only* you. I will not be repeating my father's mistakes."

"That's good to know."

Low murmurs rise up from the other occupants sitting around the table. Everyone can sense Santiago's growing displeasure, except the one man who really needs to start paying attention.

There are eleven here today. They're all that remains of *Los Cinco Grandes:* the five cartels of the Colombian drug trade, whose kingpins were either killed off, or incarcerated recently. These men are close relatives and loyalists, whose only hope of monetary survival now is to take the knee to the newly resurrected Santiago cartel.

Not Gomez Junior, though.

He's been stinking up the place with self-importance from the minute he walked in, making it known, loud and clear, that the only kneeling he'll be doing is in front of his girlfriend's pussy.

That's not even the worst of his crimes. He's ignoring Dante's niece, Viviana. She's sitting to the right of him: a fierce diminutive brunette who is quickly earning herself a reputation as a true, no-fucks-given Santiago. Gomez Junior hasn't spoken one word to her, either in deference or greeting, despite the fact that she's just claimed the crooked crown of heading up Dante's organization here in the South.

Dante clenches his palm into a fist, flips it over and taps the back of his wedding ring against the table's surface. "What about the distribution links to New York?" he asks idly.

"Latest shipment arrived yesterday evening, señor. It's waiting in cargo for Señor Sanders' men. As expected, there were no problems in transit."

"Are you sure about that?" Viviana's clear voice is like a breath of fresh air in a room muddied with gruffness and testosterone. "Yesterday, I discovered that twenty percent of the shipment had been skimmed off before it reached port. Word on the street is you cut a deal with the Mexicans in New Jersey, and we're providing the fucking retainer."

If there's one thing guaranteed to put a bullet in your skull, it's forming an allegiance with Val Carrera's Mexican cartel.

How the hell did she find out about this?

My hand reaches for the gun tucked into the back of my jeans, but Viviana's quicker. She's already on her feet. The room then watches, rapt, as she sinks her shoes into the seat of her vacant leather chair and steps gracefully onto the table.

She saunters down the center toward Gomez Junior, her slim legs working her tight black jeans like a catwalk model, her brown cowboy boots making a pretty sound on the polished mahogany. Glancing across at Dante again, I find he's already staring at me. The corners of his mouth are creasing in provocation, like he's in on another secret and he's itching to share.

Is this display part of a pre-approved plan, or is he guessing at her intentions? Viviana's a Santiago, after all. Fucked up shit runs through their veins, the same way hope and strength flows through others.

Gomez isn't such a slouching sack of scorn anymore.

"There is no deal with the Mexicans, señorita," he splutters, choking on his own lie.

"Ah, so you *have* noticed that there's a pair of tits in this room?"

She crouches down in front of him, something cold and calculated in her stance. It's fucking hypnotic. If Dante is slipping back into old habits, then Viviana's following after. There's nothing left of the scared, young girl who was on the run from *Los Cinco Grandes* with Anna last year.

"I was, ah, waiting for a more *formal* introduction, señorita," he argues weakly.

"I see…Tell me, is this formal enough for you?" She gestures to the closeness between them. "Or would you prefer me to shake your fucking hand?"

He shrugs. "I suppose this is a business meeting." He extends it slowly, hesitantly.

Wrong answer, asshole.

Viviana stares down at it for a moment—she roughs up the back of her throat and covers his knuckles in spit and contempt.

"Carajo puta!" Gomez Junior recoils in shock, and that's when she shows her true Santiago colors. A moment later, his severed hand is thumping across the table and onto the floor in a trail of red, and she's standing over his crumpled body with a bleeding Billhook machete in her hand.

What the fuck?

Gomez Junior's screams and curses are fogging up the room as he slips from his seat and onto his knees, crawling through static chair legs to reach his severed appendage. No one helps him. No one says a word.

"Let this be a lesson to all of you," snarls Viviana, spinning one-eighty in her cowboy heels to tick off each cartel associate with the outstretched tip of her blade. "Colombia belongs to the Santiagos now. You work for *us*. You steal, and you lose everything. You cheat, and we'll shove our fucking rulebook so far down your throat you'll be shitting out apologies for the rest of your life! But if you pay your dues? If you're *loyal*…?" She holds her arms out like she's embracing the whole room. "Then you'll be rewarded…Any questions?"

There's another round of silence before Dante starts clapping, redirecting all the shockwaves back to him. "Best show I've seen in ages," he says, rising to his feet. "Pity we didn't film it. I could have sent a copy to Carrera."

"Señor!" gasps out Gomez Junior from somewhere on the floor. "They're lies. All lies…your niece—"

"Just earned the respect of the entire Colombian cartel trade," Dante finishes smoothly. "Shut the cunt up, Viviana."

"My pleasure." She springs, cat-like, from the table, landing smoothly next to a gibbering Gomez Junior. She kicks him onto his back, I see a flash of the twisted rose tattoo on her shoulder, and then Gomez Junior's screams turn to ghosts as she slits his throat from ear to ear.

The meeting is over after that.

The message was received, loud and clear.

Ten men file out of the room, talking in hushed undertones. The story of what happened in this room today will filter down through the tributaries of the *Rio Grande de la Magdalena*. By nightfall, everyone from the borders of Venezuela right down to Brazil will fear the new Santiago order.

Once everyone's out, Viviana saunters over to join me by the door—cleaning her machete as she walks—her dark eyes raking over my face with a lingering trace of contempt. She's seeking holes in my façade, but my expression is a blank fortress. "Can you keep up with us, Grayson?" she taunts in perfect, accented English—softly though, so only I can hear. "You should have been onto those New York shipments. It's lucky for you the Santiago scorpion has a new sting in her tail. *And eyes in every port.* Fall behind again, and we'll leave you in the fucking wilderness."

Fury explodes in my veins as her gaze drops to the two gold rings I wear around my neck. Her mocking smile falters. *Don't go there, bitch.* Anna may be blinded by their history, but I'm not so easily duped. Trust has to be earned, and Viviana's bank is empty with me. If she gets up in my face again, she'll know about it.

"How's the shoulder?" she asks slyly.

"It'd be even better if you hadn't shot me six weeks ago," I say, sounding bored.

"You shouldn't have gotten in my way."

"I should have returned the favor." This shuts her up. "I've seen them all come before, Viviana,"—I lean in, ice-cool—"and I've pissed on all of their steaming corpses afterward. You're a new plaything. Nothing more. Enjoy your time in the sun, because one false move and you'll fall out of favor so fast, you'll lose more than a fucking hand."

"Wrong." She flashes me another grin. "I'm family, remember, and I just earned his respect." She glances behind herself at an approaching Dante. "You don't have to worry about the whole 'days in the sun' thing with me, Grayson," she adds, patting my rigid bicep in a way that makes me want to ram my fist down her throat. "After today, I'm not going anywhere."

Chapter Three

ANNA

"Irony is the most misquoted word in the English language," declares Eve, tossing her magazine onto her swollen stomach and flexing her toes in the brilliant sunshine. "Most of the time it's either coincidence, satire or bad luck."

Stretching out on the sun lounger next to her, I fight the kind of laugh that threatens to dislodge my sunglasses from the bridge of my nose. "Isn't it kind of ironic that you've used the word 'misquoted' for your outburst there, Miss Award Winning Reporter?"

A second later, the same magazine is being tossed at me.

"You always were a smart ass," she says with a laugh, capturing the strands of her long, dark hair and twisting them up into a messy bun. "Tell me, how did you end up working for Rick again?"

"I worked in one of his bars, not for Rick directly," I correct, shutting my eyes and allowing the heat of the day to soak into my skin. "How is he doing, anyway?"

"Happily corrupting every New York socialite under the age of twenty-five. Dante's flying over to see him in a couple of days."

"Is he taking you and Ella?"

"No, I'm too pregnant to fly now." She pats her stomach with a pout. "My doctors say I could deliver any day, especially as Ella was two weeks early. Besides, I haven't learned how to unpick the locks to my paradise, yet."

I follow her gaze to a horizon of serene ocean and placid skies that paint the pretty bars of her jail cell. There's only one way people come and go from this place and that's with the Dark Overlord's permission. Her husband is fanatical about his family's safety, even at the risk of crushing the ones he loves.

My thoughts stray to an old farmhouse in Texas.

There are hidden chains in the most unlikely of places.

"Drink?" Eve reaches for the pitcher of iced water on the table between us.

"I'm good, thanks." Rolling over onto my front, I sweep my long blonde hair over my shoulder to cover up a love bite and stifle a yawn. I hardly see Joseph during the day here, but from dusk until dawn he makes up for it. "Why are you hating so hard on 'irony' today, anyway?"

"Because I have a starring role in the most obvious example." She shoots me a cryptic side-eye. "And *sometimes* it gets a little overwhelming."

"You and Dante," I mutter.

"Me and Dante," she confirms, her hand straying toward her stomach again. "The reporter who hates the narcotics trade and the not-so-former cartel boss." She sighs and glances at the horizon again. "I always knew that love moves in mysterious ways, but I didn't realize it dances rings around your decency and waltzes all over your ethics. I can't excuse what he does, anymore than I can forgive the men he kills for the crimes that *they've* committed. But with everything that's happening in Colombia right now…" Her voice trails off, her next words eaten up with worry. "I thought the pact with Roman Peters would have focused that side of him more."

"You hate that he's resurrected his cartel," I say, speaking the truth she's struggling to admit.

I watch her gnawing on her lower lip.

"There's a part of me that wishes those days were over for good, but his past is a story that will always bleed a narrative into our present."

"If he really loved you, he'd walk away," I say slyly, playing devil's advocate with the devil's wife.

"I don't doubt his love, Anna." She side-eyes me again with a frown. "And I know what you're trying to do…I've come to terms with the two people I love most in this world despising each other."

"I don't despise his hospitality," I say lightly. "And his kid is pretty cute."

"You don't despise his enforcer, either," she teases. "How was Texas?"

"Hot."

She quirks her eyebrows at me. "Hot, huh?" I must have blushed beneath my tan because the next thing I know she's snaking those eyebrows sky-high. "I'd ask you for details if I didn't think Dante would lose his shit over it."

"Dante loses his shit over everything. The difference between Dante losing his shit and a normal man losing his shit is the body count."

"Joseph's not so different."

"Joseph sees it as a job, not a sport he has to win medals in."

"Well, his bedroom skills are clearly gold, if your smug smile has anything to do with it."

"Eve!" I toss the magazine back at her as she collapses into more laughter.

Time stops still and reverses. We could be two friends in Miami again, lying on South Beach and scraping by on fun— satisfied with just enough rent money and maybe a couple of dates that didn't suck. Okay, so we were empty on direction back then, but we had a future that was ours to define. There was no murder, and all the other stuff that taints our souls as much as the men's we choose to love.

But then there was no Joseph, either, and a world without my shadow is a world without light.

He never discusses his work, but I've seen the outline of the army barracks from a distance. I've seen the violent way he kills. I've kissed the countless scars on his body.

"I can't remember the last time we did this," says Eve, as if reading my thoughts. She reaches out to link her fingers through mine, bridging our two sun loungers with our history.

"Me neither," I say, staring down at them. "Oh wait. I think it was before your psycho husband kidnapped you again. Or maybe it was before you acted like a lunatic and walked into that animal's mansion."

The same animal that stole me, raped me and tried to sell me as payback for what you and Dante did.

The truth stales the air like a dirty word.

Our fingers unravel.

They stirred up a hornet's nest, and I was the one who was stung.

They set me up as bait, but the hunter outsmarted them.

"I never stopped looking for you," she says softly, turning onto her side to face me. At eight months pregnant, it's a slow process. "*We* never stopped looking for you...Joseph may have found you first, but I'm hoping that one day we can find each other again, too."

"Eve—"

"Loving Dante came with consequences," she interrupts. "I figured that. But I never thought they'd become *our* consequences. I'm so sorry for everything that happened to you, Anna."

"I know you are."

Taking back her hand, I curl our fingers into one fist. We were also two girls in the same neighborhood once—sharing cuts and bruises and bicycles and hiding out under the shelter of her father's lie.

She thinks of a past as a story. I see it as the glue in the cracks between friendships.

"I don't blame you anymore, Eve." It's the truth. "I know what you did for me. I know what you sacrificed."

I blame your husband, instead.

"How long before you're heading back to Miami?" she asks.

"I signed up for a two-day residential at Greens starting on Monday."

Back to reality.

Back to rehab.

For a time, I didn't cope so well with the survivor wasteland. After my ordeal at the hands of a gang of Russian traffickers, I found myself at the mercy of a new vice—better known as a shitty drink and drug problem. I've been clean for nearly six months now, and I'm determined to keep it that way. For a time, that will include regular, short-term residentials at the Greens

Therapy Center in Miami to keep myself on track.

"Is Joseph flying over to the States with you?"

I shoot her a combination of an eye roll and a grimace.

"Okay, stupid question..." She goes to say something else when there's a wicked wail from the baby monitor. "Dammit. Ella's woken up from her nap early. If I don't rock her back to sleep, she'll be seriously cranky for the rest of the afternoon."

"Want me to go?"

"Oh God, would you?" Eve looks pathetically grateful as I rise up on all fours to stretch out my back and swing my legs off the side of the lounger. "Sofía's on the mainland until late afternoon and I move with all the speed of a truck on a sharp incline these days...Ugh, I look like one, too," she adds in disgust, blowing out her cheeks.

"No you don't, you look beautiful," I say firmly. Eve has embraced her second pregnancy like everything else in life: quietly, thoughtfully, and with more grit and determination than an advancing army.

I reach for the pale green chiffon sarong and tuck it around my black bikini. Meanwhile, the wailing is growing in tempo. Ella will be shattering glass soon.

"Where's the nursery again?"

"First floor. Next to mine and Dante's room. If she doesn't stop crying, I'll crawl up the steps like a giant slug and rescue you."

"Chill," I say with a smile. "I've got this covered."

Padding into the living area, I allow the calm and light of Santiago's mansion to envelop me like a greeting. I may have a long list of issues with the man who owns this place, but I'd never fault his taste: white walls, white tiles, stark black furniture lines and colorful explosions of modern art reveal a sharp eye and some serious fucking blood money.

When I'm here on the island, I stay with Joseph in a separate wing of this great white house that clings to the side of a mountain. Sometimes, when I'm out for an early morning jog along the beach, I look up and feel my steps falter. In those moments, it resembles Eve and I—and how we're desperately clinging to the last few morals we have left.

Like the rest of the house, Ella's nursery is impeccably designed. While the walls are white, there are soft feminine touches in grays and pinks that are definitely Eve's influence.

The most violent colors are coming from the little girl herself. Barely a year and a half old, and looking pretty darn cross about it, her cheeks and her arms are flushed red with heat and indignation.

"Hush, Ella Bella," I soothe. "I have all the hugs right here."

Scooping up her little body from the bed, along with her soft brown teddy bear, I hold her close to me, savoring the warm weight of something more precious than gold in my arms.

"Did you have bad dreams?" I whisper into her damp forehead, absorbing the last of her hiccupping sobs into my bare chest as I sway gently from side to side, doing something so instinctive I'm not even aware of the movement until my knees start aching.

Settling into the nursing chair next to the window, I pick up a book lying on the table and start to read to her, curling my contentment around every word.

Sliding her pink thumb into her mouth, Ella gazes up at me with dazzlingly blue eyes that are all Eve's and hair as black as her father's soul.

So trusting.

So innocent.

If you screw this up, Santiago, I'll kill you myself.

He's already the reason I missed out on the first year of her life.

"I'll make it up to you, Ella Bella," I whisper, pressing my promise to the top of her head. "I'll always be here for you, and your mom and, whoever else is growing inside her."

For the next few minutes, I read, and she smiles. Her rapt silence is the sweetest melody, lulling me into a kind of peace I've never felt before. Unlike Eve, I never had this big life plan before the underworld crushed it with a swinging fist. She always wanted to be a reporter. In turn, I've been a coasting pinball with no damn direction, traveling from one job to the next—waitress, bartender, animal shelter volunteer…finding enjoyment in all of them, but no real satisfaction in any.

But this…this—

"Anna."

I turn to find Joseph standing in the doorway to the nursery. His gaze ricochets from me to Ella. I watch his expression catch fire before it's sliding into his usual apathy.

There was a declaration once, made by a pool in Colombia, when he turned words into treasure and made me believe in love and life again. Since then, there's been nothing, so I've learned to grab hold of these brief glimpses. I've learned to interpret his feelings in the blink of an eye. I've developed a patience I never thought I was capable of as I wait for him to open up to me again.

He wants this.

He hates that he wants this.

Does he hate it because he doesn't want it with me*?*

Rising shakily to my feet, I transfer the little girl to her bed and tuck a loose sheet around her and her brown teddy bear.

"She's just fallen back to sleep," I whisper, tiptoeing toward him and then beckoning him out into the hallway. "What are you doing here?"

He swipes a hand across his jaw. "Looking for you."

"Is something wrong?" I shut the door behind us, wincing at the slightest creak.

"No."

He's in one of those moods again where getting whole adult sentences with adjectives and adverbs is like squeezing blood from a stone.

"You're busy," he says abruptly, turning to leave.

"Wait, Joseph—"

"I'll catch you later."

"I really think—"

But he's already heading back down the white stone steps, leaving me trapped behind the cold, steel bars of his emotional diffidence.

Chapter Four

JOSEPH

When I walk back into Dante's office, he's already on the phone. With three quarts of bourbon in his hand and an expression that's just as sour, I'm guessing my afternoon won't be improving anytime soon.

He looks up as I enter and jerks his head at the bar.

"Keep the bullshit pleasantries for your superiors, Peters." He switches the call to loudspeaker. "Just tell me what you have on Morozov."

"He's a real piece of crap," comes the cool, uptown brogue of Special Agent Roman Peters. "Remind you of anyone?"

I fight a smirk as I reach for the Macallan. I pour out a double, knock it back in one, and then refill it—all in the span of a couple of breaths.

Roman is our FBI connection in New York. We help him bring down the kind of international human trafficking organizations that the US justice can't touch. In return, he keeps our cartel business from the more law-abiding detectives in his department. There's enough history between us to fill an eighteen-episode Netflix special, and Dante's clearly going for the bonus scenes today.

"When I want your fucking opinion, Peters, I'll ask for it. What else do you have?"

"His links to Sevastien Petrov are as ugly as he is."

The glass pauses halfway to my mouth, and then I'm slamming it back down on the drink's tray, making all the glass and silver rattle. Petrov was the same bastard who kidnapped Anna and turned her into his own personal fuck toy. We've spent the last year hunting down and eliminating the roots of his former organization. We'd believed that every man was dead.

I turn to find Dante watching me. There's murder on his face, too. If what Petrov did to Anna was bad, it's nothing compared to the abuse he inflicted on Eve when she was a child.

"Is Morozov a threat?"

"Yes."

"To me or to Sanders?"

"To our whole operation."

Fan-fucking-tastic.

That trip to Texas planted a devil's seed of unrest in my soul. There was too much past, and now it's spilling into my present. I'm edgy-as-fuck, drinking too much…*I never should have snapped the locks to that dirty box.* What the hell was I hoping to find there? Rose-tinted redemption? Blunted memories?

It's infecting me.

It's infecting my work.

My only respite is Anna and this gossamer-thin veil of contentment we've wrapped around ourselves, but even that's in danger.

Seeing her with Dante's kid was like a fortune teller waving the future in front of me.

What's left of my heart beats for her. It will never beat for another, *and never for a fucking child.* I made that deal with myself the day I lost my son. Soon after, I made another deal with the man sitting in front of me.

But I saw the look on her face.

I saw the peace.

I saw the problem.

"I'll tell Rick about Morozov." Dante's dark gaze seeks out mine again as I'm flicking the bird at my self-control and lifting my third Macallan.

"Tell him to stop screwing Senator D'Angelo's daughter as well," responds Roman tersely. "It's pissing the senator off. He's up our asses, day and night, wanting Sanders and his product gone from the streets." He stops and sighs, like it's the greatest imposition in the world. "I'm running out of places to hide the dirt, Dante," he warns. "Rick's wandering dick keeps straying into hostile territory. It's in danger of compromising our entire operation."

Dante lifts his dark eyes to a heaven he'll never get to greet. "Stop being dramatic."

"Don't say I didn't—"

"If Rick goes down for so much as a parking ticket, Peters, you lose me *and* my entire army."

"So, it's like that, is it? You ungrateful bastard! I'm starting to regret ever breaking you out of prison."

"Call me a bastard again, and I'll be shoving your FBI badge so far up your ass, your mouth will be gleaming gold."

Neither insult carries much weight. They rely on each other too much to survive.

"Did you give my niece intel about the Gomez Junior cartel shipping mess?" Dante demands.

This pricks my interest. I'd assumed he was the source.

"I've never even met your niece," comes the weary response. "Why the hell would I do that?"

"Why do you do anything? Self-preservation?"

"Tell Sanders to keep his pants zipped," snaps the detective, finally losing his cool.

"Try doing the same thing with your mouth." The call ends abruptly as Dante kicks the phone off his desk, spilling wires and twisted metal all over his cream carpet.

"Was that strictly necessary?" I murmur. We both know Roman Peters isn't the real reason for his bad temper. Any mention of Petrov is like a spark to a trail of gasoline with us.

"That man is walking a fine fucking line between this life and the next."

"He has a point, though. How *did* Viviana find out about the Mexicans?"

"The fairy godmother of cartel business deals. How the fuck should I know?"

Dante's switched to a combative mood now and I'm just the wrong side of drunk to aggravate it.

"Pour some sugar in your bourbon. I'll make a couple of calls this afternoon."

"Don't." He glances out of the huge floor to ceiling window behind him for a long moment, as if he's contemplating the meaning of fucking life. "Let her bring the connection to us. She's flying into Miami for a couple days to oversee a new shipment from Colombia. I'll send a crew to pick her up and fly her out to the island. We can talk more, then."

"You're bringing her *here*?"

I'm shocked. This island is his sanctuary. It's his home. His life. His family. It's an inner circle that once breached can never be redrawn.

"Whoever her connection is in New York, he just saved us a hundred mil. In my book, that's a friend, not a foe—"

"Then get a better library!"

There's a vicious beat as he drops his gaze to the empty in my hand. "I suggest you take that bottle of Macallan and fuck off for the rest of the day. You've drunk most of it anyway."

"Don't flash that limp dick dismissal crap at me, Dante," I say coldly. "You told me a couple of months ago—to my goddamn face—that you didn't trust her. When you first found out who she was, you traveled to Colombia to put her down. Now you're risking your family for a circus parade of *faith*?"

For a man who doesn't talk much, I just managed to load enough incitement into a couple of sentences to red flag a bull.

"Did that bullet in South America travel to your brain?" Dante rises up from his desk, all six foot three inches of killer, and I wonder—idly—if I'll be missing a hand by dinnertime. "Since when do you question me about anything?"

"You said—"

"*She changed my mind*," he snarls, enunciating every word.

"When she dismembered some lowlife for you?" My mouth twists in scorn. "That isn't a demonstration of trust. That's a fucking pay-per-view. She's Emilio's daughter, and don't you forget it. She's just as bat-shit crazy as he was. Come on, Dante... You're smarter than this."

That *really* pisses on his mood.

"What the hell are you still doing in my office?" he snarls. "Chancing a death wish?"

"I'm demonstrating what real trust is." Eating up the

distance to his desk, I lift up my shirt to show him the ugly, six-inch scar running jagged across my abdomen. "It's you knowing, believing, *trusting*, that there will never be a retaliation for *this*."

Two years ago, he'd thrown Eve off this island and into the shark-infested waters of the Miami FBI department. When I'd called him out on it, he'd carved his displeasure into my skin.

Tossing my empty glass down on the desk, I drop my shirt and walk out before I do something really stupid like going back on my word and finally returning the favor.

I spend the next few hours lost in the bottom of a bottle, chasing sundowners like I haven't had a drink in days. In reality, I've sunk more liquor since Texas than I have in a month.

I do the worst of my drinking away from Anna, down on the shoreline below the main house. She's a recovering addict and I'm not that much of an asshole to spill my vice in front of her. I'm the one who made her whole. I'll be damned if I'll be the one breaking her into pieces again.

I've taken up smoking in a bid to hide the taste. This evening I'm a real sin magnet, cooling my anger on a carpet of white sand that feels like cremation remains beneath my fingers.

"You saving any of that for me, little brother?" murmurs a voice that hasn't aged a day since a barn and a shotgun, and the start of a nightmare.

"Nah, Cash, get your own."

I slur it at the sunset, even though he's sitting right next to me. I can smell the dirt and the Old Spice he used to steal from the hardware store in McKinney.

In my head, he's wearing the same plaid shirt that Pa turned from blue to red. The left side of his face is missing and there's a strange look in the one eye that still blinks, like he knows things but he isn't telling me, just like he did back then…like the fact that our father was a paranoid schizophrenic who was always one ju jitsu away from triple homicide, or that our mother was cooking up meth in the basement as well as growing skunk in the attic to deal with the issue.

My brother.

My dead brother.

Cash first appeared to me in Texas once Anna and I were done making good in a place that holds nothing but bad. He opened the door and slid right into the Dodge's back seat as I was starting up the engine. It was almost like he'd been expecting me.

I know he's not real, but his figment won't quit. It's like he's here for a reason and he isn't leaving until he's done.

"What are you drinking?" he asks.

"Frustration," I say bitterly.

"Sounds like shit. Give me a Beamer any day of the week."

He lights up one of my Marlboro Reds like he did on his last day on this earth. I smell the smoke. I hear the grinding metal of the lighter, and just like that I'm back on the family farm I've spent my whole life running from.

For the next couple of minutes, he keeps his dead mouth shut as we stare out at a false paradise together. It's the worst conversation we never had. He's making me think things I haven't thought for years—like a hope that crashed, and a loss that burned. Stuff that as a kid I didn't know how to process until Santiago put a gun in my hand and told me to shoot it all away.

I finish the rest of the bottle, and feel the payback kicking in already. I'm craving Anna's body now to turn my vice into something sweeter.

As if by magic, a neon pink dot appears on the far side of the beach. It's clashing with a sinking skyline that's every color of murder, and traveling toward us at a steady pace. As she draws closer, I can see her blonde ponytail bouncing from shoulder to shoulder.

Prayers fucking answered.

Tossing the bottle over the crest of a dune, I stagger to my feet as Anna jogs a path right up to us. She smiles in greeting, slowing to a walk, her hands on her hips and her cheeks flushed.

"Cute twister, Jukebox Romeo," I hear Cash say.

"Nah, Cash. This twister is a *masterpiece*."

And she is—standing there, burning up harder than the red sky above. Tall and athletic, she's a color explosion all of her own: with green, river-deep eyes and long, golden hair that wraps so perfectly around my fist when I'm arching her back to the point of pain and driving my cock deep inside her.

"I'll leave you to ride this one alone, little brother," says Cash, the grin in his voice already *bon voyaging* with the retreating tide.

"What's a masterpiece?" Expression curious, Anna turns toward the ocean. "Do you mean the sunset? It's amazing, right?"

"Fuck the sunset," I growl, wrapping a hand around her damp neck and yanking her toward me to catch her next labored breath with my mouth.

She tries to wriggle away in embarrassment. "Oh God, don't kiss me! I'm a hot, stinking mess."

"You taste of moonshine," I say huskily, keeping her locked against me, her small hands curling around my biceps as she steadies herself. "And that, my *Luna*, is the second best taste of all."

"Oh, I get it." Her head dances out of the path of my mouth, and I growl again in frustration. "This is your way of apologizing for being such a monosyllabic asshole earlier."

"I don't apologize for anything. I learned that from Santiago."

Her smile falters. "You taste of cigarettes. When did you start smoking?"

"It's a casual thing." I tilt my head to one side. "Deny me your mouth again, and you'll start a habit."

A wicked smile dances across her face that does even wickeder shit to my cock. "So, if moonshine is the runner up in the taste Olympics, what's the winner?"

"Sex." I sweep the backs of my fingers across her tight black running shorts and neon pink vest.

An extra layer of color reddens her cheeks. "There's no sex here, only sweat."

"Sex…Sweat…it's a beautiful combination." A beat later, she's lying on the sand beneath me. Soft. Honest. Exposed and perfect.

Wanting me for me.

Me.

A murderer. A criminal.

"You taste of the last moments of sex," I clarify roughly. "When you're so focused on my cock making you come, that your vulnerability blows you wide open."

Judging by her breathy response, I'm doing nothing to lower her pulse rate. "Did you always have such a dirty mouth, Joseph?"

"Oh honey," I drawl, arming my voice with a couple of hundred rounds of southern charm. "This ain't the half of it."

"Shame that mouth can't drawl much else for me," she says, firing back with a light accusation. Her fingers trace my jaw, and then up into my hair. I keep it longer these days: close enough to keep hold of the killer I've become, but with hints of the man I was before. "Why did you come and find me earlier?"

Because I'm spinning, Anna, like you told me to.

One problem: I'm blowing off course.

I nearly tell her then.

I nearly give her the black beating heart of me, as well as the bleeding red. Instead, I part her legs and slide in between. Rising up on my elbows, I trap her face between my hands, the sheer size of them covering her cheeks and jaw.

"Tell me I'm enough for us."

"Joseph—"

"Don't lie to me, *Luna*," I say harshly.

"I won't," she gasps out. "I'd never—"

"Tell me!" I thrust against her, soaking up her sharp cry of surprise. "I want the truth, even if I have to fuck it from your lips. What would make us even more perfect?"

"Words," she whispers reluctantly. "There are never enough words between us."

"Words are for shit, baby. They're a fucking flea circus...it's too damn easy to lie." I kiss her again, imposing my violence on her mouth, her greedy moans doing dark and twisted things to my lust. I'm too far gone now. I'll take her through her clothes, if I have to. "What else?"

"The truth," she rasps, as I palm and pinch her nipple through her jogging vest, making her squirm and fight against my touch.

"This is all the truth we need." Reaching down between us, I push her jogging shorts and panties to her knees and rip open my zipper. "We never did dates. We're every season of fucked-up, but we save each other remember?"

Rising up on my knees, I remove the rest of her clothes, and then sink back down on top of her.

"We can't have a future without the truth," she argues breathlessly. "Let me in. Let me see all of you, even the broken parts."

"What if I can't do that?" I move my hand to her clit, trapping the swollen bud between my fingers, feeling her throb against my skin as her heels hook into the waistband of my jeans and drag the material down.

"The future—"

"You *are* my future. You're the only thing that matters." Fisting my cock, I line it up with her pussy. The insides of her thighs are slick and trembling. The scent of her is pooling lava at the base of my spine, and the need to defile is warped and blinding. I run the head of my shaft up and down her entrance, soaking up the juices, brushing against her clit again. "What else do you need from me?"

"A family of our own," she whimpers, bruising us with the one thing I can't give her.

"Marry me," I roar, driving so deep inside her my balls are crushing against her soft skin.

With each brutal thrust, I demand an answer from her, but it's on the wings of her breathless comedown that she finally gives it to me.

"Yes." Tears blur her green eyes as she wraps her fingers around the two rings I wear on a chain around my neck. The same rings I bought the day I vowed to find her, fix her, and never let her go. "Yes, I'll marry you, Joseph Grayson."

It's only when we're lying next to each other on the white sand, matching the rise and falls of each other's chest, with twilight as a flickering canvas, that I realize I'm a thief, as well as a killer and a liar.

Those tears aren't just happiness. They're confusion. They're a torn-up agreement that I back-tracked on.

I promised her something in Colombia. I swore it on my own life, and then I broke it, drunk and demanding, on this very beach when I fucked her the way I did.

That's not the worst of it.

I just sold her a future to cover up my own certainty.

She is all the family I will ever need.

Chapter Five

ANNA

I f places were emotions, Greens Therapy Center in Miami would be a black and white kiss in Times Square on V-J Day. It's relief, dressed up in a smart white building and emerald green lawns that are allergic to weeds.

I didn't always feel so warmly about this place.

Last year, when I was checking in and out of here so fast I was giving myself whiplash, it was cold and depressing—like a prison cell on death row. Turns out, self-destruction requires dedication, and I was well on my way to a PhD in screwing up my life.

All that changed when I bought a one-way ticket to Colombia and found my rebirth in sex, death and violence. I found guilt, too, but I left that behind in South America because of love.

Love.

How can a simple four-letter word be capable of such wildness and eccentricity?

I murdered for love

I love a murderer.

A man who ties me up in knots, more so today than ever before.

"Right this way, Miss Williams," says the rehab's administrator, a brisk brunette with a tight bun that's ironing out the lines on her face, as she leads me down a wide, willow-colored hallway toward my room. "Your first group therapy session commences in twenty minutes."

"Thanks so much." I pick up my pace, my pink sneakers pounding out a squeaky rhythm on the clean floor.

"The session will be held in the Beethoven Room, followed by a group meditation outside. After that, there's a specialized session on stress management in the Vivaldi Suite." She gestures to the folder in my hand. "You'll find your full schedule in there."

The communal rooms are named after famous classical composers, the same way all the decor harmonizes in themes of white and green. The sense of conformity here is as slick as the service.

Still, I need this place. I need it to keep on healing me, even though I need Joseph to explain what the hell is going on with him more.

I barely saw him during our last days together on the island. When I did, we barely spoke. The night we made love on the beach—*the night he asked me to marry him*—he stood up afterward, brushed his shirt down and walked away.

He left me there alone, and it's like he hasn't returned to me since.

My cell phone pings as the administrator directs me toward a door. Yanking it out of my pocket, I pause when I see who's messaging me. Guilt wasn't the only thing I left behind in

Colombia, but I miss this one way more.

"No cell phones allowed in here, Miss Williams," says the woman sternly. "You know the drill."

"Just this one message, and I'm done. I swear!"

Her face relaxes a little. "You can hand it in to reception on your way to the therapy session. They'll make sure to store it in the safe for you until your departure." She slots the key card into the lock and opens up. "We'll see you shortly."

With that, she drifts back into the hallway, leaving me tapping out my reply to the beats of her fading footsteps. My new ring keeps catching in the strip lights overhead, offering me short sharp stabs of happiness, followed by icy trickles of doubt. Like the fact I said "yes" to a shadow man who hides so much of himself in the dark.

Maybe he never expected me to say that word back to him.

My stomach lurches.

Stop with the second-guessing, Anna. You knew it was coming. He bought the rings years ago.

I'm only here for two days. Joseph and I have the rest of our lives to make us right.

With that in mind, I press "send".

I have news…

She replies right away.

Good?

Bad?

I miss your face, *parcera.*

Does she ever think about the faces we obliterated together? Like the rapists in her bar, and the tormentor who ordered us to shoot each other before we fired on him instead? We never spoke it aloud, but we synced our plan anyway. Me and her—after everything we'd been through—it was just…

Instinct.

Snapping a picture of my ring finger, I press "send" again.

This time her reply takes ages to come through.

Cool.

That's it?

Cool?

I stand there, staring at my cell, expecting another message to show up any second demanding all the details.

Stupid me.

I should have known not to expect rainbows and glitter cakes. I traveled to Colombia to escape Joseph, and if it was up to Viviana I'd still be running. Before I came along, he was *El Asesino*. Santiago's red right hand. Someone to be feared and avoided. Then she shot him in a gas station parking lot, and now he's the man who drew a line in the sand between me and her.

There are ten of us in the group today. There should be eleven, but there's an empty chair that's as conspicuous as a freshly squeezed zit.

Some are older than me, some are younger—it's a perfect cross-section of well-heeled addiction. There are even a couple of washed-up rock stars… Greens is the best rehab center in Florida, after all.

We're sitting in a neat circle, on chairs as hard as these first few minutes of introductions invariably are.

Not for me.

I've always been a pretty open person—a walking target, as my mom used to say. When I was a teenager, I wore my heart on both sleeves of my Nirvana T-shirt. I guess that's what broke me after I was rescued. For the first time in my life, I clammed up. I couldn't deal with it, so that shit had to speedball somewhere.

It's what makes it so painful to love a man who's a tightly closed fist. Joseph kills to relieve that pressure, but I know it's not sustainable.

And then what?

"Would anyone like to go first?"

Rina, our therapist, is one of those extreme cat-lover types in her late-fifties, with frizzy brown hair, a purple thigh-length cardigan and half-moon glasses on a silver chain. There's sympathy and toughness in her smile—kind of like a librarian with teeth.

"Yes, I will." I raise my hand above a sea of relieved expressions.

"Wonderful." Rina flicks through her notes trying to place me, then nods in encouragement. "In your own time."

"My name is Anna. I'm twenty-eight years old and I'm an addict."

I say it confidently because I own this statement now—the same way I own every bad thing I've ever done, just like Joseph taught me to.

I fought for it.

I killed for it.

I don't tell them that, though. Jeez. They'd all be running scared back to their beachfront mansions. Instead, I share the PG version of my story—leaving out the parts about the Russian traffickers and the rapes, the murders, the cartel leader and my fiancé—the Wanted Man. I tell them all the relevant parts that they can relate to, and in turn I'm rewarded with a strange sense of relief for sharing my demons with a bunch of strangers.

"That's wonderful, Anna," says Rina when I run out of steam. "Thank you for trusting us with your story." She glances around the room again. "Who'd like to go next?"

The middle-aged Soccer Mom in Gucci sweats opposite me raises her hand.

"I will."

After that, the admissions flow freely from one person to the next, circling the room like wildfire and smoking out shame. We're like soldiers united in this battle. We talk endlessly about consequences, about sadness and loneliness; about running from pain, and finding comfort in all the wrong places. After two hours of this, I feel like I've undergone the mother of all workouts for the mind and soul.

Rina's just wrapping up when the door to the Beethoven room bangs open with the kind of drama that the late composer would be proud of.

"Sorry I missed it," drawls a female voice, a million times more confident than mine—with an edge and an accent that fills the room with enigma and mystery. "Crosstown traffic was a bitch."

We all turn with interest, but it's only me who's left gaping at the newcomer in recognition.

There, standing in the doorway, looking as smoking hot as the day I met her in a bathroom stall in Colombia—in black skinnies, a tight white Tee, brown leather cowboy boots and a wicked grin—is Viviana Santiago.

Chapter Six

ANNA

She enters the room like an electric storm: lighting up the atmosphere and commanding all the attention. Acting like she's addicted to trouble more than anything else.

"You must be Elena," says Rina briskly.

"Yeah, ah, Elena. That's me." Vi shrugs at her fake name. She couldn't give two shits about keeping up pretenses. She's already daring the therapist to call her out on it.

I want to murder her for this. She doesn't belong here, and her company is making a mockery of our pain.

"I'm afraid you've missed most of the session today." Rina adjusts her spectacles and glances at her notes again. "Not to worry, we can have a one-to-one CBT after meditation."

Vi wrinkles her nose like she just offered her a colonic. "Yeah, um, sounds great."

Ignoring her less-than-lukewarm reaction, the therapist checks her wristwatch. "We still have a few minutes left. Would you like to use that time to tell us about yourself?"

"Is that the fun part?"

"*Excuse* me?"

"You know, the movie scene tragic confessional?" She straightens her face and fakes a bass. "*My name is Batman and I'm an—*"

"Yes." Rina's response thunders around the room, echoing disapproval. If her lips get any thinner, they'll be disappearing altogether. "Those 'words', Elena, offer structure and meaning. We're here to share our experiences, not demean them."

"Fine, let's do this."

All eyes are following her as she crosses the room to the empty chair next to Soccer Mom, giving me the ghost of a wink as she passes. Her raven hair is longer than before, tumbling down her back in a silky cascade, but it's the swagger in her steps that's the real revolution.

She's standing taller…bolder.

Braver.

When we first met, she was a scared girl on the run with a couple of kilos of coke taped to the inside of her dress. These days, she's Colombian cartel royalty and people run from her.

The room holds its breath as she makes herself comfortable— well, as much as you can on these stupid chairs—stretching out her long legs and giving every man in the vicinity a new focal point.

"My name is Elena," she intones, playing fast and loose with the drama again, catching my gaze and holding it. "And I'm an addict, too…"

After that, the lies come smoothly. Too smoothly. Vi didn't have to leave South America to lose her guilt. She lost it the day she aligned with her uncle, Dante Santiago.

I still love her, though. Even when I'm crazy mad at her, like I am right now. That's why I'm waiting by the door as everyone else files out for the afternoon meditation session, knowing she'll be hanging back as well.

Once we're alone, she kicks the door shut, grabs me by the waist and spins me around, filling my senses with that cool spicy scent as visions of car crashes and murder flit through my mind.

"Vi, stop!"

"Surprise, *parcera!* Did you miss me?"

"What the hell are you doing here?" I wriggle out of her embrace.

"I was in Miami when I got your message." Vi pouts at my expression, looking more like a Colombian supermodel denied lip gloss than a stone-cold criminal. *I know the lines she's crossed, because I crossed them, too.* "Santiago said that you and *El Asesino* were over here for the next couple of days. I thought you were having a dirty weekend..." She looks around the room and does that wrinkled up nose thing again. "I didn't expect to find you having an overnight in the nuthouse."

"This is *not* a nuthouse. It's a rehabilitation center. I'm a recovering addict, remember? When I say my 'movie scene tragic confessional,' I actually mean it."

"You're not an addict, Anna."

"Are you *serious*?"

She fixes me with those deadly nightshade eyes. I think it's finally hitting home that I'm not exactly overjoyed to see her.

"I figured you might be lonely in here all by yourself."

"Well, I'm not."

She catches sight of my hand and wrenches it up for closer inspection. "*Hijueputa*." *Son of a bitch.* she curses in Spanish. "That *is* a wedding band. You never said you'd actually gone through with it."

I bristle at the disapproval in her voice. "We haven't."

Her dark eyes gleam.

"Not yet, anyway," I add crossly. "But it's going to happen."

"There's still time to change your mind."

"Why the hell would I do that?" I snatch my hand back and fold my arms across my chest. "I take it you're not going to congratulate me?"

"Where the fuck are all the diamonds, *parcera*?" She lunges for my hand again. "This is, like, the most boring engagement ring in existence…"

"No, it's not. It's perfect. I'd rather have the man than a stone."

Or a man made of stone.

"*El Asesino* should stick to doing what he does best, or maybe put the bottle down once in a while."

"What the hell are you talking about? Joseph's not an alcoholic."

"And *you're* not a cokehead." She folds her arms in a mirror vision of my stance and cocks her eyebrows.

I've had enough of this.

"Go screw yourself, Vi," I mutter, walking toward the door.

"*Parcera*," she wails after me. "I was only joking." I hear the clip clop of her cowboy boots behind me as she jogs to catch-up. "When did you get so moody, all of a sudden?" She takes my arm and spins me around, trapping me with a brooding dark gaze that roots me to the spot. She's clever like that. People's hardline decisions always seem to do a one-eighty whenever she's around.

Her lips twitch and her head drops to one side. "Aren't you just a *little* pleased to see me?"

"No," I lie. "How did you get in here anyway?"

"I have an unhealthy addiction to cocaine." She flicks me that wicked grin again.

"You mean the money it makes you. Half the people in this center are probably here because of the Santiago Cartel."

"Collateral." She rolls her eyes. "I'm not stupid, like they are. I don't snort what I sell."

Was she always this insensitive?

"Well, I do," I grit out, feeling the heat blooming in my cheeks. "I guess that makes me doubly stupid."

"Did," she argues. "And I stand by what I said: you are *not* an addict."

"Well, I'm not here for the goddamn food, if that's what you're inferring."

"I'm not ghosting what happened to you, Anna, but you don't need this place to help you heal. You're the coolest, strongest woman I know. I saw your face when you fired those bullets at Fernandez—"

"Keep your voice down," I hiss, slamming my palm against her mouth.

"Chill!" She laughs, shaking me off. "There's no one about. They're all off chasing their spiritual super-highs."

"Vi, don't take this the wrong way or anything, but can you please just *fuck off.*"

"You faced your demons in Colombia." She traps my face between her hands suddenly, looking so serious, and so like Santiago, that my breath catches. "I was there when you slayed them, *parcera*. You never hesitated. You did what needed to be done. You saved me, and I won't forget that. Whatever happens, I will *never* forget that," she repeats solemnly, a strange expression crossing her face before she's jerking her head at the door. "Now, let's go have some fun before *El Asesino* takes you back to my uncle's secret island again."

Her blast of sincerity almost makes me consider it.

She always did offer temptation like a shiny, red apple.

"No, Vi," I say firmly, taking a step away to break her spell. "I'm staying here. I'm not going back to how I was before. No way."

She considers me for a moment. "Then I'm staying with you." Linking her arm through mine, she pulls me close, hip-to-hip. *Addict to cartel princess.* "How else am I going to get to speak to you these days with *El Asensio* screening my calls."

"Please don't call him that—wait, *what*?"

"You didn't know?" She blinks at me. "Checked your emails lately? Your messages? I've been trying to reach you for weeks, *parcera*, and I'm betting you haven't received any of them."

I wrack my brains for the last time we spoke. It's true. I haven't heard from her in ages.

"The moment I found out you were here, I had to see you. I was desperate. I'm sick of him keeping us apart."

I study her face for traces of deceit, but it's a picture of innocence.

"I know that you and Joseph have history, Vi, but I can't imagine him ever—"

"Are you sure about that?" she says sharply, driving her insinuation deep into my doubt. "There's something weird going on with him. I saw it for myself in Colombia last week."

My silence stretches, and her eyebrows lift in curiosity. She just spun a map of possibilities and landed a pin on the problem.

"Fuck! I knew it! What's happened? Are he and Santiago—?"

"No, it's nothing like that…" I trail off and glance at my sneakers. "Damn. We're meant to be in this meditation."

"Fuck meditation," she drawls, teasing a smile from my

Chapter Seven

JOSEPH

I watch her walking into rehab with her head hanging low and her sneakers dragging. There's no life. No bounce. She's confused as fuck as to why I'm acting so distant. She's trailing her moonshine behind her like she's bleeding that shit out.

The fact that I'm doing this to her burns like fire. In punishment, I force myself to watch until the last blonde strands of her ponytail are swallowed up by the sliding doors, just to make the guilt hurt more.

I'm still sitting in the parking lot five hours later, in a black SUV with black interior and tinted windows that bears more than a passing resemblance to a coffin. Once again, I find myself reaching for the handle to follow her inside. I want to slam her up against the wall and force an apology and an explanation into her mouth. They've been hovering over us for the last two days now. She never demanded them, but every time we touched, I felt my deception.

"Fuck!"

My hand drops to my lap again. She came here for peace, not my past. The very least I can do is leave her alone for two days.

I'm slamming the SUV into drive when a message comes through from Dante.

New York. Nine p.m.

I take a beat to process it, and then I'm hitting the brakes hard.

"Fuck!" I roar again. "FUCK!"

Re-reading the message, I grip the wheel so tight I can feel the black leather biting into my skin. New York wasn't in the plan. I had every intention of staying in a safe house near the rehab center for the next forty-eight hours and ignoring my problems with a bottle of Jack.

He calls with more details as I'm pulling out of the driveway. By then, my heart is so heavy it's hanging out somewhere near the gas pedal.

"Grayson?"

"Speaking."

"Did you get my message?"

There's a coolness in his voice that I don't appreciate today. I haven't apologized for what happened in his office, and he's not exactly known for his amnesty. We've been acting like two tigers ever since—snapping and circling—and that's the way it's staying until he comes to his senses over his niece.

"It just came through." I tell him.

There's a pause. "Williams?"

"Delivered. Leaving the center now."

"I need you in New York to take my place for something."

"What and why?"

"Eve's having contractions. I'm flying back to the island now. Peters has something urgent for us. It's sensitive, and he wants to deliver it in person."

Jesus Christ. "Can it wait?"

There's a pause. "No, it can't fucking wait, Grayson."

My hostility is catching him off guard. I've usually backed down by now.

"He's meeting you outside Sanders' bar in Manhattan at nine. There's another jet waiting for you at Opa-locka Airport."

I ring off after that. He's already pissed all over my plans enough.

It's late afternoon in Miami and the sun is dueling with the tinted windows. Even my Wayfarers are acting like a waste of two-hundred dollars. Pulling over, I call my man inside Greens. Anna doesn't take one step in the US without constant eyes on her, even when she's in rehab. She's been kidnapped twice before, and it's never happening again.

He answers on the first ring.

"Grayson."

"I'm out of town for the next twelve hours. I want updates."

"No problem."

"Any hint of trouble, I want to know about it."

"Understood. She's going into a group session now."

"Call me afterward."

Hanging up, I take my frustration out on the incoming traffic—swinging away from the curb so violently I leave a chorus of squealing brakes in my wake.

An hour later, I'm thirty-thousand feet up in one of Santiago's jets, nursing a whiskey and cursing every single mile that takes me further away from her.

Closing my eyes, I let the sound of the engines lull me down to hell. I can feel him approaching from the back of the jet, his wet sneakers leaving bloody footprints on the carpet. It's always worse when I'm alone and half-cut. They're the lock and the key, and I'm the shit security guard who lets him in every time.

"Why are you letting that twister spin all alone, little brother?"

When he speaks, his voice is coming from the seat behind me.

"Not now, Cash," I mutter, watching the droplets of rain on the cabin window streak across the glass like speeding bullets.

"Bad men shuffle the cards of love to the bottom of the deck, Joey. Guess you had them twisted bones all along, just like Pa said you did."

"Good to know I'm living up to his expectations."

The rest of my whiskey vanishes, and I pour another.

"You shouldn't have gone to Bill's that day," he chides, reaching so deep inside my walls I can feel my foundations shaking. "You shouldn't have left us all alone with him."

"Bullshit," I hiss. "You told me to run. If I'd stayed, he would have killed me, too."

But the guilt of that decision is punching me in the gut. My justification sounds as empty as my glass.

"You could have stopped him."

"Quit it, Cash!"

"Or what?"

"Or I'll be shooting myself in the head just to shut you up!"

He laughs. "You're going to lose this one as well, little brother...you're the reason she'll die."

I freeze.

"Because she *will* die. They *all* die. You're a fucking death magnet. Always have been. Santiago saw it in Afghanistan, and he's been ridin' it ever since."

"Stop," I rasp.

"Dead like your dead wife."

A fresh pain explodes in my chest. *Not now. Not here.* But Cash is all out of mercy tonight. He leans forward in his seat to deliver his next words.

"Dead like your dead *son*."

I see his face the day he was born. *A year later he was gone.*

"Dust and bones, little brother." Cash cackles. "We're all just dust and bones and we're waiting to see you again. Everyone you've ever killed—heck, there's a whole goddamn army down here."

"Shut the fuck up!" I roar, chucking my glass at the cabin wall. It shatters on impact, sending shards in every direction. The co-pilot emerging from the cockpit curses in shock.

No one moves.

Silence smothers.

"You going to clean that up?" he says eventually. "I'm not a fucking air attendant."

I consider slitting his throat, and then I think better of it.

Bending down, I close my fist around a jagged piece of broken glass, feeling the slice of satisfaction on my skin.

Pain is good.

Pain keeps me grounded.

"Keep it together, Joseph," I mutter. "This isn't the time to go losing your mind."

The next time I glance back across the aisle, Cash is gone.

Rick's already waiting for me in the VIP section of his bar, wearing a midnight blue three-piece and a smirk. There's a half-drunk bottle of Scotch in front of him, but only one glass. *Some things never change.* You have to beg for everything from this asshole. Nothing comes for free.

"You look like shit," he says when I reach the table, appraising me with his sharp gray eyes.

"And you're a piece of shit," I respond dryly, picking up the Scotch and taking a swig directly from the bottle. "But don't go thinking we're related."

"Would you like a glass to go with your liquor, or did we park our manners by the door again? I always said you were a fucking savage underneath the Captain America façade, Grayson."

I ignore the jibe. "Where's Roman?"

It's packed in here tonight and the beats are making my head swim. Rick makes as much from his bars and clubs as he does from flooding the Mean Streets with our coke.

"Running late. He'll be here in ten."

Glancing back, I find him watching a pretty, dark-haired girl behind his bar. She's nervous as hell. Her fingers keep fumbling with the bottles, and she's pouring more on the bar counter than she is in the glasses.

Not so long ago it was Anna who worked there. Maybe not in this bar or this city, but in a place that looked similar. Rick likes a uniformed banality with all of his establishments. He calls it "sin with a side of vanity", which roughly translates as extra low lighting, black marble, and tacky mirrored ceilings. I imagine his bedroom looks the same. He's such a fucking narcissist, I'm betting he can't come without watching himself.

He catches me staring at the girl and his smirk disappears. *Interesting.*

"Who's that?" I ask. "Latest fuck?"

"Not yet," he says lazily, playing with his cut-glass tumbler. "But I'm working on it."

"She looks Russian."

"Try taking off the sunglasses for once, you might see better."

"Try turning up the lights in this place, you might find your integrity."

He laughs long and hard at this, like a whore at a client who's asking for proof of her virginity. "Hold your wig there, grandpa." He composes himself. "I cater to rich college kids and Wall Streeters with money to burn, not enforcers with chips on their shoulder the size of China. They want darkness and ego to dwell in, not spotlights and reality." There's a pause. "How's Anna?"

"Mine," I say tersely.

"You sure about it?"

Jealousy wraps her wicked hands around my heart. "Lay one finger on her, Sanders, and you're a dead man."

"If I lay two, will I be in heaven?"

A beat later, I'm dragging him to his feet by his fitted black shirt. Another beat passes and a Glock is being shoved into the small of my back.

"Ease up, Danny," says Rick to the man standing behind me with my life in his hands. "No one's going to do anything stupid here—Are you, *Joseph*?" He lifts his brows at me, and I let go of him reluctantly. I'm already in enough trouble with Santiago as it is. If I go shooting up our number one dealer on the East Coast, I'm as good as dead myself. "Good boy," he says as I shrug Danny off and slide onto the booth bench opposite. "Now stop being such an uptight bastard." He takes a seat himself, straightening his shirt. "Tell Anna you need an extra blow job to chill you out."

Jealousy flares again in shades of green and red. "Mention her again in any context and I'll rip your throat out."

"You're very 'threat happy' tonight," he muses, studying me closely. "Is there trouble in paradise?"

"I don't want to talk about it."

"That's gotta burn after you chased her all over Colombia, started a cartel war for her, and got yourself shot up for the privilege." He leans over the table with his smirk back in place. "And here I was thinking you, 'made shit right' for everyone," he says, quoting my own words back to me with a twist of scorn.

I hold his gaze. "Maybe I'm making shit wrong for a change."

"Oh?" He leans back in his seat again, looking mildly interested. "Tell me more. I've always wanted to see the Iceman melt."

"Why? So you can piss in the mess on your carpet?" I chuckle darkly. "You don't keep secrets, Rick, you hold them for ransom and then triple the interest."

"Now you're just being mean."

Clasping my hands together, I blow out a harsh breath. "Get me a bourbon."

Without missing a beat, he pushes the Scotch bottle and glass in my direction. "Something tells me you're not in a fussy mood this evening."

I pour out two large doubles, one after the other.

"Is it Dante?" he asks, watching me closely.

"Is what Dante?" My hostility is spilling out worse than his new bartender's cocktail skills.

"The reason for the temper tantrum."

When I don't say anything, he flicks a silver coaster across the table at me. "How did you two meet, anyway? I've always wanted to ask."

"Afghanistan." I pour myself another drink. "Our M-ATV was blown up south of Kabul. We were the only survivors."

Rick curls his mouth in scorn. "Oh Jesus. Don't give me all that war hero story bullshit. I want to know the good stuff, like how he reeled you into this sordid world of ours. I'm betting, once upon a time, you were the star quarterback and all the pretty cheerleaders lifted up their skirts for you." He leans forward, elbows on the table again. "What happened, Texas Sun? Did the bad shit trip you up?"

"He came looking for me." I blast him back with the coldest fucking glare I have. "He was long gone from the Marines by then. He found me in a bar with dried blood on the floor, blue collars lined up like broken whiskey bottles at the bar, and a jukebox full of Springsteen."

He winces. "Sounds hell."

"He walked in alone, and an hour later he was walking out with me."

"How did he turn you?"

I think of a morgue, two bodies, and no fucks left to give.

"After what we did in Afghanistan," I say harshly. "I was already turning."

"How many people have you killed for him, *El Asesino*?" he murmurs. "A hundred? A thousand? It doesn't stain his soul, but with you—"

"Quit with the questions," I warn, "or I'm making you one more."

Rick holds his palms up in surrender. "I'm just looking after my business interests. You two are a bromance for the ages. Your connection is bone-deep. If one of you falls, you both do, and it looks to me like you're on the fucking edge, Grayson."

"Bull*shit*."

"If you stumble and Santiago's leash slackens, we all suffer. After Eve, you're the only one who can keep him in check. If you're a savage, he's a fucking monster."

"I'm nowhere near the edge, Sanders," I say, forcing the lie. "All I am is jet-lagged, not drunk enough, and a thousand miles from my woman."

"You could have just said that in the first place."

"I've never had a way with words." I raise the glass to my mouth again. "How about you? Did you wake up one day with a kilo of his coke in your hands?"

"I followed a red dress." He flashes white teeth at me.

Well, what d'ya know? Same as me.

"I should have known a woman was involved."

His grin widens, but there's a bleaker story in his gray eyes. "I made her a promise."

I know about promises. *I know how to break them.*

Just then his cellphone beeps. He glances sideways at it. "Roman's arrived," he says, scooping it up. "He's waiting for us in the car downstairs."

Chapter Eight

JOSEPH

The detective's face is bathed in shadow as I swing into the backseat next to him. Rick climbs into the passenger seat upfront. His man, Danny, is driving. Rick tweaks the stereo until New York City Cops by The Strokes is blasting out of the SUV's speakers.

"Your sense of humor never fails to amuse me, Sanders." Roman's words are so dry, I'm surprised his voice doesn't crack. "Has Santiago called you out about D'Angelo's daughter yesterday?"

"No." The volume dips momentarily. "And it's none of your business who keeps my dick wet. She's obliging, and I'm very much obliged…wait, I have a better one."

Undercover of the Night by The Stones starts playing.

"Are you done?" The detective's composure is in danger of being left on the corner of Cedars and Ninth.

"Not even close."

We pull away from the curb, the shadows falling away from Roman's face as he turns to talk to me. Handsome. Expressionless. There's not a dark blond hair out of place. His shirt is crisp and white, new on today, and his shoes are so polished they gleam orange-gold in the passing streetlights. He's everything a good undercover agent should be. One difference. He plays for us, not them.

"Grayson." He hands me a red file. "Thanks for coming at short notice"

"What's this? Fan mail?"

He glances at the back of Rick's head, waiting until he cranks the music back up before leaning over. "There's a very good reason I dragged you all this way."

I nod once, understanding immediately.

"You asked me to look into those…*connections* in Miami."

We share a look in the darkness before the flare of Rick's lighter kills it. I'm dicing with death by going behind Dante's back with this, but I know that Roman doesn't trust Viviana Santiago, either.

"You found something?"

"I have," he confirms, flipping open the file for me as I switch on the torch app on my cell. "It's tenuous, but it's there."

There are pages and pages of business transactions and papers for an organization called The Vindicta Corporation.

"What's this?"

"On the surface, Vindicta is a shipping company with an annual turnover of eighty million. They were only founded a couple of years ago, but since my father's death they've been buying up lines and property all over the world."

Roman's father was a shipping magnet himself, and one of Russia's most feared *Pakhan*. Roman still operates his father's company under an umbrella organization that disguises his true name. He's the only FBI agent with a net worth of a hundred billion, but the money doesn't mean *jack* to him.

"Why the fuck is Santiago interested in shipping companies?" asks Rick, turning the music down.

"Go back to playing your songs, Brooklyn Boy," I murmur. "Leave the hard stuff to us."

Roman laughs, a sound that's rare from him. Rick says nothing, but I know that his retaliation is being stored up and multiplied for a later date.

"It's Dante's business." I relent with a double lie. "Shipping channels in and out of Miami need consolidating."

"Then this is Miami shit, not New York shit. Why the hell am I even here?"

"We required your scintillating conversation and views on world politics," drawls Roman.

"Not when I have D'Angelo's daughter waiting for me," he counters slyly.

"He wanted you to have this." The detective hands him a second red file. "The Italians are planning a second hit on you. No time yet. No place. But it's coming."

Rick looks unimpressed. "The Italians wouldn't be stupid enough to strike twice in the same week. I've killed twenty today alone in reprisal for their attempt last night. They've had their fun. As long as Don Ricci learns to stick behind the Bowery and Canal Street, I see no reason to start a turf war."

"You're not listening to me, Sanders," says Roman patiently. "They have someone else on the inside. I suggest you switch up your nighttime habits again. Keep them guessing. Don't visit the same club twice in a row—"

"Yadda, yadda, are we done yet?" Rick tosses the file onto

the front dash, unread, and flicks his cigarette ash out of the window.

"There's something else, but Dante will fill you in."

"I can't wait."

The car slows to a crawl. We're outside the Barfly again. Danny exits first, and then Rick. He turns back to rap on the window.

"You coming in?" he asks when I open the door a crack.

I shake my head. "I left Anna in Miami. I need to get back."

"All alone in Little Cuba?" he taunts. "How careless. Give her a kiss from me."

With that, he's slamming the door in my face before I make good on my threats.

Roman tuts in frustration. "If that man wasn't so good at making money…"

"Dante trusts him. He's not going anywhere."

There's a pause. "I heard what happened in Colombia."

Roman sounds concerned.

Roman never sounds concerned.

"Dante's blinkered by the curiosity of his own family bloodline. It won't last. Tell me everything about Vindicta."

"They have a strong fleet, and they own at least ten percent of the warehouses and container docks along the East Coast."

"Mexican?"

"No."

"Russian?"

"Quite possibly."

"What's this got to do with Viviana?"

"You said she had a mystery contact in shipping. I'd planned to start with the big players and work down. Until I found this." He takes the file from me and flicks through the pages to the last one. "This is a recent export agreement with Vindicta for Gomez's business. For years, he exported coke into the US disguised as cocoa beans with a rival company—Aba Shipping. Or they did until your girlfriend blew the back of his head off, and Viviana did the equivalent with a knife and his only son."

"Fiancée," I murmur without thinking. "Anna and I are getting married."

"Congratulations," he says, with a note of sincerity in his voice. He knows, first-hand, what she went through because his twin sister, Natasha, suffered the same fate. She never came out alive, though. She never had a man to fix her, and then fuck it all up again.

Since Natasha's death, Roman's family have made it their mission to destroy human trafficking. Since his father's murder, Roman has thrown his rage, his grief and everything else at it.

"So let me get this straight: Gomez swapped Aba Shipping for Vindicta to smuggle their coke into the US?"

"Yes, three years ago, but it was a bogus deal."

"Explain."

"Look at the figures." He taps his finger on the bottom line. "They may as well be stamped with Mickey Mouse logos, for all the sense they make. Exports costs are usually double, *triple*, what they'd agreed on. My guess is it was a tradeoff for something much bigger. Both Gomez Senior and Junior betrayed the Santiago cartel, which gets me thinking—"

My cell starts buzzing in my pocket. It's my guy on the inside at Anna's rehab.

"I need to take this."

Roman nods. "Go ahead. I'll wait."

"Simon."

"Did you get my messages?" He sounds rattled and pissed.

"What messages?" I demand.

"I left you about a dozen."

Wrenching the iPhone away from my ear, I check the screen. There are hundreds of missed calls, emails and messages—

"There was a surprise arrival in the group session."

"Who?"

"Viviana Santiago."

My stomach drops. "What the *fuck*?"

"Bitch waltzed into a group session like she owned the place, which judging by the size of the bribe she made at the front desk, she more or less does. They've been inseparable all evening."

Fuck. Fuck. Fuck.

Since Colombia I've been monitoring Anna's calls. I've been trying to carve out some distance between her and Viviana.

I should have seen this coming.

If I wasn't so drunk all the time trying to deal with my own shit, I might have.

She's my priority. Not me.

"Where are they now?"

"In the cafeteria having dinner."

"Don't let them leave together under any circumstance. I'm flying back to Miami now."

Hanging up, I kick the door open and stand there in the middle of Fifth Avenue, breathing fumes. It's the height of summer in Manhattan—a melting pot of heat and humidity. This New York minute is saturated with it.

Viviana played me.

She fucking played me.

She slid right into the gap I left by Anna's side like a bullet into a well-greased chamber.

Roman exits the car after me and leans against the side of the SUV with his hands in his suit pants' pockets. *Does he think I'm close to the edge too?* I wouldn't blame him if he did. I can't stop pacing.

I spin around. "I need to get back to Miami."

"So I gather."

"You need a ride?"

He shakes his head. "My car's parked over on the next block." He takes a cautious step toward me. "When Dante asks about this, tell him we met because of the rumored hit on Rick."

"No problem." Dragging my thoughts back from dark places, I wave the red file at him. "Viviana's making chess moves I can't read anymore, but I can't take this to him without more proof. You know what he's like. He'll blow the back of my head off just for Chinese Whispering the word 'conspiracy'."

"There's something else I haven't told you."

I pause. "Do I need another drink for this?"

"Probably. When Anna first met Viviana, she was up to her black eyes with the Fernandez cartel—"

"She owed them money," I interrupt, tersely. "We know this."

"Fernandez also had a new export agreement drafted with Vindicta before he died, and it's even more bullshit. If we checked all of the business dealings of the former *Los Cinco Grandes,* I'm betting we'd find a pattern."

"Get to the point, Roman," I say irritably. "I'm leaving in thirty seconds."

He shoots me a frosty look. "Viviana told Anna she was in debt to the tune of fifty-thousand. Something about her cousin's bar in Santa Perdida."

"Manuel," I confirm, remembering the brave young soldier

who'd died protecting Santiago's wife.

"There was no debt."

It takes a second for his words to register. "*What*?"

"There was no outstanding money on that property. She lied. She sold it the day after Manuel's funeral."

"To whom?"

But I know what he's going to say.

"Vindicta."

My head is spinning. "Wait a minute. You're telling me that a multi-billion-dollar shipping corporation bought some shitty provincial bar in *Colombia*?"

"The deal was brokered by Fernandez's attorney. The paperwork is all in that file."

I stare at him, sifting through the ground zero of his bombshells, but all I'm getting are twisted fragments.

"Did you ever study Latin in high school, Grayson?" I hear him say as I reach, blindly, for the door handle.

"No pussy, no point." Yanking it open, I throw myself into the driver's seat. "Italian, yes, French, definitely. But Latin? No woman wants to be seduced by a dead language."

"Well, here's something that'll make you hard; 'Vindicta' is Latin for 'revenge'."

I pause, his insinuation hitting me like a slap to the face.

"What the fuck are you saying? You think something big is onto us?"

"Something or someone?" I watch him pop his elbow on the open door, my own concern mirrored in his face. "I'm not confirming anything at this stage. But it's a strange name for a company, don't you think?"

Chapter Nine

JOSEPH

I'm halfway to Teterboro Airport when Highway Patrol adds a splash of color to my nightmare in shades of flashing blue.

Glancing in my rearview mirror, I'm met with a wall of it, stretching out across every lane of the I-95. Even the cops want in on the action. Five seconds later, their sirens fill the air with angry wails, and I'm cursing Rick for not leaving his fucking playlist behind.

Did I get careless?

I'm so used to slipping in and out of the US undetected, I'd half-assumed they'd given me diplomatic immunity for being such a cocky bastard. On reflection, I doubt they give that out to the second Most Wanted man in America without an under-the-table bribe the size of Santiago's island.

Was I sold out?

There's a growing consternation in my mind, one with brown leather cowboy heels, a blood-soaked machete, and lying eyes.

That fucking bitch.

Slamming my foot to the floor, the SUV surges forward like a line-back going for a super catch. I barely shift in my seat as I weave in and out of the deadbeat middle laners, nudging one-thirty. I'm running on a hunch, and that hunch is leading me all the way back to Miami. Anna needs me there, and nothing, not even an army of the State's Own, is going to stop that from happening.

I've already crossed the Hudson, but there are still six miles of heart-in-the-mouth to go. I'm deep in New Jersey which is Mexican Cartel territory. One wrong move, and I'll have two sets of guns pointing at my head.

Without missing a beat, I reach for my cell. Eli, our pilot, answers on the first ring.

"I've got company," I tell him, taking the next exit and running a set of red lights—losing three cop cars in the process.

He blows out a cigarette breath. "How many?"

"Looks like a couple of departments of NY's finest just got a day outing."

There's a pause as he assesses my likelihood of staying out of jail tonight.

"Think you can get here in one piece?" he asks, picking the right option.

"Damn straight I can."

"We're fueled and waiting for you, Grayson."

"Be ready. I'm coming."

My next call is to Roman.

"I'm thinking of taking up Latin," I drawl, needing a drink so bad I can taste the burn at the back of my throat. "Vindicta was a warning we should have seen coming."

He reads between my cool lines right away.

"What's happened?"

"I have a parade of blue behind me a mile long."

He curses loudly. "Where are you?"

"Blowing through New Jersey like a fucking hurricane. We've got a leak, and my money's on Colombia."

"Shake them off, then call me back. I'll do what I can from here."

"Watch your ass, Roman," I warn, coaxing one-fifty out of the SUV, flying so hard down the I-95 I'm like a G-6. "If you get rumbled, our entire anti-trafficking operation goes up in smoke. We need every resource we have blowing Vindicta wide open. This stuff just got personal."

"What about Dante?"

"I'll deal with Dante," I say grimly.

I'm speeding through some backstreet shithole when I spy a large parking garage. Swerving into the security bay, crashing through the barrier, I spiral up to the top floor with the speedometer barely dipping. The whine of cop cars is still trailing after me, but this SUV is top of the range and they're not even tasting my gas fumes yet.

Pulling into the only spare space, I kill the engine and grab my gun. By the time their Toyota Tacomas reach the SUV, I'm already three floors down in the exit stairwell, my boots pounding out the "fuck you" anthem of survival.

Bursting through a doorway into a side street, I rejoin the main road at a flat sprint. There are a couple of cars parked nearby. The closest, a cherry-red Chevy, has a kid and his date swapping saliva in the front seats. I wrench the driver's door open like I'm a mean-eyed Papa with a baseball bat.

"What the hell?" The kid's expression is teenage outrage,

until he sees my gun. "Hey man," he whimpers. "We don't want any trouble."

"Get the fuck out of the car then," I say calmly, turning to his date. "You, too, sweetheart. Take your first base elsewhere and leave me the keys."

Fifteen minutes later, I'm climbing aboard the jet and swapping looks with Eli.

We're in the air before the cops are even dusting prints off of the SUV's steering wheel.

That's how fucking good I am.

I'm on the phone to Simon as soon as we're in the air. When his cell rings out four times in a row, my hunger to reach Miami turns into an obsession even bleaker than the sky outside. Heavy storm clouds are rolling in from the east, but there's danger lurking in every corner of the horizon.

Exhaling on a curse, I reach for the Macallan in front of me. That edginess I've felt since Texas just morphed into something that tastes like unease.

I need Anna safe in my arms.

I need her to be okay.

I just fucking need her.

Taking a deep swig from the bottle, the liquor settles like burning oil on my tongue. Our story is a mess. It's a love without convention. We were founded in her ruins, before she laid siege to my ice castle.

If I lose her, I lose myself.

Or what's left of me.

After leaving Simon another message, I tap out the number

for the rehab center as the aircraft shivers and shakes. The sky outside my cabin window splits with white light. Moments later, a clap of thunder joins the party.

"Green's Therapy," chirps a voice. "How may I direct your—?"

"I need to speak with Anna Williams." I cut the receptionist off mid-flow, shot-gunning that sweet little birdy with my harsh demand. "She checked in yesterday."

"Is this a personal call?"

"I'm her fiancé."

A dark, cloying need to possess her rises up inside me. *I'll kill anyone who tries to tear us apart.*

"I'm afraid we don't accept these types of calls for patients," she trills. "We discourage any contact with outside influences, except on Wednesdays and Sundays."

Outside influences? They should be more worried about the one inside their own four walls.

It's only Tuesday. In the next twenty-four hours, Anna could be killed, or worse.

"Listen ma'am, I don't have time for your bullshit rules."

"I understand that, sir," she says patiently. "Perhaps if you leave a message with her therapist…?"

"Fuck her therapist," I roar, hanging up and finishing off the rest of the bottle.

Unclipping my belt, I stagger up the aisle toward the cockpit. Eli and his co-pilot, Andy, glance up as I enter.

"Grayson."

"How far are we from Miami?"

Eli adjusts a dial on the MFD and switches back to autopilot. "Two hours, give or take the air temperature and density."

"Any updates from the ground? Have the cops figured out

my exit plan yet?"

"No advisories have been issued." He checks the altitude dial again. "We're already cruising at thirty-five thousand and clean as a whistle to Air Traffic, but if you want, we can jam the transponder—relax," he adds with a grin. "This is Santiago's jet. He and his own have more lives than a pussy farm. As far as I'm concerned, we're home, dry and coasting."

Just then the aircraft gives a violent lurch, mocking his casual immortalization of us.

"You sure about that?" Swinging into the Jump Seat behind Eli, I buckle up as the aircraft jerks again, acting like a virgin bride on her wedding night. I have a bad feeling I can't explain. It's a rising fever, and the only cure is waiting for me in Miami.

"Hold on to your cock and balls," shouts Eli, switching back to manual to nudge the plane down a couple of thousand feet. "Turbulence is a cranky bitch in this airspace. It can hit you like a…" He trails off when he catches sight of the fuel dial.

"What's wrong?" I'm picking up on his muted disbelief as we hit another fun pocket that rattles our bones.

"We're nearly out of fuel," he mutters, tapping the instrument. "That's what's wrong."

"Thought you said this thing was loaded?" I say, betraying no emotion whatsoever.

"I did. It was… Andy? Check the reserves."

"Empty," comes the clipped response.

Motherfucker.

"How far can we glide this thing?"

But Eli's already on the radio to air traffic control about a return to Teterboro. That tells me all I need to know. The man who flew Fighters during the Iraq War is spooking.

Outside, the storm is a gathering maelstrom of hell.

Visibility is at zero. The rain drops lashing horizontally against the jet's windscreen are like bullets. Another streak of lightning highlights the swirling vortex of black and gray cloud in front of us.

I don't give credence to fear. After everything I've been through, I don't much care for it, but the acridity filling my mouth reminds me that my heart is split in two now. I share it with another—a woman whom I swore to keep safe from that very emotion.

As the jet dips for a third time, Andy suddenly creases over his side of the MFD with a low groan.

"Fuck, Eli," he rasps, clutching at his stomach. "I don't feel so good."

"Take five," the pilot barks, not even looking at him. "Grayson, step in."

Andy lurches past me and out of the cockpit. The sound of his retching is drowned out by another clap of thunder, this time so close and so loud I can feel its vicious reverb in my soul.

"You ever co-piloted before?" Eli asks, keeping the joystick as steady as he can as he checks the primary flight display to his left.

"Not for a while," I admit, settling in the spare seat beside him. "But it's like screwing a hot woman, right?"

Another flash of lightning illuminates the flight deck. Eli's staring straight ahead, his lips peeled into a snarl, but his right hand is inching toward his stomach.

Bang.

The unlocked cockpit door crashes open, flooding light into the small space. Beyond it, Andy's passed out in the aisle in a pool of vomit. Eli turns to see him, and we catch each other's eye on the downswing.

"Teterboro," I say, thinking fast. "What the hell were your movements back there? Did you eat? Drink—?"

"Nothing. Nothing!" Eli scrunches up his face as another wave of pain hits. Whatever the poison is, it's fast acting. "Wait… One of the fuel guys was handing around his hip flask—"

"Goddammit!" I roar, as the word "sabotage" floods my veins with putridity. I was someone's target tonight, and they're not stopping until I'm six feet under. "What did he say to you?"

"Small talk." He creases up in agony again.

"What was your story?"

"We made some shit up about you being a celebrity who'd flown in for a TV interview."

The jet gives another lurch and Eli manages to drop us down to twenty thousand feet before he's bending-double over the controls.

"Grayson—"

"Go!" I order, pulling him out of his seat as a high-pitched whine fills the cabin.

"Out of fuel," Eli gasps, falling to his knees. "We need to land her now."

"Where are we?" Taking control of the joystick, I drop us down another thousand feet and switch the alarm off.

"Somewhere over Virginia," he croaks from the floor.

"Only eight mountain ranges to dodge." I drop the jet again, too fast this time, and she groans out in pain as well. "Tell me more about the man at Teterboro."

All I get this time is a grunt.

"Eli?"

"I was ragging him about being a Lakers guy." Eli crawls a couple of meters through the swinging door to reach Andy's body. There's white foam rimming the unconscious man's mouth.

I watch him check his pulse. When he swings his gaze back to me, I see the dawning comprehension in his eyes.

"I can't feel his pulse, Grayson…I can't fucking feel—"

"Describe him to me," I say harshly. "Concentrate, Eli."

"Tall." He doubles over again, gasping. "Tan-skinned, like Santiago. Same accent."

"You mean he was Colombian?"

He nods before vomiting his guts up. "Jesus Christ. *This ache*."

"Suck it in, Eli. Breathe that shit out."

"Am I gonna die too, Grayson?"

It's a closing scene rhetorical. There's an acceptance in his voice already.

Yes.

"No." The lie comes so easily I almost convince myself. "I'm putting this jet down the first chance I get. Tell me how to kill the radio and transponder."

Eli vomits again and wipes his mouth. "Gray box next to the navigation display. It's a homemade device. It jams radar, radio, black box, the lot."

I crank the dial to the Max without a second thought.

"He gave me his card."

Eli's voice is so weak now it's barely a whisper.

"The fuel guy?"

He nods before vomiting again. His time on this flight is nearly done. "Jacket pocket."

Holding the joystick steady with one hand, I find what I'm looking for in a screwed-up black Bomber next to the seat.

White card.

Gold letters.

Black deliverance.

Dig your grave.
Suffer the consequences.
Vindicta

Fuck. Fuck. Fuck.

I quickly stuff it into the front side pocket of my jeans. When I turn back to Eli, he's already passed out.

What follows next is a hollow core of silence as my fate is sealed and Santiago's jet becomes my tomb. There's no point calling for help. I've killed every transmittable signal in and out. It's just me, all alone in a dying aircraft, with no fuel and little faith.

Ten-thousand feet.

Nine-thousand feet.

Eight-thousand feet.

I tick off each altitude drop. It's a countdown to my End Game. The storm has nixed any hope of a smooth glide. We're a broken ship at sea, being tossed about by wind and gravity.

Seven-thousand feet.

Six-thousand—

"Goddammit!" I roar again, the word bursting from me as my composure cracks. I try in vain to pull the aircraft up as her nose starts to dip.

It wasn't supposed to end this way. Not after I finally found her, loved her and made her mine.

"Falling into hell so soon, little brother?"

Cash slides into the empty co-pilot seat and waits for his presence to be acknowledged.

"Five-thousand feet," I holler, not giving him the satisfaction, gripping the shuddering joystick so hard it's close to snapping off.

"The ending won't be so bad," I hear him say, with a shrug in his voice. He brushes dried blood off the thigh of his blue Levi's. "No worse than getting the side of your face blown off by Pa."

"I'm not dying today, Cash," I mutter through gritted teeth. "I've got a twister waiting for me."

Four-thousand feet.

"Not dying? You sure about that?" He laughs, a sound that's full of dirt and scorn. "You've no fuel, no pilot, no chance…"

At that moment, the clouds part and there she is: shining so fucking bright and silver she's blasting hope into my midnight hour.

"I'll be seeing you real soon, Joey," Cash whispers, rising from his seat to join the other dead bodies behind me.

Three-thousand feet.

Two-thousand feet.

I see a scattering of lights below as I execute the landing gear. The horizon is a jagged silhouette of a mountain range that's going to rip us apart.

One-thousand feet.

I wait for my life to flash before my eyes, but all I see is her.

Messy.

Unconventional.

Ice breaking.

Her.

Breathe. Want. Mine.

Boom.

Chapter Ten

ANNA

"You can't marry a mantra, *parcera*," Vi says, pushing the almond flour pancakes around the plate with a fork. "There are only so many times you can tell yourself it's going to be okay, or that one day he's going to magically open up and tell you his tragic life story."

"I like mantras," I say with a frown, watching the pomegranate seeds commit suicide from the top of her stack. "They keep me sane in a world full of hate and madness."

She gives up on the pancakes and takes a sip of her soya milk and berry smoothie, making a face as she swallows it. She's still wearing the same white Tee and black jeans she arrived in, but they never look out of style. She's far too cool for creases.

"What happens when you forget the words?" she says slyly.

"I find the notepad that I wrote them down on."

"Nope, you find yourself chained to a bad reality." She's full of self-confidence as she places the glass back down on the table.

Presumption is just another good hair day to her, and it's making the edges of my temper fray.

"Joseph is *never* a bad reality to me, Vi."

"Mm, if you say so."

"Enough!" I drop my spoon into my untouched granola and lean back in my chair, my shoulders catching the sunshine trail from the skylights above.

I wish I hadn't told her about that weird night on the island with Joseph, or about the ocean of distance that floods the spaces between us. She's been dog-without-a-bone relentless about it ever since. Her anti-Joseph lectures are almost as bad as my anti-Dante ones, and it's making me lose my appetite.

"You going to eat that?" She points to my overflowing bowl.

"All yours." I wearily push it across the table at her.

"Thanks."

It's our second morning here already. Joseph is picking me up in a couple of hours, but I don't feel calm or together in the slightest. Vi's a livewire who never sleeps. Her constant questions are like interrogations and her views are doctrinaire at best.

In short, the whole residential has been a disaster.

"*Pinche puto. Motherfucker,* this is even worse than those pancakes," she mutters, spooning up the granola with another of her sourpuss faces.

There's a loud noise from the kitchens behind us.

"What was that?" Vi tenses, as if she's expecting carnage to come spilling out of the door.

"It's only a dropped pan." I frown at her. All around us the rehab cafetiere is emptying. Fading voices, food debris, and crushed recyclables are the only evidence of a busy breakfast period. "Why so jumpy?"

"I don't like loud noises."

"Chose the wrong profession then, didn't you?"

She rolls her eyes as I mimic the action of a firing gun. In the end, she fell so naturally into the Santiago cartel business, it was almost like a calling.

"Is he coming to set you free?" she says, resuming *my* breakfast.

"Joseph? Yes. He's picking me up at midday. Can we *please* stop talking about him now?"

"All I'm saying is you can't make judgment calls about a man like *El Asesino*." She shrugs in that careless, cavalier way of hers. "The same way you can't break down a wall with your bare fists."

"Maybe you're right." My gaze wonders again, drifting back to the kitchen door. *I miss his stillness. I miss the certainty he brings to my brave new chaos.* "But sometimes the unexplainable is the only thing left that makes sense."

"*Parcera*—"

"A bad reality, to me, is a place where I don't feel safe."

"That's no reason to stay with a man like him. Get a dog."

"I don't want a dog, Vi." I stop and take a short breath before I lose it. *How do I explain that to love a shadow is to love all of his darkness?*

"Dogs are more endearing." She shovels another spoonful of granola into her mouth. "They talk even less than he does, though."

"That's a matter of opinion." I flash her a small smile, trying to lighten the mood. "Look, I know we're not a typical love story. I get that. We're dirty, raw and bruised. We put the 'D' in dysfunctional, and we wear it like homecoming crowns. But I *feel* him, Vi…" *God, I feel him so much.* "Even though I don't really know him."

"You *feel* him?" She laughs, as if I just told a bad joke. "Is that a sex reference? I don't need to know how big his dick is, Anna."

"Do you know how amazing it is to sit here and feel *anything* after what happened to me?" I say, bristling. "To feel is to love, to laugh, to dig your toes into the warm sand...to wake each day dying to live, not living to die."

The mocking grin slips from her face. Mine is a story I've hinted at, but never shared.

"I was taken," I blurt quickly, before my courage slips back under the table.

"Taken?" She drops the spoon, her sharp gaze homing in on me again.

"Last year."

"Who took you?"

I stare down at the table's surface, seeing black instead of white.

"*Parcera*?" she says, more urgently. "Who took you?"

I see his face so clearly—the pinched skin, the cruel mouth. The memory still cuts like a knife, hemorrhaging fear and self-loathing.

"They were waiting for me in my apartment. I was on the phone with Eve, Dante's wife, when they—" I shut my eyes and feel her hand slipping over mine. Encouraged, I spit the next words out of my mouth before they have a chance to poison me. "He was Russian. Bratva. Some enemy of Santiago's who decided to break me on his quest to breaking him. They used me up. Sold me. But Joseph tracked me down to Amsterdam. He never gave up on me. He freed me from a place that was worse than hell, and that's something I..."

Her hand tightens painfully, before pulling away. "What was this man's name?"

"Does it matter?" I open my eyes to find her unusually still. There's a raw violence shadowing her expression.

Just like Santiago.

"He's dead now anyway."

"His name, *parcera*."

I shiver.

"Sevastien Petrov."

The widening of her dark eyes is unmistakable. I see it all— the shock, the pain—before her composure slams shut on her secrets like a pair of French shutters in a storm.

Recognition.

But that's impossible.

My heart starts thudding painfully. "Vi, did you know—?"

"No." Her answer is final, leaving no room for contradiction.

Instinct. *She's lying.*

She reaches across the table to cover my hand again. "I've never heard of him, but I'm glad he's dead. If he wasn't, I would have tracked him down myself. Did Santiago—?"

I shake my head. "Petrov died in jail. Probably on his orders. He hurt Eve years ago, and your uncle isn't one for letting go of stuff like that without serious consequences."

"Did he…hurt you badly?"

"Yes."

There's another flare. It's briefer this time, but just as revealing. And then she's nodding, like she fully expected me to say this.

Nothing weird there, Anna. Human traffickers aren't known for their civility and kindness.

"*Hijueputa.*" *Fuck,* she curses, pulling a vibrating iPhone out of her back pocket. She hovers it under the table, just out of sight, and flicks the home screen up.

"How the hell did you manage to smuggle that in?" I hiss.

"Shush, I need to read this."

Intrigued, I lean across the table and catch a glimpse of a three-digit number before she's yanking it out of view.

154

"What's that?" I ask, sinking back down into my chair.

"The code to the safety vault here," she says, without missing a beat. "I'm organizing a heist. Wanna join?"

More lies.

"I'm good, thanks."

"Think you can keep it a secret?"

"I'll keep yours, if you keep mine."

"Always, *parcera*." She forces another grin. Rising to her feet, she pockets the iPhone. "What time is that stupid group session again?"

I glance at the clock on the wall, not bothering to check the contempt. She doesn't belong here, and she never will. She takes her guidance these days from her uncle, a man devoid of altruism.

"Twenty minutes."

"I'll meet you there."

"Hey, where are you going?" I call out, but she's already left the cafeteria.

———

My departure time comes and goes uneventfully.

Too uneventfully…

In fact, it's non-existent.

I'm still sitting in the reception area with my bag packed and my sunglasses perched on top of my head like an insult, staring out at a whole lot of sunshine and nothing.

No message.

No voicemail.

No Joseph.

Nothing.

He better have a good explanation for this. The *tick tocks* from the clock above the front desk are starting to sound like the opening chords of a really shitty break-up song.

Do you even break up with master criminals?

I'd figured it was a lifetime deal with him. Like an arranged relationship with no get-out clauses. I've draped it around me like a comfort blanket because the thought of taking a single breath without him makes a mockery out of living.

"Has he messaged you yet?"

Vi's slumped in the willow-green chair opposite, watching me like a hawk. She's pretending to read a fashion magazine, but she hasn't moved past the contents page for thirty minutes.

"Not yet." I stare down at my newly returned cell and attempt to telepath it back to life. "You don't have to wait with me, Vi."

She grins. "Oh, I wouldn't miss it for the world."

That just pisses me off even more. She wants me to give him hell about this, but it's never going to happen. All I want to do is bring that hard body in close and take his shelter.

It's twelve fifty-five. He was meant to pick me up at midday, and my panic levels are fast approaching the red zone. If he was stuck in some meeting for bad men, he would have sent another bad man to pick me up. He'd never leave me stranded on this white island, surrounded by the rough seas of uncertainty.

That's not Joseph's style.

"I'm calling, Eve," I mutter, finding her number and lifting the device to my ear before Vi has a chance to talk me out of it.

The call rings out as well.

"Shit."

I try again. More nothing. Meanwhile, there's a commotion going on over by the front desk. Five of the team are crowding around the receptionist and talking in hushed voices. There's a fast clicking of high heels as Rina cannonballs down the hallway toward the living quarters, her frizzy brown hair flying.

I glance at Vi, who's pretending to ignore that as well.

"What's going on?"

"How the hell should I know?"

"Don't go all 'moody pop star' on me, Viviana."

"Some guy was found hanging in his room an hour ago," says Soccer Mom, leaning over the seating divide to whisper, "suicide," at me like it's an insult.

"Are you *serious*?" I'm shocked. "I've stayed here loads and nothing like this has ever happened before."

"Medics have already called it. The cops are on their way."

Cops?

An unpleasant shiver zips up and down my spine. I feel bad for the poor guy, but I'm on a wanted list myself somewhere—a girl with an old life and an old surname. Joseph definitely is. He's got his own headline and graphic, and I'm damn sure Vi's international rap sheet is nudging into the CIA and DEA's viewfinders.

Vi slaps her magazine down on the coffee table. She's clearly thinking the same as she motions me away from Soccer Mom.

"We need to go."

My heart lurches. "What if Joseph's delayed? What if he's on his way and we miss him? I can't let him turn up and be greeted by a pair of handcuffs, Vi."

"That would never happen," she scoffs. "He's a *pinche puto, motherfucker*, but he'd read the signs a mile off."

I let the insult go.

"Call Santiago. They're bound to be in contact."

She tosses her black hair away from her face. "I don't have direct access. Only *El Asesino* has that..." She stops and thinks for a moment. "I can maybe try to get a message to him some other way."

"Please," I beg. "I'm really worried, Vi."

"Don't be, he'll warn him, *parcera*." She glances over my shoulder to the front desk where more people are gathering like flies around a shit storm. "Listen, I'm due to fly out to his island this afternoon. He's organized a jet for me. It's ready and waiting at Opa-locka Airport. We can go there together. *El Asesino* can meet us there."

I hesitate.

Why the hell am I hesitating?

"We need to leave *now*, Anna," she urges. "The cops will be here at any moment. They'll be asking all kinds of questions..."

"Okay. Fine."

Grabbing my bag, I shoot a sad face at Soccer Mom. Any other form of goodbye seems wrong with a dead man down the hallway.

Following Vi out through the sliding doors, we cross the forecourt to an idling black SUV with tinted windows. It's been there for ages. I noticed it an hour ago.

Deep down, I know that this is the right decision. So why

does another shiver hit my spine when Vi ushers me into the back seat and slams the door behind us?

Why does it feel like I'm sealing my fate?

Why do the two men sitting up front in their black jackets and dark cartel-esque sunglasses make my stomach hit the soles of my dirty pink Chucks?

Chapter Eleven

ANNA

"I need to use the restroom."

We've been traveling in awkward silence for over forty minutes and the tension has gone straight to my bladder.

I watch the men exchange glances before Vi unleashes a string of vicious Spanish at them. Whatever she says has their heads jerking back to front and center. Case closed. There's only one person in charge here, but it doesn't soothe my churning stomach.

"We're ten minutes away from the Opa-locka, *parcera*. Can it wait?"

"Nope." I shuffle about in my seat to make a point.

Scowling, she taps the driver on the shoulder. "Next diner you see, Matias."

I watch her scroll through a new message on her cell. She's blatantly ignoring me again now, but I'm not so easily overlooked.

"Can I ask you something?"

"We're stopping like you wanted, okay?"

I watch her coolly for a moment. "Maybe you should swing by the restroom yourself, Viviana, and dump whatever crawled up your ass and died."

She grits her teeth but doesn't comment. I'm starting to think she has a split personality.

"Who are these men?"

"My security in the US," she mutters. "They're Santiago's."

I must be a born-again poker player because I'm learning to read her like a book. She holds your gaze when she lies, but her right-hand lightly brushes at the tangled rose tattoo on her shoulder. It's like she has ninety-nine problems, but the truth ain't one of them.

It's making me think bad thoughts as we hit post-lunchtime traffic just south of Westview. Shitty, horrible things that I'd tucked away at the back of mind and forgotten about. Like how she sold me out to that creep Alberto Fernandez on my first day in Colombia. How if my broken past hadn't compelled me to fire that gun and save us, we'd both be dead now.

I try to counteract them with a good memory, but after the last two days I'm struggling.

"Is Santiago *really* flying you out to his island?"

It blurts out of my mouth like volcanic ash, polluting the atmosphere even more.

"Why? Does it bother you?" Vi lifts her dark brows at me. "I'm leading his operation in Colombia. I'm his fucking niece, Anna...I should have been invited there weeks ago."

The car slows to a crawl as we swing into the lot of an old diner and park in a bay underneath a flapping red canvas.

"Well, you must be doing something right," I concede, sick

of fighting with her. "It's like a reverse Alcatraz. It's harder to be admitted than to escape."

She smiles, but it's not a smile that comforts me.

I don't want her near Ella.

I don't want her near Eve.

I glance away, staggered by the intensity of that thought. Our friendship used to be a living breathing animal, and now it's lying wounded on the ground somewhere.

"Hey Anna?" Her casual tone puts me on high alert as I reach for the door handle. "Can I borrow your cell?" She holds up hers with an apologetic grimace. "My, ah, battery is dead and I need to make that call we spoke about."

She's going for the liar lotto win today.

"Sure." I hand it over reluctantly. I'm not sure what the heck I was planning to do with it in the restroom, but options would have been nice. "If Joseph calls, come and get me."

She smiles that damn smile again. Her right hand brushes her shoulder.

"Of course, I will."

The diner's interior is sad and tired. There are only a couple of occupied tables, mostly truckers wearing faded baseballs caps the right way round. The yawning waitress who points me in the direction of the restroom fits the place to a "T".

The restroom itself isn't so bad. At least the walls aren't smeared with shit. *At least Vi isn't in the next stall ready to mindfuck me into unzipping a nightmare from her skintight dress.* I'm grateful for her taking charge of this situation, but I'm starting to wish we'd never met.

I'm just finishing up when the door opens. Heavy footsteps trail into the end stall, making me panic I've stumbled into the men's room by mistake. I wait a couple of moments before flushing and exiting, still fiddling with the top button on my skinny jeans which is refusing to cooperate.

If I hadn't been so distracted, I might have seen his reflection in the mirror. I might have ducked away from the dirty hand now clamped across my mouth, as that dangerous combination of blood, sweat and determination hits me like a tidal wave.

Before I can scream, he's spinning me back into the stall and kicking the door shut behind us. "Be quiet, *Luna*," he growls, his deep cadence as familiar to me as the beats of my own heart. "Don't say a word, and maybe we can get the fuck out of this diner alive."

Tears burn—part in relief, part in horror. I blink them back furiously because I never want to blur the sight of him again. His huge, masculine body is dwarfing me; I'm lost in unfathomable gray-blue eyes. I inhale all of him—from that strong stubborn jawline to the mouth that will one day tell me all of his secrets.

He looks like he's been to hell and back and bought more than the T-shirt. His handsome face is barely recognizable. It's bloody, beaten and streaked with dirt, and one eye is bruised over completely. His jeans and denim shirt are clean on, but they smell of a cheap cologne he'd never wear. I know right away that they're stolen.

We stare at each other, both breathing hard, as hurt, faith and forgiveness swirl like invisible smoke between us.

"Fuck, it's good to see you." He presses his forehead to mine. "I had to get back…I never thought…"

Gently tugging his hand away, I pull his mouth down to mine, because I can't wait any longer for something I'll never tire of.

Our lips connect, but the kiss never deepens. Instead, we stay like this. Immovable. Resuscitating each other with the simplest of touches.

This is what I was trying to convey to Vi earlier. This nearness. This fatal pull between us that fizzes my senses and detonates in my soul—a craving without a name that feels so unequivocally right.

I don't know who snaps first, but suddenly my mouth is full of him—his tongue twisting wicked shapes around mine, his fingers fisting around my blonde hair. He's demanding and violent as he purges our forty-eight-hour absence with his hands on my body.

Breaking away, he smears salt water into my cheeks with the pads of his thumbs. "No tears," he murmurs. "Not yet."

Emotion swells in my throat as I trace an outline around the ugly gash on his temple. "What the hell happened to you?"

"I survived," he says bleakly, before his expression freezes and he's slamming his hand down on my mouth again. Seconds later, the restroom door opens up.

"Anna?" Vi's voice echoes with impatience as she strides further into the room, her cowboy boots *click clacking* their frustration on the floor tiles. "We need to get going. Are you done?"

Joseph yanks us away from the locked door as her footsteps approach. He shakes his head at me, demanding nothing but trust from his expression.

I nod.

Message understood.

I trust him with my life.

Relaxing, he removes his hand to let me speak, shooting me a final warning look.

"Nearly," I croak out. "Sorry for the hold-up…Bad stomach." I wince at my crap excuse as she comes to a stop just beyond the stall door.

"We can visit a drugstore on the way," she offers.

"Yeah, sounds good."

There's a long pause. It's a three-way, silent stand-off. I watch in horror as Joseph slowly pulls out a gun from the back waistband of his jeans. *What the fuck is he doing?*

"Shall I wait?"

"Erm, not unless you want me to put you off eating freaky health food for the next hundred years."

Vi chuckles. "Okay. I'll meet you out front."

Joseph waits until we hear her speaking to the waitress outside before returning his gun to his waistband. "Well done, baby." He swipes a casual finger across my still-glistening lips that makes my pussy clench. "I'll explain everything on the way."

"You mean you're actually going to *talk* to me?"

I can't help it. It just slips out.

His jaw clenches. "You really want to do this now?"

"No, I—"

He mutes me with another savage kiss. "I love you, Anna Williams...I fucking *died* for you. That should be enough."

Survived or died? Which is it, my shadow?

"What—?"

He swallows up another reply and thrusts his hand between my legs. I moan into his mouth as he roughly cups my heat, his own response low and ravening. "We'll talk, and then we'll fuck," he states, eliminating my choice in the matter. "I need to claim this body again, *Luna*. I need to fill you up with my sin all damn night—to take you at sunset and still be fucking you at sunrise."

I'm seeing, breathing, *hearing* only him. I reach for the thick bulge at the front of his jeans and he growls, grinding his erection against my palm before shoving it away.

"We're coasting on borrowed time. We need to go."

I drag myself back to the dingy restroom. "Just tell me why we're running from her."

"We're not running from her. We're running from the men she works for until we can figure the game plan out and destroy them."

A vicious shiver rattles through me. He's so careless with his murder.

He unlocks the stall door and tucks me behind his huge frame. "My car's parked out back."

"Do you have proof about Vi?"

"Are you fucking questioning me?" He turns sharply and backs me up against the restroom wall with my jaw between his fingertips. "I had a man inside Greens who was looking out for you, Anna. He was so deep undercover—so convincing—that the therapists wanted him on an extra special dose of methadone. Care to guess where he is now?"

"Dead?" I whisper.

"Dead," he confirms.

A horrible thought spreads inside me like a rash.

"What room was he staying in, Joseph?"

He frowns "Why?"

"Tell me!"

"154."

My breath catches.

He pounces.

"You knew him?"

"I saw that number in a message on Vi's cell."

"Convinced yet?" he says bitterly.

I nod, those damn tears burning the corners of my eyes

again. *She killed him. She fucking killed him as I sat in the cafeteria next to a bowl of half-eaten granola.*

"Tip of the iceberg, *Luna*," he says, taking in my reaction. "Wait 'til you hear about all the other good stuff she's been up to."

"Did she do something to you? Is that why your face is looking like one of Santiago's torture victims'?" My anger is leaking out of me in a lava-like rage now.

"Confession time is in a motel room a couple hundred miles from here." He glances down at my side. "Where's your bag?"

"In Vi's car."

"I'll buy you another."

He's limping badly as he drags me down a dark hallway toward a side door. I barely have time to taste the sunshine before he's pushing me into the driver's seat of a dark blue Toyota Corolla that's as banged up as he is.

He falls into the seat beside me with a grimace. "Drive."

The pain and urgency in his voice makes me fumble with the keys. I hit pay-dirt on the third attempt. Sliding the car into reverse, we're speeding out of the parking lot with Vi's black SUV still stationary in my rearview mirror.

She'll be pissed about this, but it's nothing compared to the way I'm feeling right now. She knew Joseph was my fucking heart and soul, but she hurt him anyway.

"Slow down, Anna."

"Shit, sorry." I lift my foot from the accelerator. "Pure rage was driving there for a second."

"Keep to the limit." He takes a swig from a small, brown script bottle, swallowing way more white pills than he ought to. "We don't want any attention."

"Is this vehicle hot?"

"Boiling." He's slumped in his seat, his eyelids drifting. There's a spreading patch of crimson across his left thigh. "But Roman took care of it."

Who the hell is Roman?

"Where are we heading?"

"I'll know when we get there."

"That's kind of vague, don't you think? I figured you were the master of the exit plan."

The corners of his mouth twitch. "As long as there's a church and a priest, I'm good."

My foot slips again and the car hits a rapid eighty. "You want us to get *married* today?"

"Slow down," he barks. "Besides, it shouldn't be such a shock."

"You asked me to marry you four days ago!"

"Men like me don't have the luxury of forward thinking, Anna. We stick to the present."

"Do I get a choice in this?"

"Nope."

"You arrogant maniac." I suck in a ragged breath. "Those pills must be really messing with your brain, Joseph Grayson. You can hardly stand. How the hell are you going to walk down an aisle?"

"I'll crawl if I have to." He slides a large palm up the inside of my leg, his voice dropping to a seductive octave that's instantly dirtying up my thoughts. "Hands and knees, baby...all the way to the ultimate prize."

He's reached the top of my thigh now and I nearly run a red light. I'm still wet and needy from earlier.

"Why now?"

"Why not?"

"Hmmm, let me see…." I lift a shaky hand from the steering wheel to count off the numerous reasons. "We have a bunch of defecting Colombians after us. You've said about ten sentences to me our entire relationship—most of them in bed. And your weird proposal doesn't exactly fill me with confidence over the forthcoming state of our marriage."

"I really want to taste your pussy right now." The car jerks forward again. "Maybe your asshole, too." He's eyeing me like I'm a condemned man's last meal.

"Stop trying to change the subject," I splutter, but I'm squirming in my seat. "I'm still mad at you. You jammed a ring on my finger and then ignored me for two days."

He stares straight ahead, his jaw ticking.

"Care to explain?"

"No. Did you play with yourself in rehab?"

"You're kidding, right?" I shoot him the mother of all WTF side-eyes. "You mean in between all the intense meditation and the hot stone yoga classes?"

"That's a 'yes'."

"That's a 'hell no'."

He starts toying with the button to my skinny jeans. "Touch yourself again without my permission and we have ourselves a problem."

The button's toast.

The zipper follows.

"For a sick man, you have serious priority issues," I mutter, trying to push his hand away, but it's not going anywhere. "Were you just guzzling Viagra?"

He laughs, a rich unfamiliar sound that flattens the last of my defenses. "Darlin', I couldn't get any harder for you if I tried."

"Can we maybe deal with your alpha urges once you're

feeling better?"

"My 'alpha urges' are doing just fine." His southern drawl is even more languid when he's high on whatever the hell he's taken. "What color panties are you wearing?" He tugs hard at the lace trim and cocks his head to see. "Black. Nice."

"Same color as your Dodge."

"Same color as my soul. Shall we stain it further?" His fingers slip inside the material and rest tantalizingly close to my throbbing clit.

"Do you *want* me to crash this car?" I say helplessly.

"No more crashes this week, thanks." His fingers disappear, and I'm left grieving their loss. "Make yourself come," he orders.

Yes please.

"No way!"

"I wasn't asking."

I hate my sharp, shallow breaths when he's all bossy and macho like this. I may as well be naked on a bed with my legs spread. He's pushing all my lust triggers right now.

"One more word out of you, *El Asesino*, and I'm pulling over and screwing you to sleep, just to get some peace and quiet."

He barks out another laugh. "Well, you know my dick is hard and waiting."

"*You know* that this is officially the longest conversation we've ever had."

He muses on this for a moment. "Maybe some of the old ways hit the ground and burst into flames around ten p.m. yesterday evening."

I have no comeback for this.

What I do have is a spark of hope.

We leave Miami and follow the US-27, up through the lush, rolling core of the Sunshine State. Eve and I took a road-trip this way once, long before shadows and devils corrupted our bodies and minds.

Joseph's finished talking about sex and epiphanies. He passed out sometime between South Bay and Clewiston. His huge, masculine frame is crumpled up against the passenger door, with his head resting on the window.

He looks peaceful this way; less enigmatic. I wonder if he dreams in bricks and mortar, or if his walls come tumbling down like everyone else's. *Does he see his wife? His son?* He's never mentioned them to me, but I know they exist. The same way I know that he was a war hero with Santiago in Afghanistan before he switched to the wrong side of the law.

These are all sound bites I've picked up from others. Different pieces of the same jigsaw puzzle that only he can slot together for me.

Taking a sip from a warm bottle of water, I run a hand across my aching neck muscles. The sun is like a high school bitch today and I'm constantly in her glare. My T-shirt is clinging to my spine and my bra straps are cutting angry red marks into my shoulders. Still, I'm here. I'm living. I'm not chained in a basement or caged in a sick display for a trafficker who dealt in human misery.

Three hours pass, and then four.

Seconds feel like days.

Minutes, centuries.

I'm dreaming of a hot shower and a cheeseburger and fries, which has me flicking the bird at McDonald's signs and wondering how I find myself in these crazy situations in the first place. I'm half-tempted to steal a cigarette from a crushed pack I found in the glove box and set fire to an old habit, but I stop myself just in time. One false move, one misstep, and I'll be tumbling back to a place that doesn't deserve me.

I'm better than that now.

He makes me better.

The radio keeps looping Taylor and Ariana, and it's driving me nuts. I switch it on and off so many times my hand is getting its own sweat on.

I think about Eve and Ella. Joseph must have told Dante the truth about Vi by now. There's no way she'll be setting foot on his island, but my best friend and her daughter are still vulnerable in a universe where the innocent suffer first. I don't know what Joseph's plan is, but we need to return to the island as soon as possible.

"Pull off here." His voice is thick with sleep as he rights himself with a grimace. He tips another couple of those white pills into his mouth and coughs them down without water. "Do it, Anna. Next exit."

We're somewhere close to Haines City on the outskirts of Orlando. After hitting a couple of minor towns, we see a roadside motel with vacancies.

"There," he says, pointing.

Pulling into the parking lot, I kill the engine. "I'll go get us a room key."

I'm reaching for the handle when I feel a heavy hand on my arm.

"I'll do it."

I lift my brows in dispute. "Since I'm the only one of us who *doesn't* look like a filthy fugitive, I'll go."

He glares at me, and then he's grabbing me by the neck and pulling me close. "You have no fucking idea how filthy I really am," he murmurs, his sexy-as-heck declaration warming my already overheated skin. "But I'm in the mood to show you."

"You can start with a bath," I whisper, feeling the hunger and possession in his touch and fighting the urge to climb him like a tree.

"Pay cash. Be nice." He lets go of me, frowning as he hands over a wad of tens and twenties. He hates this dynamic. There's only one person in the world he takes orders from, and it's not me.

"I'm always nice," I say, exiting the Corolla with a smile. "Are you going to watch my ass as I walk away?"

He leans across the transmission to smolder me up with another look. "Damn straight I'll be watching. That ass is my dinner."

Summer honeysuckle grows thick around my fears.

"At least your sleep didn't shrink your hard-on."

"If you're longer than five minutes in reception, you'll be finding out either way."

Our room is a bad seventies pastiche with a twist of neglect. There's way too much wood paneling and the cream fringing around the lampshades is patchy and fraying. It's also cold-as-hell, which is a good sign that the air conditioning works.

Joseph is limping worse than ever, but I'm too scared to ask why. As we cross the threshold, he's carrying a large bottle of vodka and a medikit he took from the trunk. Kicking the door shut and fixing the bolt, he pulls the curtains together and chucks everything onto the nightstand.

"Take a shower," he orders, brushing my temple with a kiss.

I watch him pick up the empty ice bucket and slam it down next to his supplies. His gun follows.

"Let me help you."

"No need. I can loop stitches like a pro."

"Do you need to see a doctor?"

Stupid question. Of course, he needs to see a damn doctor.

He fights a smirk as he unbuckles his belt. "Thanks for the offer, Nurse Williams, but I got stitched up pretty good yesterday. This is a clean-up job. I busted one in the diner earlier."

Some balled up emotion inside me expands and fills. I walk over to him and throw my arms around his neck—wanting his sweat, his strength, his mysteries.

"Don't die," I mutter, pressing the side of my face into his chest, scratching my cheek on his shirt buttons. I hide my vulnerability well, but when he busted the lock to my first cage, he busted them all. Since my mother died when I was sixteen, I've pretty much been on my own. I only had Eve, until I had him.

He stills, and then his arms come crashing around me. "Not today. Not yesterday. I'm here for as long as you want me."

"I think I want you forever." I reach for his belt to finish the job, unhooking his top button and unzipping his jeans. "What about you?" I don't look at him as I say it. His face is a mask, and I'd hate for this to be the first time it cracks. "Is this marriage what you really want?"

Wrapping his fist around the ends of my blonde hair, he tugs my head back to scorch me with his gaze. "The things I want, *Luna*?" he says with a growl. "They're things that a man like me should *never* want."

"Like what?" I whisper.

"Like you sharing my name, my life, a house on a fucking hill with 'The Graysons' stamped all over the mail box."

What about your child growing inside of me?

As if sensing my question, he drops my hair and steps away to remove his jeans. His movements are slow and deliberate, and soon I see why. There's a deep laceration on his thigh. It's at least six inches long, with splashes of dried blood and purple and yellow staining the edges. Neat stitches have been sewn into the swollen skin, except on one small section where the wound is a gaping hole of tissue.

He doesn't need a doctor. He needs a hospital

"Look away if you're squeamish." He sits down on the side of the bed and unscrews the bottle of vodka. Taking several deep swigs, he pours the rest over his thigh. "*Motherfucker,*" he hisses, scrunching up his face in pain.

I watch the streams converge and drip down his leg before I'm snatching the bottle out of his hand. "Here, let me do it."

Running into the bathroom, I grab a couple of clean towels, and then I kneel down in front of him to mop up the worst of the spillage. Next, I pour a generous amount of vodka onto one of the towels. Trying not to throw up, I dab at the wound, cleaning it as much as I can.

"How are you not flinching?"

"This isn't my first pain rodeo, sweetheart," he says through gritted teeth as he shrugs out of his shirt, temporarily distracting me.

"Eve said she saw you take a bullet when Dante's brother kidnapped her. Then there's the time Vi shot you—exactly how much lead is in your body, Joseph Grayson?"

When he doesn't answer, I graze a trail across his sun-kissed skin, noting the fierce tribal tattoos on his chest, the numerous bullet hole scars, the vicious white welt across his stomach…it's a map of endurance for a road less traveled through a dark and dangerous land.

"How did you get that?" I point to a jagged scar just above his hip.

"Shrapnel. Afghanistan."

"Was it a bomb?"

"A bomb that caused a road crash."

"What happened?"

"They held us captive for thirty days."

My head jerks up. "You and Santiago?"

He grabs the half-empty bottle of vodka from the floor and nods. I watch him take another couple of swigs. He's staring straight at the wall, like he's fighting memories in his head.

"Did they torture you?"

"Well, we didn't sit around all day playing cards with one another."

There's a note of bitterness in his voice. And pain. *So much pain.*

"Is that when he asked you to work for him?" I remove the bloody towel from his thigh and examine the wound. It's smoother now. Neater. All the crustiness has gone.

There's a pause. "That came afterward."

Sitting back on my haunches, I reach for the medikit.

"You sure you want to do this, Anna?" His gray-blues are burning a hole in my face again.

"Something tells me this won't be the only time I see you shot, stabbed or roughed up." I say wearily. "Just tell me what to do."

Tell me how to heal you, Joseph Grayson.

"There's no needle driver in the kit. You'll have to thread it yourself."

"Roots suturing. Awesome." I hold out my hands and he splashes neat vodka all over them. "Who did this?" I ask, leaning over the wound to inspect the stitches. "It's really tidy."

"A Good Samaritan."

I glance up through my eyelashes at him. "Male or female."

His lips quirk. "Male. And he wasn't half as tempting with his face so close to my cock. Just pull the wound together and keep the suture about half a centimeter from the edge." He straightens up and brings the bottle to his mouth again. "Now excuse me while I drink the rest of this vodka and pass the fuck out."

"What's the worst pain you've ever been in?" I hover the needle over the wound, wanting something—*anything*—from his past before I start.

"Seeing you in a cage in Amsterdam." There's a pause. "The death of my son."

I freeze, my heart hammering. There's a sloshing sound as more vodka is tipped down his throat. It's a liquored-up full-stop to the first line in his story.

"Three stitches should do it, Anna," he murmurs.

Three stitches and the truth.

Chapter Twelve

JOSEPH

Past

I sat on the steps of the front porch until they came for me. I sat all day and all night, watching the crows circle above Pa's dead body in the doorway of our barn.

I hoped that he was hurting real bad wherever he was in hell right now. I wanted to know that when the crows got bold and greedy and started feasting on his eyeballs, he felt every one of their nasty, stinking pecks.

He'd blasted a hole the size of my head in the screen door, so the flies were swarming thick and black over Ma's body in the hallway. I pretended the rank smell was coming from the dead chickens littered all over the drive. Pa didn't just try and take out his entire family that day. He took out all of our livestock, too. He spared no one except me, and even that was a fluke.

Eventually this place would become known to the locals as Dead Animal Farm. Teenage kids would dare each other to smoke weed in the ashes of my past. That night it was a graveyard, and

I was a twelve-year-old kid working the all-hour shift.

I didn't have the courage to peek inside and see Cash's body. I didn't want to accept that hurt just yet, so I figured it was best if I stayed put and didn't move.

It was best not to move.

And I didn't, not even when the temperature dropped, and my shorts and T-shirt were as useful as brown paper packaging left out in the rain.

For twenty hours it was just me and the tin soldier I'd been playing with in the barn earlier that day. I'd pulled it out of my pocket and balanced it carefully on one bare knee. I couldn't stop staring at it. He was small, green and mean-looking, and he wore the same expression on his face that he always did.

Nothing affected him.

Not even this hurt.

At some point, sitting there, I became that tin soldier. I made myself swallow my feelings. I adopted the same remote expression that would see me in and out of kid therapist rooms for the next four years. Tin soldiers were supposed to fall down and get back up again. They were caught in a loop of indestructibility, until you lost them or some stupid high school bully like Brett Chambers stole them out of your locker.

I was the only survivor of Pa's madness, and I was going to close myself off from thieves and loss so I'd never feel this way again…

Time moved.

The day ended.

When the sun set, I saw blood.

When the sun rose, I saw violence.

In between, the stars were scattered bullets. But the moon was different. She looked like the hole in the barn door that Pa

122

Chapter Thirteen

JOSEPH

I wake to light and dark, and a head swimming in cheap liquor. The first thing I do is reach for the loaded gun on the nightstand. Bad move. The pain in my leg hits me like a bullet to the balls.

"Holy fuck!"

Hissing out more bad words through clenched teeth, I grab the small bottle of Vicodin and knock a handful back—washing them down with the lukewarm remnants of the vodka. The pain is red, brutal and blinding. It's taking everything I have not to throw up.

Lying back with a groan, and a head like lead, I close my eyes and try to get a handle on the sickness. It's a waiting game now until the Vicodin kicks in and I can resume some kind of functional normality.

It could have been worse.

Spine crushed. Skull smashed. Dismembered.

Dead.

I was lucky. So goddamn lucky.

I'm indestructible, remember?

The dying jet dodged the Blue Ridge by a hair's breadth. It smacked down in the middle of a field in a spluttering fireball that consumed the back end, but not the cockpit. I caught a break when I skimmed a forest, losing both wings. I cheated gravity, and then the cabin cracked in half. When I finally landed in three feet of cow's shit, it was the joystick that made ground beef out of my leg.

It's night outside. Anna's gone, but she's not long left the room. I can still smell her flowery scent and her fucking moonshine. I'm not worried about her. She's a smart woman, I know she won't have gone far. Still, I count the minutes regardless. Time is a fucking charade when she's not in my arms.

It's just me, my growing painkiller addiction, and the steady rumble of cars on the road outside.

No ghosts.

No Cash.

He hasn't reappeared since the plane crash, and I'm hoping it killed him off for good.

I'm just sinking into the mattress in a happy chemical haze when the lock on the door starts jiggling. Anna spills into the room, her river-deeps glazed with exhaustion and her messy topknot scattering tired gold strands all over her cheeks and forehead.

She looks whole.

She looks perfect.

Her gaze falls on me and her face lights up.

"You're awake."

"You're fuckable." I drag myself into a seated position with a grimace. "Two rights make for a wicked time."

She grins. *I've never seen her grin before.* It spins her gold into something even more precious. "Extra cheesy, I like it. It goes nicely with this…" She produces the pizza box from behind her back with a theatrical, "Ta-dah!"

Surprisingly, the smell doesn't make me want to gag. In fact, I'm fucking starving. When I was pulled from the plane wreckage, my thoughts were singular and desperate. I was so hell-bent on reaching Miami that minor shit like eating and drinking were forgotten about. Santiago doesn't even know one of his jet's went down in flames yet.

"What's the time?" I ask.

"Nine-ish. You passed out about three hours ago." She kicks off her Chucks and walks her long legs over to me. Despite the hurt, the meds and the hangover from hell, my cock still pays attention. "I know you said we're not the kind of couple that has dates and stuff, but I figured we could do it our way."

"The best way."

"The *only* way." She chucks the steaming box down next to me and curls up at the foot of the bed. Leaning over, she flicks the lid up. "Hope you like margherita."

"Everyone likes margherita."

"Except the tuna topper anarchists."

"They're not fucking human anyway." Taking her arm, I haul her up the bed and settle her astride my waist.

"Careful! You're leg—"

"Is soaked in Vicodin." I tug at her hairband, setting a golden waterfall free. The way it tumbles around her face, framing perfection, crushes something inside my chest.

Her T-shirt follows, and I'm left palming her generous breasts through a veil of black lace.

"God, that feels so good." She tips her head back and moans softly as I roll her hardening nipples between my thumb and finger, torturing my cock just as much as I'm torturing her.

"Lose the jeans," I say huskily, tugging at the top button to help her along.

When she returns to my lap, she's dressed like a goddess in her black bra and panties. It takes all my willpower not to rip them to shreds. Taking her face between my hands, I'm just as turned on by the delicate jaw beneath my fingertips and the trust she gives me.

I could so easily break her into pieces again.

"I thought we were going to talk first?" she chides softly, shuddering as I drop a hand to tease her clit with my thumb.

"The schedule got rearranged."

I lean forward until my chest is pressed flush against her breasts, and then I hold her there, my palms flat to her shoulder blades until I can feel our hearts beating for and against each other.

Seeking out her lips, I taste her sweetness and light. She's golden, inside and out. And I tarnished it. *I fucking tarnished it.*

"I never asked you for your permission the other night," I murmur against her mouth. "But I'm damn well asking for it now."

She pulls away, her face creasing in confusion.

"I vowed in Colombia I wouldn't be like those animals—"

Realization dawns and she stares at me in horror. "How could you even *think* that?"

"I know what I am, sweetheart." Ignoring the agony in my leg, I tip her onto the mattress and follow her down. Pushing her legs wider apart, I settle in between them, indulging in the sensation of her wet heat against my straining cock.

"Joseph, listen to me." This time it's my jaw resting between her hands. "You and I, we own our bad. It's what you taught me, remember? We own the highs and the lows, the kills and the blood-stained victories, but we still have choices. You've crossed some dark and dangerous lines, but you will *never* be like those men...*you will never be like those men to me.*"

"Anna—"

Reaching between us, she slides the crotch of her panties to one side and widens her legs. "This isn't an invitation," she whispers. "It's a request and a declaration. Fuck me clean. Fuck me dirty. Fuck every lunar phase out of me. This is my lifetime supply of permissions."

Grinding against her hand, I growl my approval. "Tomorrow we're finding a church and a priest..." Then, lining my cock up, I drive inside her as she arches into me with a strangled groan. I nearly lose my shit when I feel how tight and wet she is.

"We don't need them," she whimpers as I start to move, making each thrust so slow and so savage I'm stealing the air from her lungs. "We don't need a piece of paper to tell us what we already know."

"You deserve it. You deserve everything."

"I take you..."

Thrust.

"I take all of you..."

Thrust.

"Forever and always."

Thrust.

Her words make a home in the ruins of my heart. She's right. She became my wife the moment she fell into my world.

"This bed is our ceremony." I shift my hips to fuck her deeper. "The moment you start milking my cock—the moment you scream my name—you're mine until death comes for the both of us."

Her walls are trembling, so I pick up the pace. Soon, I'm pounding into her so hard, her breasts break free from her bra.

"You saw me," she gasps out

"I'd set this world on fire for you."

"You turn for me."

"I'd die for you."

She reaches paradise first, tipping her head back and screwing up her eyes as her inner muscles clamp down on my cock.

A beat later, I'm coming so damn hard I see stars.

Her legs fall from my waist in exhaustion as I lean over to give her one last lingering kiss.

"That's one way to do it," I say, nuzzling into her neck

"Our way," she says, and I feel her smile against my cheekbone.

"Welcome home, Mrs. Grayson," I say, smoothing her messy hair away from her face.

"Welcome back, Mr. Grayson," she replies softly. I open my mouth to ask her what she means when she adds, "Please can we return to the devil's island now? I'd like to make an announcement."

"Sure. Once I figure out a way to get there." Sliding out of her pussy, I roll onto my back, gritting my jaw as the pain comes rushing in again.

She shimmies onto her side to watch me. "Can't we just take Santiago's plane and jet-stream our way to freedom?"

"Not unless you have a secret degree in aviation engineering." I reach for the crumpled pack of cigarettes and matches on the nightstand, sparking up a Red right where I'm lying. Taking a drag, I flick the dead match onto the floor. "His jet's somewhere in Virginia."

"Then fly it here."

"Not when the wings are lying in a forest in North Carolina."

I take another drag and wait for my words to register.

"Did it *crash*?" She sits up slowly, her voice a shocked whisper. "Don't you dare lie to me, Joseph."

"I never lie to you."

"Oh my God…"

I give her a moment to take it in as I smoke nicotine until I'm sucking fingers and air. Eventually, she lets out a breath— sounding like she's been holding it in forever.

"How are you still *alive*?"

"Luck."

"It's more than that, don't you think? Shit, did Viviana…?" Her voice rises to a horrified pitch.

"She's connected."

Anna shuts her eyes as I fire the final bullet into their dying friendship. "How did Santiago take it?"

I don't answer until I've chain-smoked my way onto another cigarette. "He doesn't know."

"He doesn't *know*?"

It's like I dropped a second bomb.

Jumping off the bed, she tugs up her bra cups. "You have to call him, Joseph. Right now! He needs to know!"

I narrow my eyes at her reaction, thinking stupid things. Crazy things.

"He has three other jets," I say coldly. "I doubt he has a favorite."

"Why didn't you call him?" She's acting hysterical now, spinning around in circles and picking up random items of clothes and chucking them at me.

"I didn't realize you cared so much about what he thought."
I swing my legs off the bed with a groan. I can feel another page
turning in this fucked-up storybook of a week, and I'm going to
need a ton more liquor to deal with it.

"It's not that…" She pauses in front of me, her delicate
features pinched and scared. "Viviana told me she was flying
out to the island today. She would have arrived by now. If she's
capable of bringing a plane down, she's capable of anything."
She starts pulling on her T-shirt. "I have to warn Eve!"

Fuck.

"Calm down." I catch her as she starts spinning around the
room again, and pull her in close. "I'll find a way to contact him."

But she's rigid and dubious in my arms.

"I had to get to you, Anna. Nothing else mattered more than
that."

"Why is she doing this?" Her voice cracks. *Betrayal is the
cruelest revelation of all.* "I thought I knew her. I thought after
Colombia…"

"No one really knows anyone, *Luna.*"

I think of a night full of angry stars. A boy. A tin soldier.

Letting go, I dress as quickly as my fucked-up leg will
allow. "We need a cell and a laptop."

Grabbing my gun, I'm limping out of the door before she's
asking the obvious question.

Chapter Fourteen

EVE

The griping pain takes another vicious swipe at my stomach. I clutch at the edges of the white dresser with both hands as I wait for it to pass, imagining a baseball bat hitting the hurt away with a perfect arc of a swing.

Damn. That one was even stronger than the last.

"If you're going to give birth on the fucking floor, can you at least take it into the bathroom?" Dante's watching me from the doorway, arms folded. Face impassive. "I'd prefer to keep this bedroom sacred for other things."

"*Sacred*?" I pause my panting to consider his stupidly inappropriate word. "Nothing that ever happens in this room is *sacred*, Dante."

"It is at the start of the night, my angel. It sets a precedence to corrupt and defile."

"Don't be such an asshole!"

I know it's only frustration that's making him act this way.

For a man who gets off on control, this situation is his worst nightmare. He manipulates my body to accept his darkest, filthiest desires. What he can't do, however, is manipulate the same body to give me my perfect, tick box birth plan.

I can't excuse these contractions away as Braxton Hicks anymore. My doctors were right. This baby is coming two weeks early, whether I like it or not.

"You only get to insult me in labor, my angel." He saunters over to plant a dangerously warm kiss on the back of my neck. "After that, it comes with a harsh punishment."

"I don't want to talk about sex," I mutter as he slides a large hand across my fit-to-bursting stomach, pulling me back into his heat and his hardness. The pain is easing, but it's a temporary relief. That wave will be overwhelming me again soon enough. "And if you think I'm letting you anywhere near me after this birth, you're very much mistaken."

He chuckles into my hair. "I'll hold you to that, *mi alma*."

"Are you still timing my contradictions?"

"No, I've been distracted by other things."

Jesus Christ. I love Dante with all my heart, but I wish Anna was back from Miami to help me with this. She's going to be so upset. She missed Ella's birth, and I know she really wanted to be here for Thalia's.

Thalia.

I'm about to give birth to a new baby girl.

Shudders of panic start to intermingle with the pain and exhilaration.

"Can I get you anything?"

"Some alone time?" I say with a sigh. "Preferably *without* my husband?"

"One more strike and you're out, Eve."

"Don't you have someone awful to torture? If not, I suggest you go take a long walk off a short pier."

"Orders *as well* as rudeness?" He pulls me even closer, not to hurt but to caution. "Careful, Eve...I'm keeping a note of all of this."

"Be nice," I grit out. "Or I'm going downstairs and having this baby on your desk."

"Didn't we conceive her there anyway?"

"No idea. You've screwed me a billion times on every available surface in this house. I wouldn't mind a new location."

"You're not leaving this island, *mi alma*," he murmurs, knowing exactly what I'm hinting at. "You're too much of a target."

It's the usual argument. I rattle the bars of my cell and he brushes my fingers away. I'm aching to see the world again, and he refuses to entertain the idea.

"That's always your response for everything, isn't it? Oh *shit*." Another contraction swamps my body, pitching me forward against the dresser again.

He holds me close until it passes, riding out the pain with me—whispering sweet Spanish endearments that contradict the type of man the underworld thinks he is. The one they all fear. The myth. The legend...

I know what hides beneath his layers of darkness. I found the source of his pain. I embraced it and I made it my own, and then I brought it to his surfaces, and we grieved it together.

Only I know the real Dante Santiago.

Only I know about his regret.

He never knew his eldest daughter, Isabella, and it tears him up inside. It colors every decision, every kill. Her remains are buried on the north side of this island and he visits her grave often. In the last few weeks, he's gone there every day. There are reasons for this, and I'm still waiting for him to share them with me.

"How far away are the doctors?" I whisper.

"Thirty minutes. They're in the air. If their expensive Lopez Loafers aren't climbing those stairs in the next hour, I'll be returning them to the mainland, along with their dismembered feet."

He says it lightly, but his nonchalance belies the truth. He takes a sadistic pride in carrying out *all* of the threats he issues.

Please God, don't let there be any more delays. I need those damn doctors here with me. I'm brave, but I'm not that brave.

When the pain eases off, I gently push his hands away. "I'm going to give Ella a quick kiss before her nap time."

"Hmm."

He's busy checking a message on his cell. He raises the device to his ear as I step into the hallway. "Bring her up to the house," he orders, following me out. "We'll talk in my office… wait, Eve."

I turn, and he catches my mouth in an all-consuming kiss. "This won't take long, my angel," he says, muffling the cell against his chest as he runs a cool finger down my cheek. "I'll be back before you know it."

"With the doctors," I say pointedly.

"Or dismembered feet," he confirms grimly.

Another contraction creeps up on me as I reach the nursery door. Not wanting to scare Ella, I huff and puff it out in the hallway before entering the room.

My firstborn is sitting on the nursery rug, chewing on a toy giraffe. Our nanny, Sofía, has already changed her into a pair of clean PJs with bright yellow butterflies. The lights have been dimmed, and the curtains are closed. It's a warm, safe cocoon that makes me feel exhausted suddenly.."El-*la*," I call out softly.

Her head turns at the sound of my voice, her black curls bouncing. She drops her giraffe in delight. Squeaking impatiently, she holds up her arms for immediate attention.

This is another reason why I love my dogmatic, murdering bastard of a husband I reflect, scooping her up into a bear hug. He gives me the most beautiful children in the world.

"How are you, señora?" asks Sofía, testing the temperature of Ella's milk on the inside of her wrist. "How far apart are they?"

"No idea because Dante forgot to count."

She laughs and guides me to the nursery chair. "That man... always distracted by your beautiful mama," she coos at Ella. "Here, let me take her."

Giving Ella the squishiest, mushiest kiss, I reluctantly hand her over. "Sweet dreams," I whisper, overcome by that wicked tiredness again. The contractions seem to have lessened. All they've brought me this time is chronic back ache and fatigue.

"Close your eyes too, señora," instructs Sofía, tucking Ella into her bed and passing her the sippy cup of warm milk. "You have a long night ahead of you. I have this covered."

My thoughts drift to the soothing sounds of Sofía's voice. She's reading a silly children's story about two tiger cubs in the jungle who won't stop fighting, one called Devious, and the other, Trouble. I never get to hear the parable's message because I'm fast asleep in minutes.

————

I haven't dreamed about my father in years.

I haven't allowed it.

In truth, he doesn't deserve it.

I didn't shed a single tear when his body was found mutilated in a ditch outside of Houston. To me, he'd died the day he admitted trafficking my six-year-old innocence to a known Russian pedophile called Sevastien Petrov. In return, he'd stuffed his empty soul with money, and bought himself a one-way ticket to the place where pure evil burns the longest.

My mind refuses to recall a single moment of my time in Russia, and for that I'm thankful. There are barriers that not even the greatest therapy can breach, and I'm happy to fortify them every day with contentment and love.

I sometimes wish I could block out every part of my childhood in the same way. Memories come with feelings that can trip you up and hurt you when you least expect it, and I have a ton of those.

One night, not long after Dante broke the news about my father to me, I stood on the beach below the house and threw a single white rose into the water. It wasn't to signify forgiveness. It was too late for that. Instead, I was mourning the moments in my past that were now stained with his guilt.

The birthdays.

The Christmases.

The day I graduated from college.

He was there for all of them.

I see that rose again now. My father is holding it out to me, but his face is all blurry. One half of the rose is dripping crimson blood and the other is charred-gray and wilted, like two halves that will never be whole.

When he finally speaks, it's with an accent from my nightmares.

"*My brother's whore, I presume?*"

I know those words.

I know that memory

Before I can piece it together, I'm back in the safe, dark bubble of Ella's nursery. My little girl is still asleep. Her head is turned to the side, flattening her black curls. Her brown bear is tucked under her chin.

"She's cute," says a voice suddenly.

My breath catches sharply in surprise. There's a woman standing in the doorway. She's silhouetted by the mid-afternoon sun so I can't see her face, but I can tell she's beautiful. It's there in her stance—exuding the kind of confidence I'd kill for. The rest of her is tall and slender, with curves in all the right places.

"C-can I help you?"

Am I dreaming still?

"I came to say 'hi'."

Her voice is laced with an accent that's heavier than Dante's.

I go to pull myself up from Ella's nursery chair when a fresh contraction hits me like a runaway train. "Ooh crap," I wail, doubling over.

"You okay?"

It's a reflex response. *She doesn't give a damn.* She hasn't budged from the doorway, and there's an icy detachment to her voice that reminds me so much of—

"Shit!" Instead of easing up, the contraction seems to be gathering momentum. "Where's Dante?" I manage to gasp out.

"On the phone in his office."

"To my doctors?"

"No idea."

Great. I'm stuck in labor with a stonewalling stranger.

"Can you call him, please?"

"Yeah, I will in a minute. It's not like you're crowning or

anything." She glances at Ella again and my Mama tiger instinct kicks in harder than any labor pain.

I want her away from Ella.

I want her gone from that doorway.

I go to stand, to slam the door on her, and then a second contraction is crashing down on top of the first one with no let-up.

Oh, boy.

I drop back into the chair because standing is impossible now.

"Sofía…"

"Is that the maid?" She runs her fingers up and down the door frame. "Yeah, she's making me lunch. I had a really shitty breakfast and I'm starving."

Looking up at her through blurred vision, I take in her brown cowboy boots, tight black jeans and a white T-shirt with the tails of some intricate green and red tattoo peeking out of one capped sleeve. Her skin is tan, and her loose hair covers her shoulders in wavy black silk. She's hot as hell, but she's burning up with trouble.

I know a threat when I see one. Not to my marriage, but to the life we've carefully constructed.

Why has Dante allowed her into our home?

I can't stop thinking about the two-tone rose from my dream as her head turns toward Ella again.

"Let my daughter sleep," I beg her.

"She's adorable."

She's mine.

Something lurches inside me, like a ship going down in a storm. A beat later, warm liquid is gushing down my legs and onto Ella's rug, and the urge to push is so overwhelming I let out a scream.

"Eve!"

Dante's voice comes bellowing up the stairs, followed by the sound of heavy footsteps.

The woman retreats back into the hallway, leaving me with a spicy scent that turns my stomach to thorns. "It's going to be okay, Eve," she croons, blasting me with her insincerity, but I'm too focused on not giving birth in front of my daughter to care anymore. "Her waters just broke," she informs Dante as he strides past her and into the room with a face like homicide.

"Ella," I croak.

Our daughter has woken up from all the commotion and is wailing noisily.

Scooping her out of bed, he holds her close to his chest, and murmurs more of those Spanish endearments—moving so naturally, he's contradicting his dark legend again. She responds, as she always does in his arms, with giggles and smiles. His hands can kill and soothe in equal measure.

The stranger can't take her eyes off him. It's not lust, though, I realize. It's shock. As for Dante, he doesn't seem in the least bit surprised to find her here.

"*Oh Dios mío!*" Sofía cries, rushing onto the scene, still wiping her hands on the front of her blue dress.

"Take Ella downstairs," he orders, and I moan again, this time in relief.

"I'll go get some towels or something," says the stranger, drifting away.

"Bed," he snaps at me, his strong arms lifting me up. I'm trying so hard not to push, I've bitten through my bottom lip.

"Who the hell is that woman?" I gasp out, as he helps me onto the mattress.

"Lie back."

"I'm serious—"

"Try expending some of that fucking curiosity on this birth. You're going to need it."

His flat cadence fills my chest with panic. There's no light in his expression. No sweet promises of painful retribution if I misbehave.

"Where's Whit? Where's the Obs. guy?" I cry, balling my fists around the white bedsheets as he grabs Ella's pillows and slides them under my head.

"He's not coming."

Panic moves up to my throat. "W-what do you mean?"

There's a pause. "The plane went down soon after take-off."

"Down?" I whisper, horror-struck.

"All five onboard were killed."

He's completely emotionless as he says it, which only spikes my fear. When Dante shuts down like this, his monster is roaring into life.

There's something else he's not telling me. Something worse. His dark eyes are as hard as flint. His face, like stone, but there are emotions moving just below his surface that he's struggling to conceal.

Grief.

Rage.

I clutch at his hand as another contraction blasts me into the pain stratosphere. We ride it out together, with him never flinching as I crush every bone.

I try again. "What is it?"

"Not now. We have a baby to deliver." He yanks my white dress up to my waist.

"Oh my God! Are you kidding me?" My voice rises

hysterically. "You take life, Dante. You don't birth it!"

"Well, we don't have any other options until a new physician arrives. It could be hours."

This can't be happening.

I feel the mattress dip beside me. His mouth finds mine, his tongue snaking out to lap up the droplets of blood on my lip. "You can do this, *mi alma*," he murmurs. "After what I've put you through, you can do fucking anything. You're a Santiago, remember?"

I nod, holding his dark gaze as I suck in lungfuls of air to help conquer the rippling ache. "You need to tell me what the hell is going on, Dante."

"No."

"I'll crush your other hand to a pulp…"

"After."

After?

I can't hold back any longer. My body is taking over. I bear down so hard I feel like my spine is going to crack.

"I'm scared," I whisper, in between desperate pants.

"Don't be."

"Will you stay with me?"

"Always," he says fiercely, rising up to smash our mouths together again. "Now push."

Chapter Fifteen

VIVIANA

Children are a flaw I'll never be burdened with.
I've known this all my adult life, so it's not like the primal screams echoing through these empty hallways are having any sort of sway over my decision.

Parents fail.

Children suffer.

I've seen it time and time again at Gabriela's sanctuary in Leticia. I've watched all the broken hearts arrive at her front door, dragging their equally broken *niñas* behind them.

It's all so *tragic.*

I've no interest in perpetuating that story, not when there are so many other uses for a life once it's been handed back to you, like death and deceit, anger and revenge. It allows for moments such as these, when my lips are whistling out tunes of black satisfaction.

Circumstances bent our way today. The doctors didn't need

to die, but who am I to pass up a chance to make Santiago suffer? They were an integral part of his team, and we're picking them off, one by one. He'll see the pattern soon enough.

His house is a maze of twisting passages, but I know exactly where I'm headed. I've dreamed of being on this island for years, and here I am.

I've beaten the odds and cheated my way into the devil's lair, and, as such, I'm deriving a stupid amount of pleasure from being able to wander unchecked.

I let my fingertips trail along the smooth white walls as I walk, speculating on his color choice. It hasn't escaped me that most things in this house are white, including his wife's clothes. I was taught to expose and exploit weaknesses, and I believe I've just found one of Santiago's:

He longs for light, even when he can't escape the dark.

When I think about it, it's not such a stretch of the imagination. The devil was an angel once. Why wouldn't he yearn to climb back up Jacob's Ladder, given half the chance?

After checking that the maid is busy with the daughter in the kitchen—and collecting myself a sandwich on the way—I pause outside Santiago's office. I already have the security passcode so gaining entry is easy. All the cameras are out. We've had a contact on this island for the last six weeks. What we didn't have was complete access to his inner sanctum...

And now we do.

Stepping inside, I let the door slam carelessly behind me. No one will notice. Santiago's wife is still screaming the place down.

I was only in here a few minutes ago discussing product embargoes for those still resisting our cartel's new stranglehold, but the room looks different. The huge, circular space with the black leather couches and the glass desk seems even bigger without his soul-sucking presence around. It's darker too, despite the floor to ceiling windows spanning one wall. The sun has disappeared behind a rare dark cloud on an otherwise spotless horizon.

Do you play chess, Santiago?

He set this board. We made the first move. Now, the king is about to be checkmated, and I'll be the black knight responsible.

I work quickly to plant the listening devices, in between casual bites of my sandwich. Chicken mayo isn't my favorite, but it's better than all the health food crap I've had to endure over the last two days. When I've finished, I can't resist leaning back in his chair and throwing my cowboy boots up on the desk. Pulling the phone system toward me, I dial out a number I know by heart.

He answers on the first ring.

"Viviana," he croaks, sounding even more robotic and inhuman today. The latest surgery didn't work. His body is slowly failing him. Only adrenaline spikes of revenge are keeping him alive. "Is it done?"

"It's done."

He cackles slowly. "And where are you now, *mi vida*? Drinking his expensive liquor in celebration? Fucking his men?"

"Sitting on his throne, surveying a kingdom that will fall in days."

Alcohol doesn't interest me. Men, even less so. My desires revolve around one thing, and one thing only:

Power.

More specifically: *to never feel the loss of power again.*

He cackles again, but it soon turns into a hacking cough. There's a pause as his nurse adjusts his oxygen levels and makes him more comfortable. "My daughter, The Queen of Duplicity. Once he is gone, you will have your kingdom. I swear it."

"I want the island and the house in Leticia, too."

"You shall have all of that, and more. Tell me, why did you linger in Miami for so long?"

"To ensure that the fiancée stayed in the rehab facility."

It's a poor excuse, and we both know it.

"False friendships are a distraction, *mi vida*," he warns. "She will hate you most of all after she discovers what you've done. She's been a pawn in this from the very start."

"Hate can be overturned," I say smoothly. "Vengeance cannot."

"Just remember that." There's another round of coughing. "I hear the doctors suffered an in-flight malaise?"

"We wired the plane to explode ten minutes after take-off."

"Is the whore taking the news well?"

"Not particularly," I say, adjusting my position. The sandwich is starting to give me indigestion. "Her labor is proceeding quicker than planned."

"Perhaps we will be celebrating more providence by nightfall?"

"How so?"

"When she dies in childbirth."

My stomach ache worsens. I can imagine him licking what's left of his mangled lips as he says it. I have no problem destroying men, but women are a harder limit.

I think of Anna again, and my mind slams shut. Papá doesn't know she escaped yet. My team are still looking for her in Miami. I pushed my agenda too hard and she ran, but in time she'll come back to me.

"And Grayson?" he asks, gasping for breath. The more

excited he becomes, the less his body allows for it. *I guess even fun has an expiration date.*

"He's scattered all over some field in Virginia, Papá."

Santiago's wife's screams are so loud now they're permeating the steel walls of her husband's office.

"I want body parts," he rasps. "I want them in a red box with a bow. A birthday present to my brother is long overdue."

"As soon as we find something, I'll let you know."

A bomb wired to the wings of a jet was too good for *El Asesino*. His death would have been too quick. I'd wanted him to taste the bitterness of loss in those last few minutes as he fell from the sky. I'd wanted him to choke on it. I'd imagined him gasping and spluttering like my father does as he hit the ground in a fireball, the skin peeling from his bones. It's the least I could do after he kept my *parcera* away from me.

Resting the receiver in the crook of my neck, I pull out her cell from the pocket of my jeans and start scrolling through the messages to her dead fiancé, deleting each one in turn. I'd hoped to plant a poison between them during our stay in the rehab facility, but my *parcera's* damn stubbornness failed to hear the truth in my words.

I listen to my father wheezing for breath again.

"How long will you stay on the island?"

"I'll be leaving around nightfall."

"To Colombia or Miami?"

"Colombia."

As much as I'd like to return to Florida, I need to keep up this charade until the time is right.

"You've done well, *mi vida,*" he says thickly. "I'll notify Vindicta of your excellence. Our Bratva comrades will be pleased. Message me when you're back in the homelands."

Home for him, but never for me. Colombia sold me nineteen years ago. She's nothing but a liar and a disgrace.

"Feel free to leave a parting gift on the island of your choosing." He sucks in another painful breath. His energy is almost spent. He'll sleep for the rest of the day. *"You have more than exceeded our expectations, mi vida,"* he repeats huskily.

I couldn't give a damn what they think. This is about me and an enemy, and a wrong he can never make right.

I've never been under any illusions about the type of man my father is. It just took me a little longer to see myself in his image. From the day he sought me out, I've accepted his evil. I've even understood it. When you're betrayed by a blood relative, it changes the shape of your soul, and we recognized that in each other. It turned us both into ambush predators, who destroy their prey with stealth and cunning.

Hanging up, I lean back to inhale the smell of victory amidst the leather and cedarwood. There's another scent underneath it, though. It's one I wasn't expecting—something sour and unpleasant. *Hijueputa. What is that smell?*

Regret.

I find myself thinking about Santiago and the tender way he comforted his daughter. The devil has many forms, but I never expected him to be a father. A husband. A friend.

He longs for light, even when he can't escape the dark.

On cue, the sun re-emerges from the clouds above the pacific, flooding the office with dust dances and verity.

He's a formidable opponent.

He won't go down as easily as my father predicts.

I drop my feet from the desk. There's no point in staying. My work here is done. The next time I step foot in this office, this will all be mine anyway.

I'm halfway to the door when the phone on his desk starts ringing.

I pause. *Could it be the man we're so eager to find?* The missing link to Santiago's organization—the lone FBI agent who hides himself deeper in the dark than the Shadow Man himself?

I let the call ring out, but it springs into life again. Pretty soon, it's a constant loop of noise that's in danger of catching Santiago's attention.

Could it be confirmation about El Asesino's *body?*

It takes me three steps to cover the distance to the desk.

I'll pick it up and listen.

I won't say a word.

I lift the receiver, and then a dead man starts talking to me.

"Jesus, Dante, pick up your damn phone once in a while! I've been calling your cell for the last half hour."

The dead sound restless, angry, and very much alive.

The room starts spinning. *This can't be.* We had pictures of him climbing into the jet. We had pictures of him departing.

"Dante?" he repeats impatiently. "Dante, for fuck's sake. I know you're pissed with me, but carve another hole in my stomach later. Your family is in danger."

I tuck that information away as a new plan falls into place.

"Dante—"

"I can hear you, Joseph Grayson." My voice is clear and untroubled as I pull the rug clean out from under him. "I trust you had an unpleasant flight?"

There's a pause, followed by a curse. "What the fuck are you doing in his office?"

"Being warmed by the Santiago fires and sharing his bourbon." I laugh pleasantly. *The crueler the lie, the more agonizing the sting.* "I believe Eve and Sofía are cooking me a 'welcome to the family' dinner tonight. It's *Paella Valenciana*. One of my uncle's favorite.

"Stay away from them!" he roars.

My laughter turns into a taunt. "I knew that cold composure would crack, sooner or later. Every man has his pressure points."

"And every woman has a price. Who the hell are you working for?"

"I'm working for God. How are you still enjoying life?"

"Divine intervention...enjoy the last few minutes of yours."

"I plan on enjoying it for a lot longer than that. I warned you in Colombia you'd be left behind in the wilderness, and there you are."

And here I am.

"Who do you think he's going to believe, Viviana. You or me? History shouts louder than bullshit."

"This is a pointless argument," I say as the wails of a newborn baby filter under the door. "Whatever you think you know about me—"

"I know plenty. Enough to have Santiago rip your spine right out of your throat."

"No, you don't. Not anymore. You're going to keep your mouth *shut*."

He pauses. Calculates. He's another man I'll never underestimate. "And why would I do that?"

Think big, Vi. Think shocking. No matter how much it repulses you, because it will never come close to what Santiago did.

"Because if you don't," I warn. "I'm going to take the same machete I like to play peek-a-boo-limb with, and I'm going to introduce it to Santiago's newborn baby girl. Perhaps you can hear her now?" I pull the phone away from my ear and hold it up for him to listen. *Fuck... It's even louder than its mother.* "Stay on your side of the pacific, Joseph Grayson, and my machete stays clean and dry."

"I could call him now, and you'd be dead before you took your next breath."

"But not my contacts who have instructions to carry out the task in the event of my death," I lie easily. "Our spies are everywhere. Even on this island."

"He'll torture the truth out of you."

"I'd die before I said a word.

"You're so full of shit!"

He's past the point of anger. He's tasting what me and my father taste now.

"Care to test that theory? Care to have another death on your conscience?"

"I'll kill you extra slowly for this, and so will Anna."

Anna.

"So, that's where she disappeared to." *That smell...it's that fucking smell again.* "Did you have a sweet reunion in the restroom stalls?"

She chose him over me. How could she? The hurt is blinding, squeezing my insides harder than any labor contraction.

I go to reciprocate it, to wound him with another threat, when I hear a voice in my head that I haven't heard in a long time.

"Never show your enemy the red of your wounds—bunny rabbit—or they'll keep painting it until it's impossible to conceal."

I stifle a gasp, wrenching the phone receiver away so he doesn't hear it.

That voice with the thick, treacly accent that scarred the side of my neck as he raped me over and over again.

Breath, Viviana. Breath.

He's dead.

He's gone.

"Here's what you're going to do," I say, clawing back the power in this call. "You're going to switch your cell off for the next fifty years, or Santiago will be attending his daughter's funeral, not her intended baptism. "

"Fuck *you*!"

"Temper, temper," I drawl lightly. "Do you need another drink to calm down? Does she know you're an alcoholic yet?"

My cell beeps. It's my team in Miami sending me a security camera screen grab of Anna and Grayson climbing into an old blue Toyota outside the diner with the license plate on full display.

Checkmate, again.

Another message arrives, hot on its heels.

Tracked them to a motel outside Haines City.

A tight smile stretches round my teeth as I tap out my reply.

I only want the girl alive.

If he won't die promptly, my men will bleed him out.

"Did you know that there are parts on a man's body where you can stab him and he'll not die for hours?" I say, casually. "As long as you avoid the major arterial areas, you can keep on wounding him, over and over."

"And your point is…?"

"You come at me, and I'll come back at you so hard you'll be begging me to end it."

He laughs bitterly. "It's good to know we're thinking along

the same lines."

"I'm sitting in his chair right now, you piece of shit." I let out a contented sigh. "I have my feet up on his desk, but they'll soon be under it. Care for a picture?"

"You can't keep it up, Viviana…"

I allow my laughter to linger long and hard. "Watch me."

Slamming the phone down, I tap out a message to my father.

Change of plan. I'm staying here for now.

Ingratiation is a colorless land that I'll keep on conquering. *This island isn't done with me yet.*

Chapter Sixteen

JOSEPH

I listen to the dead tone, thinking how appropriate that fucking description is.

Dead in the water.

Dead out of ideas.

I'm the man with a plan, but tonight I have nothing.

"Joseph?"

Anna's hovering on the other side of the bed, biting her thumb nail down to the quick. I can't bring myself to tell her how deep the rivers of betrayal flow.

"Joseph, please," she urges. "Is Eve okay? Ella…?"

"We need to go." Picking up my gun, I chuck the empty vodka bottle into the trash and grab the keys. The Vicodin is still working its magic so at least I'll be able to drive.

"Where?" she says dully, sensing the truth but not wanting to accept it.

Ignorance is bliss, sweetheart.

I've never felt rage like this before. It's glazing my insides. It's melting my self-control. Only her presence is stopping me from tearing this fucking motel room apart.

"New York."

"*New York?*" she gasps out. "But that's a fifteen-hour drive from here."

"Best we get started then."

I limp toward the door and feel her hand on my arm. "She's there, isn't she?" Anna mutters. "That's who you were talking to just now. She made it onto the island." She sits down hard on the bed, her face draining of color. "This is all my fault. If I hadn't become friends with her—"

"She played us all," I say grimly, switching tack. "She would have forced that friendship on you, whether you'd accepted it or not. You were a target the moment you stepped off that plane."

Sometimes the hard truth is better than a soft lie.

She nods and stares at the floor. "I saved her life, Joseph. I saved her fucking life!"

"Which is probably what saved *you*." Taking her hand, I tug her to her feet. "Dante isn't just a sharp guy. He's a ruthless bastard. A trained killer. He'll figure it out, if he hasn't already."

Hell, I almost sound convincing.

"Try him again," she begs.

"I can't."

"Fine, then give me the cell." She flings her hand at me, her green eyes flashing. "I'll call Eve."

Goddamn. *Who knew her defiance would make my cock this hard?* I stare down at her, fighting the urge to roll her onto her back, rip her jeans and panties down and make her so full of me she's choking on my name. Somehow, in the middle of perdition, she's managing to make me fall even harder for her.

"Stop aiming those wicked greens at me, sweetheart," I warn, flicking a strand of blonde off her face, "or we won't be going anywhere."

She flushes. "Time and a place, shadow," she mutters, keeping her hand outstretched.

"You can't call her," I say, ignoring my throbbing cock. "Viviana and her people have already infiltrated the island. She has spies everywhere. We need to find another way."

"Which is?"

"I have a contact in New York. He can fix us up with a new jet. We need to get back to that island and talk to Dante, face to face."

"Is it that Roman guy?"

"Where did you hear that name?" I catch her chin between my fingers in a vice-like grip, making her cry out in shock. "Did Viviana mention it?"

"No, *you* did," she fires back, pushing me away, her green eyes flashing for a whole other reason now. *For a second there I'd almost fooled her I was a nice guy.*

"When?" I demand.

Her brows shoot up, daring me to call her a liar. "If you must know, you were off your head on meds."

I grit my teeth so hard, the pain ricochets into my skull. "You need to take that name and bury it, Anna. Kiss the headstone goodbye and forget about it."

"Who is he?"

"Did you hear what I said?"

Our glaring contest is interrupted by the slow crawl of headlights across the gray curtains. A car is pulling into the motel. Usually that would be pretty normal, but it's past midnight and the place is dead.

Grabbing her hand, I yank her toward the wall by the window. Flicking the edge of the curtain back, I see a shiny new SUV parking up next to all the old Fords and the Chevrolets.

"Into the bathroom," I say, over my shoulder. "There's no other exit. We'll have to kick the window frame out."

She's frozen to the spot as I drag the mattress off the bed and pin it against the door, closely followed by the table.

"Anna, go!" I roar, pulling out my gun. "We have five minutes before they discover which room we're in."

There's a flash of gold in my periphery as she runs next door. A moment later, there's the sound of broken glass. I flick the edge of the curtain back again and watch two men enter the front desk area opposite. Twenty seconds later, there's a muffled shot and they're walking out again studying the check-in book for a couple of new arrivals with fake-sounding names.

These assholes aren't playing around.

Half-jogging, half-limping to the bathroom, I find Anna knocking out the jagged remains of the window glass with a trash can wrapped in a towel.

"Stand aside."

Balancing on my bad leg—ignoring the knife-like agony—I kick out the rest of the frame, the rotten wood caving in like molding clay. There's a knock at the motel room door as I'm helping Anna out. Clicking the locks to the bathroom, I swing my legs out to join her.

The motel backs onto a steep slope. Keeping close to the building, wading through empty coke bottles and darkness, I lead her around to the side and back to the parking lot, just as the two men are attempting to kick our door down.

"Who are they?" she hisses.

"An after-fuck delight from Viviana, I can imagine."

"She wants to kill me too now, huh?"

She wants to kill us all.

I make a quick scan of the lot. The SUV is parked opposite. The door light is on and I can see another man in the driver seat. *Bingo.* Meanwhile, the others have forced their way through my flimsy barricade and are shooting their happy welcomes into the bathroom door.

"Stay here," I tell her.

"Wait, Joseph—"

She sounds scared. Unsure.

Whirling around, I grab the back of her head and smash our mouths together. It's brief and rough, but it does the trick because she's arching into me right away. *I need you present, Anna, not drifting.*

"I guarantee in one minute we'll be on that road and doing seventy outta here."

It takes less than that.

Within ten seconds, I've dragged the driver out of the SUV and he's rolling around on the ground with a bullet hole in his shoulder.

Hitting the gas, I reverse back up to her.

"Move!"

She's in the vehicle by the time the men reappear in the doorway of our motel room. We're already hitting the road as the first wayward bullet skims the trunk. The second doesn't even hit the target.

Typing "New York City" into the GPS, I re-route it to keep us off the main roads. We'll need to change vehicles at some point. They'll be hacking into the police systems to follow their own plates. Anna's not speaking, and I don't interrupt the silence. There's a lot for her to process tonight, and she'll talk when she's good and ready.

Reaching for the crumpled pack of smokes in my pocket, I slot one between my lips and, joy of joys, find a lighter in the glove box.

I smoke.

She frets.

I need to get hold of Roman.

She needs to understand that the rules have changed.

"Why is Vi doing this?" she asks quietly, after a couple of miles have passed.

"I can't answer that," I say, shrugging. "But Santiago blood never flows clean. Her father, Emilio, was a psychopath. Looks like she inherited more than just his name."

Anna falls silent again and I chase the white lines on the road—thinking forward, not back. Roman must have missed something. Despite what I said, I'm not convinced it's an old family rivalry that's being passed onto the next generation. It's too organized. *Too calculated.*

"How did she know where we were?"

"Security footage from the diner. That's where I would have started."

Her head tips forward suddenly, her fair hair glistening silver in the moonlight. She's shaking and she can't seem to catch her breath.

"Anna?"

"This is so fucked up," she gasps out. "So fucking fucked up. The way you just killed that m-man."

Goddammit.

Spying a rest stop up ahead, I pull over, skidding across the gravel in a show of stones before slamming my foot down on the brake.

"Come here." Ripping off her seatbelt, I force her into my lap and into my arms. She's drifting again, and I need to pull her back before it's too late.

"Get your hands off me!" She's fighting my embrace, drumming her small fists against my biceps, her blonde hair whipping at my skin.

"I didn't kill him, Anna," I say calmly, taking it all without flinching.

"All these guns and killing and running...why is my life one crazy scenario after another? Why is everything so messed-up!"

"Because I made you love a man more messed-up than any of it," I roar, grabbing her wrists.

"And I made you love me right back!"

We glare at each other, and then suddenly my mouth is full of gold—soft, warm, violent and precious. Our tongues are like crossed swords, fighting and fucking, as I kick the driver's door open and drag her out with me. Flinging her across the hood of the SUV, face down, I slam a clenched fist between her shoulder blades as I rip at her jeans and panties. The balmy night air is almost brutal in its humidity, but not as brutal as how I'm about to be with her body.

"Not here," she begs, splaying her palms flat against the paintwork. "Anyone could see!"

"We haven't passed a car in twenty minutes," I snarl, reaching for my belt. "Do you think I'd let another man catch a glimpse of what's mine? Besides, this won't take long."

"Wait! Joseph…"

"You can't fucking feel me right now, *Luna*, so you leave me no choice. I need you with me, not fighting me."

Dragging my fingers down through her soft folds, I drive one and then two inside her—pumping mercilessly before sliding them out and smearing her wetness all over the shiny head of my cock. This is a savage angle for her. She won't be walking right for days. *But, my God, she'll feel me afterward.*

"Shit," she whimpers, widening her legs as much as she can, flicking me a scared look over her shoulder. "Are you seriously going to—?"

"Damn right I am."

Keeping her pinned to the car, I force my cock into her tight velvety heat until I'm seated as deeply as her small body will allow.

"It's too much," she chokes out.

"You like it, though?" I lean forward to wrap my hand around her soft throat, feeling the frantic swallow as I slide in even deeper.

"Yes," she groans, almost pitifully.

"You'll like this even better."

She groans again as I pound her into the metalwork with three vicious strokes, before I'm yanking her hair back and ramming my fingers into her mouth.

"Bite down, baby. That was just a warm-up. Now, I'm really going to make it hurt."

It's hot and dirty. Fast and unforgiving.

Bad men fuck rough, and we take without mercy.

When she comes, her spine arches in pleasure. Her muscles clamp down on my cock and I'm shooting my load into her with a twisted groan.

We collapse forward together in a tangle of limbs and hastily pushed aside clothes. Brushing strands of blonde out of her face, with my cock still buried inside her, she turns to look at me.

"I always want to feel you, Joseph," she pants. "No matter how many arguments we have or what crazy situations we find ourselves in."

Her face is mostly in shadow, but her lips are a glistening promise.

I could almost fool myself that it's true. Instead, I let my cock slip from her body.

"Get dressed," I say, fixing my belt as I climb back into the car.

"You don't believe me?" A beat later, she's sliding into the passenger seat, still adjusting her jeans.

"It doesn't matter what I believe," I say, starting up the engine. "Life is a frozen lake in Michigan. One minute it's solid, the next it's broken, but we keep on skating anyway."

"Broken like the driveway at that old farmhouse in Texas," she muses.

At this, I say nothing.

Chapter Seventeen

VIVIANA

The sunset is a war between fire and death, and they're dragging the whole damn horizon into it.

I'm still deciding on a winner as Santiago hands me a double whiskey.

"It's one of the reasons I bought the island." He gestures at the crimson battlefield, before adding dryly, "The skyline should always imitate your work."

That, or your severed conscience.

"How did you find out about this place?" I ask, knowing the answer already. I know every movement he and his bitch wife made after they left my father for dead in Miami three years ago.

"A British arms dealer owed me a favor. I took it in part-exchange." He leans back against the balcony's white stone wall—the Man in Black—and offers me a toast. His dark eyes are gleaming with something unreadable. "To new, ah, beginnings?"

"To new *daughters* and new beginnings," I correct, faking

graciousness as I raise the glass to my lips and take a sip.

Santiago doesn't comment. He doesn't even take a sip of his bourbon. He just stands there, his face an unmovable mask, studying me—trying to crawl inside my brain like a rat within the walls of a house.

A nasty thought hits me. *Did this hijo de puta just spike my drink?*

The glass drops from my mouth as I search his face for evidence. The corners of his mouth are curving, but it's not a pleasant smile.

"Problem with the whiskey?"

"I prefer ice," I say, my heart hammering.

"My mistake," he says idly, but he doesn't offer to remedy it.

"*Pendejo*," I mutter under my breath. Being in Santiago's company is like juggling knives. You're constantly on edge, whether you're on the verge of destroying his kingdom or not. One false move and his blades are fatal.

Holding his gaze, I return the drink to my mouth and drain the contents. If my uncle is the dark cartel prince of psychological warfare, I'm the doyenne of giving it back, two-fold.

"Your father was a cunt," he declares, turning to look at the sunset again.

I give a bark of relieved laughter. "I've been told that by many."

"I should have killed him sooner. How much do you know about him?"

"Next to nothing."

"How old were you when Gabriela found you again?"

"Eight. She hated my father too. She never spoke about him. Manuel, even less so."

At the mention of my half-uncle's name, *his half-brother*, his head jerks slightly. I search for a morsel of guilt on his face, but there's none.

Manuel never should have gone to work for him. If he hadn't, he'd still be happily running his bar in Santa Perdito and hacking internet codes on the sly. He was a computer genius, but none of that mattered to Santiago. He put a gun in his hand and a bullet in his brain.

"Where would you like to eat, *señor*?" The maid appears on the balcony, looking expectantly at us.

"In my office please, Sofía."

"Certainly *señor*. Dinner will be served in twenty minutes." She turns to leave.

"Eve is resting," he calls out. "Please ensure that she eats something when she wakes. Tell her everything else is in hand."

A giggle escapes my mouth, drawing two pairs of eyes in my direction.

"Something amusing?" Santiago asks.

"Forgive me," I say, straightening my face. "Your choice of words reminded me of our meeting in Colombia last week."

He gives me another cold smile, before pointing to my glass. "Come. We'll find you some ice downstairs."

The journey is a lesson in staccato small talk.

Santiago seems more detached this evening than he was earlier in the day. Something's weighing on his mind, so I go through a checklist in my head: The baby is healthy. The wife survived childbirth—perhaps he's pissed about two of his jets blowing up? *El Asesino's* "death" would have hit him hard as well, though he's yet to mention it. I've been monitoring calls in and out of the island this afternoon and so far my threat has worked. Joseph Grayson hasn't been in contact with Santiago once.

As we reach his office, I set myself a challenge to lighten up my uncle before I light him up. Sort of like a bonfire prelude to the firework display.

"Have you chosen a name for your new daughter?" I ask as he taps in the passcode.

"Thalia."

He stands aside to let me enter.

"Beautiful."

He follows me in, rashing up my skin with his close proximity. *My body hates him as much as the rest of me.*

"It was my choice," he adds. "It was my mother's middle name."

And my grandmother's.

"Is your wife—?"

"She's fine."

"And the doctor?"

"An unfortunate business." He gestures to one of the black leather couches before heading toward the bar.

"Any leads?" I ask, taking a seat as he starts throwing ice cubes into a fresh glass with unnecessary violence.

"A couple."

In goes another.

"One in particular."

And another.

When he hands me the glass it's full of vodka, not whiskey, but I don't make a big deal of it. I watch him sink into the couch opposite and cross his legs, looking every inch the enigmatic six-foot, dark-haired marauder that he is.

"Cheers," he murmurs.

This time he drinks long and deep, his gaze dipping to my

untouched vodka once he's done.

"Something wrong?"

"Not at all." I flash him a smile that's about as fucking genuine as his. "Tell me about this lead. Shall I follow it up?"

He grimaces. "We'll come to that in a moment…do you like my coffee table?"

His change of topic catches me off guard. I find myself leaning in, convinced I've misheard.

"The coffee table," he repeats patiently. "Do you like it?"

I drag my gaze up and down the swathes of polished mahogany. *It looks like every other fucking coffee table to me.*

"Um, was it expensive?"

"Very. My wife bought it for me as a birthday present. It would take an act of uncontrollable rage for me to bring myself to tarnish it."

Something flashes in his expression.

Something that makes me want to run and hide.

Shutting that thought down, I take a large sip of my vodka and nearly choke. *This is what the* pendejo *does, Viviana.* Once you're in his inner circle, he fucks with you for his evening's entertainment.

"I enjoyed what you did to Fernandez in Colombia," he muses, stretching one arm out along the back of the couch, twisting his wedding ring with his thumb. "It reminded me of something I would have done."

"Done?" I say, picking up on the past tense.

"Do."

He makes it sound like a threat.

"We share the same blood." I shrug and take another sip. "If someone fucks with us, we fuck them back twice as hard."

He doesn't respond. Instead, he lifts up one leg of his black pants and unveils a hunting knife strapped to his calf. "It's not a Billhook Machete, but it does the trick." He lays it down flat on the coffee table in front of me. "I used to pin my enemy's hand to the table, extracting the information I needed before firing a bullet between his...*or her* eyes."

He's still holding my gaze when there's a knock at the door.

"Come in, Sofía."

"*Señor.*" The maid sweeps into the room carrying a silver tray and dome. She places it down on the coffee table in front of him, barely glancing at the knife.

She must have seen some shit here over the years.

"I hope you're hungry, Viviana," he murmurs, reaching for the lid as the maid moves to stand behind the couch.

She's so close to the back of my head I can smell her sickly-sweet floral perfume. "What are we having tonight again?"

"Exactly what you requested, *señor*," I hear her say politely.

"Excellent."

He lifts the lid, and my smirk drops.

Before I have a chance to stumble to my feet, I feel a rope being pulled tight around my neck. Stars burst into my vision. My drink goes flying as I desperately claw at it, panic spreading like wildfire. I can't suck enough air into my lungs.

I knew he wouldn't go quietly.

"Don't." Santiago's voice is even colder than the vodka I just dumped all over my lap. "Don't make a mockery of the family name, any more than you've done already."

My eyes find the silver tray again. There's nothing there except a black iPad, and my just desserts for my own arrogance.

"You betraying *puta*!" I hiss at Sofía, tipping my head back to alleviate the pressure. She's not looking so docile anymore. Her pretty face is stretched into a snarl.

How did this happen?

Confusion is a spinning wheel I can't stop. She was our contact here on the island. She gave us the security codes. She killed the cameras...

Except she didn't.

No.

"You're a disgrace, *zorra*!" she hisses back, spitting right in my face, leaving a trail of wetness dripping down my left cheek.

Meanwhile, Santiago has risen from the couch to take a seat on the edge of the coffee table in front of me, collecting his knife on the way.

I try to kick him in the balls, but his knife delivers two quick slashes above my kneecaps.

"*¡Hijueputa!*" I scream. *Son of a bitch.*

"Stop struggling or I'll score you again."

The wounds aren't deep, but they're enough to make me behave. I sit there like a statue, breathing hard, blood trickling down the inside of my jeans. Pure hatred burning in my eyes.

"Let me tell you a story about loyalty," he says in the same measured tone that he'd read a fairytale to his daughter with. He rests his elbows on his knees and balances the knife perfectly on one finger, staring down at it for a moment. "Two years ago, I let a man into my compound. I gave him food from my table. I even let him fuck my housemaid..." His lips quirk momentarily. "Turns out, he was working for your father." He flicks his wrist, catching the knife smoothly, the blade pointing downward and poised above my thigh. "I killed him with this. Slit his throat from ear to ear outside that same warehouse where your Papá died. I vowed that day to choose my people more carefully. Grayson and I made steps to ensure that their devotion was absolute before they ever received a dime of my money." He cocks his head to one side. "Do you really think I'd entrust the care of my wife and children, my most precious of hearts, to someone who wouldn't willingly *die* for us?"

His gaze lifts to Sofía and he nods his approval. "Sofía came to me the same day you approached her…six weeks, was it?"

"Six weeks," confirms Sofía, yanking sharply on the noose. Panic blooms again before she loosens it a notch, allowing air back into my aching lungs. When this is all over, I'm going to rip the *puta* apart.

"I know that you threatened her mother and sisters in Colombia, so I've had them watched every minute of every day since then. Whatever hell you promised to deliver them, not a single drop of blood would have been spilt before my men took you down."

His revelation gives another hard spin to that wheel.

"Why didn't you just kill me as soon as you found out?" I rasp.

"I've asked myself that a lot recently," he muses. "It's been a hard secret to keep, and it's gone against every basic instinct." Holding my gaze, he clenches his fist around his blade, making me wince in horror. Moments later, a steady trickle of crimson is dripping from the edge of his hand and onto my jeans.

He never flinches once. *Does this man not feel pain?*

"Did you know I had another daughter, Viviana?"

"You're full of shit!"

I know everything about you, Dante Santiago. I know how you masquerade yourself as some anti-human trafficking Avenging Death Angel, while fanning the flames of the industry and selling girls on the sly. Papá told me all *about you.*

"You *will* respect him," cries Sofía, jerking sharply on the rope.

"Isabella would have been the same age as you." I watch his eyes turn a darker shade of black. "She might have even looked like you. That's if your father hadn't taken it upon himself to sell her into sexual slavery to punish me."

The ground gives way.

No.

Papá told me to never believe a single word he says.

"You kept me alive because I reminded you of your *daughter*?"

His lips quirk. "I was hoping some of her good would shine through you one day, but you kept crushing it with this inherited hatred you have for me. Unfortunately, my patience has run out. You made a bad move threatening the safety of my wife by blowing up her doctors' aircraft." He releases his fist from the knife and holds up his bloody palm. "That's when I knew you were not of my blood, Viviana. You were of *his.* You are nothing but your father's daughter, and I should have killed you months ago."

"I don't believe you," I croak.

"I couldn't give a fuck if you believe me, or not. You'll be dead in a minute anyway." He chucks the bloody knife onto the table. "I know why you came here. You want the name of our FBI insider, and you were willing to walk into a lion's den with dead meat wrapped around your shoulders to get it."

"It's only a matter of time," I splutter. "Once we blow your insider's cover, your whole organization will crumble. We know most of your intel comes from him."

"Better keep that secret extra safe then. As for yours..." He jerks his head at the iPad lying uncovered on the tray. "That's the security footage from the office earlier. There's no sound admittedly, but I'll trace the calls." He pauses for a moment to let this sink in. "I hope you didn't make yourself too comfortable at my desk, Viviana...not when I'm about to nail you to it."

He lunges for my hand as I unleash a string of hate in Spanish. His grip tightens and I yelp in pain. "You laid the foundations well. You built a house out of your deception, but I'll always be the big bad wolf who blows it down."

"*¡Hijueputa!*"

"You were arrogant. Complacent. Did you think I'd let a sea snake slither into my world without knowing everything about her first? Did you think I didn't hear what you said to Grayson in Colombia?" He's crushing my bones now. The agony is breath-stealing. "Killing Whit Harris and his obstetrician was the stupidest fucking thing you could have done."

"You're the stupid one, Santiago," I spit, scrabbling for ascendency before I die a horrible death. I'm under no illusions of what my uncle is going to do to me. "You let me wander these hallways straight to your daughter's nursery."

"What you fail to realize," he says, sounding bored, "is that you were watched at all times. By cameras, by two-way mirrors. The moment you lifted a finger to her, a bullet would have taken it clean off."

I blink as reality comes crashing down. The player didn't just get played. She was never in a fair game to begin with.

"Eve smelled your deception the minute you walked in."

"And Grayson?" I wheeze, shooting him a mocking smile. *My only weapon left now is words.* "I hear your aircraft was scattered across three counties."

"He's not dead, Viviana." He wrenches my cell out of my pocket and holds it up. "I know that he survived the plane crash, but there was a moment there—a brief *enlightening* moment— when you made me believe that regret was a rose with sharp thorns. For that, the punishment is…" He lunges forward again to grip my chin, forcing me to look at him. "He and I are blood brothers," he snarls, his mask slipping. "You hurt him, you hurt me. You fuck with my family? You better be saying your prayers at night. Do you have any last words before I make your existence a misery?"

"I hate you," I wheeze.

His expression resets to chilly indifference.

"I *will* make you suffer, Viviana. Give me the name of who you're working for, and I'll make it quick. You have my word. I don't enjoy torturing women, especially on the same day my youngest daughter is born." His grip on my chin intensifies, but it's hard to distinguish the pain from my throat and wounded knees anymore. "Is it Benni Morozov?"

Not exclusively.

"Which bastard sent you?"

Fear is an animal holding me fast in her jaws, but I'll never betray Papá.

"You may have outsmarted me, *uncle*, but you'll never win this."

"I'm not a patient man, *niece*—"

"*He learned to take death as an old debt that sooner or later should be paid*," I whisper, misquoting Einstein at him.

"—Nor do I like repeating myself."

"Dig your grave. Suffer the consequences. *Vindicta!*"

I'm choking out my final battle-cry when there's a noise at the office door. From Santiago's abrupt reaction, it could only be his wife.

He drops my chin and rises to his feet. "What is it *mi alma?*"

She never speaks, but whatever she conveys on her face is enough for him to leave my line of sight right away, barking out a terse order to Sofía.

"Keep her here. Reece is on his way."

"Yes, *señor*." Sofía shakes the noose threateningly, briefly cutting off my air supply again, but for the first time in ten minutes I spy a crack in the window of opportunity.

I'm no match for Santiago, but his maid is as good as dead.

Chapter Eighteen

ANNA

The call comes through as we're crossing lines into New York State.

It wakes me from a sleep where actual rest is considered unconstitutional, especially in a seat with no recline option and when your best friend is in mortal jeopardy. Not many words are exchanged, but his opening exclamation of, "Jesus, thank *fuck*," is enough for me to sit up and take note.

"That was Dante," he says, tossing the cell into my lap when he's done.

I watch him light up another cigarette. He's been chaining all night and my lungs are full of his new habit.

"Is Eve okay—?"

He nods. "She's safe. They all are."

My eyes flutter shut in relief. *Thank you, universe.* "And Vi?"

"Running for her life," he says, flicking ash out of the

window. "She escaped from the house, but she won't get far. Not on that island."

I wait for the pang of...*anything.* But there's zilch. I guess our friendship is officially dead.

"How did Santiago find out about her?"

He doesn't answer at first. His grip shifts on the steering wheel and I notice his knuckles are ghostly white. In Joseph speak, it means he's seriously pissed about something.

"He knew all along."

I go very still. "He *what*?"

"For the past six weeks."

In my head, I can hear the sound of something valuable breaking. Something that was formed a long time before he saw me on a crowded sidewalk outside a nightclub in Miami.

"Did he give you any reason why he didn't—?"

"Not yet, but I have an idea."

I glance at the passing blur of brown houses and green trees. It's a cruel existence to wake up one day and discover a lie so great it's spread through your entire life like a disease. Vi was so much smarter than we ever gave her credit for.

"Eve had the baby."

"She did?" Anger turns to frustration and disappointment. "Damn, I missed it. Are they okay?"

"Baby is now." He leaves me hanging as he changes lanes. "Her blood sugar levels dropped. She started shaking. Looked like a fit. Happens with newborns sometimes when they come a couple of weeks early..." He trails off, leaving me to fill in the blanks of his past with a question. *Did his son suffer the same thing when he was born?* "She's being monitored on the island, but it looks like she's stabilizing."

Thank you, universe, times a billion.

"What happens now?"

"We get on a plane and fly home."

Home.

For some reason that word sounds hollow, like a chocolate egg with no treats inside. It's Eve and Dante's home. Not ours.

Hollow.

Like Joseph's brusque responses that he's okay when we arrive at Teterboro Airport and park up next to another of Santiago's aircraft.

If it were me, I'd be suffering a serious case of PTSD after surviving a plane crash mere days ago. Not him. He's too damn cool about it, limping slowly up the steps without a trace of a doubt. I know that wanted assassins and mercenaries are wired differently to other people, but it worries the hell out of me. I know better than anyone that internalizing shit makes it leak out in other ways.

There's only so much a man can take until he breaks.

There's a medic waiting for him onboard. I sit across the aisle as he gets fixed up for another busted stitch. And then I watch, pretending to be asleep, as he pops Vicodin like candy and drinks an entire bottle of whiskey during the flight.

Santiago emerges from his big white mansion as soon as the car pulls up. He stands there on the porch, hands in his pockets, sunglasses glinting—a man as still as the nights on this island. A shiver zips up and down my spine. I wouldn't be Viviana right now for all the money in the world. He'll hunt her down to the ends of the Earth, and then he'll push her off it with her throat slit and a knife in her chest.

"Mrs. Grayson." He greets me with that dangerous drawl of his as I climb the steps, with Joseph falling into step behind me. "Welcome back, and congratulations. Your husband sent me a message about your news."

"Likewise," I say tersely. There's no love lost between us, but we grate along for the sakes of my best friend and the man standing in my shadow. "How's Eve?"

"Waiting for you indoors." He angles his head to acknowledge Joseph. "Good to see you in one piece. Shame about my jet, though."

"Shame you weren't on it to enjoy the ride, you fucking cunt."

Wow. My head whips round in shock. I've never heard him speak to Santiago like that before.

Joseph climbs the last two steps until he's level with us, and then he puts in an extra stride that encroaches well into Santiago's airspace. "The next time you want to play fast and loose with my life, leave my goddamn wife out of it."

Santiago doesn't comment, but two dark eyebrows rise above the rim of his sunglasses. "Would you like to hear the reasons before you—"

"Fuck your reasons!"

Bam.

Joseph's left hook sends the devil reeling sideways. He hisses out a bad word in Spanish and clutches at his jaw, ripping off his sunglasses.

"Joseph, stop!" As much as I'm cheering on my husband on the inside, Santiago's bloodlust puts the fear of God in me.

"You knew, you bastard," he snarls, pushing me out of the way. "You knew Viviana wasn't legit for six weeks, and you let it roll out at your own pace. I never would have been in New York gathering intel on her if you'd kept me in the loop. I never would have been on that plane in the first place."

I go to intervene again when someone grabs my wrist and tugs me into the house.

"There's no point, Anna," I hear Eve say, closing the front door on the new equivalent of World Word Three. "I've seen them blow up like this before. It's a summer storm. It comes in hard and cleans all the dirt away. I've already given Dante hell for not telling Joseph about Viviana. He knows he has it coming."

"But what if he retaliates?" I pause when I realize she's only half a day past giving birth and she's standing in front of me in a loose-fitted white sundress. "And what the hell are you doing out of bed?"

Outside the shouting is getting louder. There's a loud thump as something heavy hits the door, rattling the locks and the frame.

Eve doesn't even flinch. "Not if he wants to stay married… and in answer to your other question, I'm taking advantage of the miracle of two sleeping children." She breaks the tension with one of her daybreak smiles, looking shattered but beautiful. "God, I missed you." She pulls me in for a hug.

"You feel weird without a baby bump," I mutter into her hair.

"You feel weird being married." She lets go and slides her arm around my waist. "While our husbands work out their differences, come and meet Thalia."

The baby wakes as soon as we enter the nursery, mewling like a kitten and then bleating like a lamb when she realizes that her dinner isn't ready.

Eve unbuttons the front of her sundress and scoops her up.

"Joseph said she's been sick," I say, sounding worried.

"I think it was the shock of being delivered by Dante." She

laughs and eases into the nursing chair as I collapse onto a soft gray couch opposite. "It was a tough time, but she seems okay now. They're still taking blood every couple of hours."

I watch her plant a kiss on top of Thalia's head, who is predictably gorgeous with a gazillion dark curls already.

I want that, I think. *I want that more than I ever thought I did.*

"Her birth was all kinds of dramatic." Eve's smile wavers. "I caught Viviana standing in the doorway staring at Ella right before. It really freaked me out."

My stomach drops. "Did she try anything?"

She shakes her head. "Dante says he was having her watched the entire time, but of course *I* didn't know that. It was a weird moment. She looked like she was part threat, part curious."

"Joseph says she only made friends with me in Colombia to get to Santiago."

"Perhaps…" Eve falls silent for a moment. "But even best laid plans get blown off course by other breezes. I imagine she didn't *plan* to get raped by Fernandez's men in that bar, or for you to save her the way you did. I doubt she intended to find any sort of a friendship with you at all."

I think about a table in Colombia, two guns and a decision. Then I remember the sound it made as her men fired bullets into our motel bathroom door.

"Are you making up excuses for her?"

"No, not at all. Dante will find her and make her pay for what she did to you and Joseph, and I won't be standing in his way. I'm just saying that someone else was tweaking her puppet strings, and you cut a couple in South America. You confused her. The fact that she even has the ability to feel that kind of emotion makes me feel sorry for her."

"When did you get so goddamn *wise*?" I say in awe.

She laughs again, and switches Thalia to her other breast. "Not a lot else to do on this island except think…I had this weird dream, though." She scrunches her face up at the memory. "I haven't even told Dante about it yet."

"What dream?"

"Emilio Santiago was in it…I heard his voice."

"A voice can't hurt us, Eve," I reassure her. "Not when it's coming from a dead man's mouth."

"It was coming from my father's mouth."

"Are you *serious*?" I'm shocked. I haven't heard her mention him since his death. "Can you remember what he said?"

"Not really. I remember how he made me feel, though." Thalia's milk-drunk and comatose as she switches her to her shoulder and gently pats her back. "Scared for the future. Nervous…" Her gaze drifts toward the window. "What do you think it meant?"

"That your crazy pregnancy hormones were on the rampage again," I say, rearranging the soft toys on the couch next to me into size order, feeling a little uneasy myself.

"I killed him, Anna," she says quietly. "I killed Emilio Santiago, and I don't regret it, either." She nuzzles into Thalia's little body. "It's a shitty, awful thing to admit to when you're holding pure innocence in your hands."

"Sometimes we make choices we never thought we'd consider," I say, thinking of the men I've killed myself. "Fate conspires like a wicked domino queen and we all fall down."

"Now who's the wise one," she teases, buttoning up her dress.

There are heavy footsteps on the stairs. Joseph appears in the doorway, filling the space with six-foot-two of tan Texas granite. There's a bleeding gash across one eyebrow and his top lip is split, but his gray-blues are calmer seas than before.

"I came to say 'hi' to the new arrival." He leans against the frame and crosses his arms, and I find I can't drag my eyes away from him.

"Does she still have a father?" says Eve lightly.

The corners of his mouth quirk. "He's downstairs fixing what's left of his face."

"You know why he kept the truth from us, don't you?"

There's a pause. "Yeah, I know."

But I don't.

I swing my gaze between them, but no one wants to enlighten me.

"He told me to say Rick Sanders is flying out tomorrow evening."

"Oh, jeez, more immoral men to introduce to my newborn." She lifts her eyes to heaven in mock annoyance. There's a weird moment afterward when I think she's going to ask Joseph if he wants to hold Thalia, but then changes her mind. "Tell me about your wedding," she blurts instead. "Did you bribe a local priest?"

"It was, ah, pretty small," I say, thinking fast.

"Intimate," Joseph drawls, flashing me the ghost of a smirk.

"No witnesses—"

"That we know of."

"That's it?" Now it's Eve's turn to ping pong between us. "God, that's almost as unromantic as mine."

Joseph holds his hand out to me. "Come."

There's no explanation of where he's taking me, but I rise to my feet anyway. He leads; I follow. Shadows track the movement of the sun, and right now he's all I can see in front of me.

Once we reach our bedroom, he bends down and sweeps me

into his arms.

"What the heck are you doing?" I yelp, as I'm swallowed up by hard muscle, Texas sunshine and whiskey.

"Honoring tradition."

"In someone else's house?"

It's a leading question. We rarely talk about the future. It's one of our forbidden topics, along with most other stuff.

"S-sorry," I stutter. "I didn't mean to—"

"Where would we move to?" he says slowly, as if he's considering it.

"A house in the jungle with tigers in our backyard."

"And elephants," he says, playing along.

"A treehouse," I tip my head back and laugh. "With rope ladders and everything. You could be Tarzan with blue jeans and a loaded .41."

"My .41 is always loaded around you." He's laughing too now—that rich rare sound that tugs an even wider smile from my lips.

Walking me into the bedroom, he lays me down on the bed. I wrap my legs around his waist before he has a chance to stand up.

"Uh-uh. You're not going anywhere."

He doesn't take much persuading, crashing down on top of me with a groan.

"We need to sleep, *Luna*."

"Then sleep," I say, pulling him even closer.

"Like this?"

"Like this, until I can't breathe anymore. You're kind of heavy."

"Death by siesta. Can I take all your clothes off first?"

"You can, but I doubt they'd be much sleeping going on if

you did."

"Hmmm."

His eyes are closing. Gently pushing him away, he's fast asleep as soon as the back of his head hits the mattress.

I lie there, watching the rise and fall of his chest—pressing pause on a beat of calm after a symphony of madness. I never had an image in my head of the man I'd marry when I was older. I wasn't one of those girls in high school who doodled dreams and imaginary surnames. I was too busy dealing with the emotional fall-out of my mother's illness. I just hoped he'd be generous with his love, and that he'd wrap his arms around me at the end of the day and tell me everything would be okay.

"She's cute," he murmurs suddenly, his eyes still shut.

"You're a brave man mentioning other women in your sleep," I warn, cupping his semi and squeezing.

His lips quirk. "I meant the kid. She looks a bit like Caleb did."

"Was that your son?" I say hesitantly.

"Yes. Turn over."

I do as he says, my heart pounding. He pulls me into his hard embrace, holding me hostage in the best possible way, and we lie as still as sleeping lions.

"I don't talk about him because he belongs to a man I left behind," he says eventually, warming the nape of my neck with his secret. "He was a man who took his pain and turned it into something dark and dirty. My son's memory is safe in the past where I can't stain it with the murderer I've become."

"You're still allowed to grieve for him, Joseph," I whisper, sliding my hand over his. "The same way you're allowed to grieve for everyone you've ever lost. You kill bad men. That doesn't mean you have to kill all your memories, too."

"It's a bad man's penance."

"Stop giving that title so much power. You're so much more."

There's a long pause. "I don't want any more kids, Anna."

I flinch, as if struck. "You can't—"

"I know what you said on the beach, but I can't give that part of myself to you. I learned my lesson with Caleb. My bloodline is fucking cursed, so it ends with me."

"Joseph—"

"I'm done talking about this."

"Just tell me why you think it's cursed?"

"Enough." He rolls away and rises from the bed.

"So that's it?" I sit up in disbelief. "That's the only explanation I'm getting?"

"I made you whole—"

"And then you punched this decision right through the heart of me!"

It's the brutal conclusiveness of his words that spur my tears of frustration. It's the goddamn unfairness of it all. My emotions will always be front and center, while his are back behind that wall again, no matter what he said to me in Florida. He made this choice, and there's no coming back from it.

"You said you needed the truth from me, Anna." He's standing at the foot of the bed, running his hand through his hair in frustration. "Well, here it is. You knew from the start I was flawed and every shade of fucked-up."

"You say it like I had a choice!" I shout back. "You wanted me. You claimed me. It was a watertight contract, but you forgot to mention the clauses!" I swipe at my tears angrily, overwhelmed by an urge to hurt him as much as he's hurting me. "I hate that you keep me at arm's length, like you do everyone else. You drop clues, but they never lead anywhere, and I'm so over it, Joseph."

"Good to know," he says coldly, heading for the door. "Thank fuck we never made this shit legal."

Chapter Nineteen

JOSEPH

It's been twenty-four hours since I lost her.

Physically, she's still present. She still smiles when someone talks to her. She still passes the fucking butter across the table when someone asks her to. But I know her, and I know what I've done. I was so focused on fixing her past, that I failed to pay attention to the Happily Ever After.

She's right. She deserves a better explanation than what I gave to her, but that means smashing the tin soldier and he's still tightly wrapped in my fist.

Last night, when I'd finally stumbled back to our room more drunk than I'd ever been in my life, she was curled up on the far side of the bed pretending to sleep.

Pretending.

Fucking pretending.

And I don't know how to make us real anymore.

There's an aircraft approaching on the horizon. Her landing

gear flashes silver in the afternoon sun and she's spelling out trouble. Dante is just as irritated about what's arriving here in the next few minutes as he is about the lack of Viviana's dead body. Once he'd spat out his reasons for keeping me in the dark, he'd told me how she'd overcome Sofía in his office.

Since then, it's like the sea snake has slithered back underground.

Every outhouse has been searched, there are cameras covering every square mile…if she got reckless and decided to swim for it, she should have been washed up on the beach by now.

And then there's *this*. Rick Sanders bending the rules in his favor as usual.

Shifting my weight against the jeep, I adjust my baseball cap as the aircraft taxis to where I'm standing at the edge of the turn pad.

"Sanders," I say in greeting, as a familiar pair of black Oxfords hit the ground in front of me. He's not rocking his usual slick self, though. He looks like he's been sleeping in his midnight blue suit for a week.

"Grayson," he drawls, his shrewd gray eyes flickering over my face. "I hear you're an honest man now."

Only with my wife. And look where that got me.

"I doubt that applies to any of us," I tell him. Removing my sunglasses, I can't resist adding, "Still sore you lost the race?"

Oh, how you'd fucking laugh if you knew I was losing it, too.

"You won the sprint, but I'm acing the marathon, asshole," he bites back sharply. "The rewards are so much sweeter." He reaches for the hand of the woman standing behind him and tugs her into view. "Nina, meet Joseph. He's not much of a conversationalist, but he gets the job done."

I grit my teeth, sweeping a practiced gaze over the woman, taking in her bruised eyes and her soft brown curls. She's wearing a crumpled black silk dress with a cum stain on the hem. *Fucking Sanders. Thinking with his cock, as usual.*

She's the same woman I saw behind his bar in Manhattan, which prompts me to repeat the same accusation: "She looks Russian. You sure you've done your homework."

She blushes.

Rick scowls.

"Romanian," he snaps. "And a simple 'hello' wouldn't go amiss, or don't they teach you manners back in Texas?"

Not as much as they teach you how to run when your crazy Pa is pointing a loaded shotgun at you.

"You crossed a line, Sanders," I warn, reaching back into the car for the bug detector. "You know his rules."

This woman is an outsider, and after everything that's gone down in the past few days Dante isn't in the most benevolent of moods. She's in for a rough ride. He doesn't want her here and he'll be going out of his way to make that sentiment clear.

"And how is King Midas?" Rick motions for the woman to lift her arms to be scanned. "Is he busy counting out his billions, or have we been granted an audience?"

"He's down at the base. He'll be back shortly. Step forward for me, Miss Costin. This won't take long."

"Go ahead, sweetheart," he encourages.

She does as we ask, flinching like an unbroken filly as I sweep the device over her body and black bag. She reeks of sex and some smokey perfume, and for a dizzying moment I want Anna so badly the tin soldier nearly slips from my fingers.

Rick clucks impatiently at me. "A bit 'overkill', isn't it?"

Ignoring him, I open the Jeep's door. "Okay, you're clean," I tell her as she slips inside the vehicle. "Not that fucking clean, though," I murmur to Rick as he goes to follow her. "I can smell you all over her, Brooklyn Boy. Not the smartest move screwing some broad on his jet."

Rick stills and straightens. For a moment I think he's going to hit me harder than I hit Dante yesterday. *Well what d'ya know? He likes this woman far more than he's letting on.*

"Do you really think I'd entice 'some broad' into the devil's lair?" he says eventually. "Anyway, what the hell were we supposed to do for six hours plus? Play chess?"

"You're playing with his patience," I warn, sensing the storm clouds gathering over this evening. "And there isn't a whole lot of that to spare right now."

"I thought fatherhood was meant to bring joy and happiness? Good thing I bought him a gift."

It didn't to him.

Rick's ex-wife recently dropped the bombshell that his three-year-old son isn't his. That kind of revelation does more than shatter a man's ego; it sends him running into the arms of the nearest bartender to tape it back together.

A bartender who still looks Russian.

"He told me about your kid," I blurt, without thinking. "Tough break. I'm sorry." I mean it genuinely, but he doesn't take it that way.

"Shove that fake sympathy up your ass, Grayson," he snarls. "Go bore your new wife with it. I'm not interested."

"Jesus," I mutter, taken aback by his reaction. "Try and keep the attitude zipped up with your pants for the next hour, or so. Eve's back at the house, and she's expecting you."

I'm locked in Dante's office for the rest of the day, with too much bourbon and heated speculation.

The Italians are giving us hell in New York, and it looks like they have generous benefactors to fund their mischief. Dante's convinced it's a Bratva uprising led by Benni Morozov, the guy with links to Sevastien Petrov's old organization. He's convinced that he's the same bastard who's behind Vindicta and Viviana, too.

I'm still placing my bets.

To me, it's a chain of events that's too personal—designed to strike at the heart of us, and then ripple outward to affect the cartel and our other business interests. The defection of his niece is big news already. Our stronghold over South America is starting to look shaky. Dante's dragging his heels, but he knows, sooner or later, he'll have to make the move out there. Either that, or he promotes one of *Los Cinco Grandes* to oversee and enforce Santiago Cartel law on his behalf.

There's one problem there. Loyalty is in short supply, and he doesn't trust anyone beyond the confines of his island anymore.

We debate and we drink like we've always done, but Vindicta's motives have us chasing our tails and fraying our tempers. It's formed a discord within our organization that doesn't escape any of us.

I don't see Anna again until dinnertime.

I find her sitting alone at the oval table on the balcony terrace, staring out at the ocean with thoughts that are just as deep. She's wearing some kind of purple sundress and she's tied her long blonde hair into a high ponytail. The end result is lots of exposed tan skin on display and a twitching cock in my pants.

Unable to resist, I drop a kiss on her bare shoulder to announce myself.

She flinches.

I regret it.

"I've been looking for you," I say tersely.

"And now you've found me." She stares out at the ocean again.

"We need to talk."

She sighs. "I think it's a little late for clichéd conversations, don't you?"

Holding my temper, I yank out the chair next to her. "It's time to deal with this and move on, Anna. You're my wife. We won't have kids, but our lives will be—"

"Sure." She swings her face toward me and it's just as expressionless as mine usually is. "Whatever you say."

My hand clenches into a fist. If everyone else wasn't kissing cheeks and ass just beyond the bi-fold doors, I'd be bending her over this table and making her feel me again, reminding her that we're so much more than the listing ship she thinks we are.

"I need a fucking drink," declares Rick, stepping out onto the balcony with his nervy little sidepiece and Eve in tow.

We stand to greet them—coasting by on manners, if not a single ounce of enthusiasm. Eve crushes Anna into a hug and tugs her toward the other end of the table as the dark shadow of Dante appears next to me.

"You were right to get Roman to look into the bartender," he murmurs, handing me another bourbon. "I don't like the look of her."

"You don't like the look of anyone, Dante," I scoff. "Paranoia will mess you up better than my left-hook."

"Bullshit. You feel it as well. Look at her. She's too on edge. She can't even choose what fucking wine to drink."

He's right. Rick's waving two bottles at her, and she's dithering like it's a choice between a hard fuck with a ten-inch cock or a nine.

"Red or white?" Dante snaps loudly, losing his cool.

"W-white," she stutters up at him, looking terrified.

It's Anna who swoops to the rescue.

Shooting Dante a withering look, she steps in front of him and smiles down at the woman. "Hi and welcome to paradise," she declares, adding an extra layer of sarcasm for my benefit. "I hear you're from New York and you're fabulously sexy and smart. I'm Anna. Come and sit at the other end of the table with us. The men will talk business, and I've no desire to ruin such a gorgeous evening by listening to the next chapter in the Death and Depravity Chronicles."

Dante lifts his eyebrows at me, but I ignore him.

The evening proceeds with the same malevolent undercurrent.

Dinner hasn't been served yet and I'm already half-cut. Dante's not far behind. We're matching each other, glass for glass, like a couple of high school kids at their first party. I would have killed any other man who put me and Anna in harm's way like he has these past six weeks, but Eve's right. I know the truth of why he did it. This is all about his first daughter, Isabella. *The one he failed most of all.*

I share the complexity of his grief. I know how it blinds your judgement and curbs the monster. He thought Viviana could be turned in time, but he was wrong.

Meanwhile, Rick's on his second packet of smokes, and his eyes won't leave the bartender. Benni Morozov is the name on our lips, until the sound of broken glass captures everyone's attention. Rick's girl has managed to spill an entire glass of red over her white dress. There's a pause in conversation as Eve, ever the gracious host, leads her inside to change.

"What the hell was all that about?" Dante demands.

"You, being an intimidating dick, as usual," says Anna loudly, making Rick laugh.

I turn to give him a death stare and he flicks a subtle middle finger at me. I'm considering whether or not to throw him off the balcony when I see her reaching for a glass of water.

"Can I get you a drink, baby?"

She flashes me a smile because she's in not-so-polite company. It never reaches her eyes, though. "I'm going to bed. I'm not that hungry."

"I'll see you up."

We don't speak a word until we reach the bedroom, and then I'm crowding her up against the wall and slamming my palms down either side of her head.

"This ends now, Anna!"

"Your refusal to talk about anything, or our marriage?" She glares up at me, breathing so deep that the soft swell of her tits is hitting her chin on the upbeat.

"You're making this harder than it needs to be."

"And you're a stonewalling, dream-breaking bastard!"

"Fuck!" I ram my fist into the wall, but she doesn't move away.

"You stopped turning for me, Joseph," she accuses shakily. "I begged you not to do that, but you did it anyway. This is all about you now. Not me."

"What the hell are you talking about?"

"I don't want to feel anything with you again if it means feeling this...*raw*."

"You want to *feel*?" I challenge, palming her jaw. "Give me five minutes and your naked body, and I'll make you fucking feel me, Anna."

"You can't fuck me," she hurls back. "You don't fuck broken, remember?"

"You're not broken. You're hurting and you're stubborn!"

"I want to go back to Miami."

"No goddamn way!" I roar.

"I'm not like Eve, Joseph," she argues. "You don't get to throw me in another cage and expect me to sing happy songs about it."

I open my mouth to respond when the sound of shouting reaches us from downstairs.

"Shit." Letting go of her jaw, I stride over to the window. Two floors below, Dante has Rick up against the balustrade by his neck. "*Shit!*"

I reach the balcony terrace just in time to catch the fall-out. Rick's holding his bleeding mouth, glaring hate and fury. Dante's pacing with a near-empty bottle of bourbon in his hand and blood on his knuckles.

"Roman Peters just called to add a little extra spice to the entrées," he informs me with a snarl. "We were right. The bartender is a Morozov whore. She's his fucking *daughter*."

Rick picks up the nearest wine glass and hurls it against the side of the house. "This is my final warning, Dante. The only man allowed to call her that is me!"

Tipping my head back, I hiss out a low, slow, "*fuck*" at the starless sky. As predicted, the storm clouds have gathered overhead. Even the moon is in hiding.

"You have exactly thirty minutes to taste the color of her fear, Sanders," I hear Dante say, "or I'm doing the honors myself. I want her intel, and then I want her dead."

Rick's gone from the room by the time I drop my head.

"We can't kill her with your kids asleep in the same house, Dante."

I'm not sure how much sway I'll have over the decision, though. Right now, he's a poster child for barely restrained violence. I'm half-tempted to go and wake Eve up to help me calm him down.

"See what Rick extracts from her first. She's hurt his ego, so he won't go easy on her. Now, give me some of that bourbon…" I hold out my hand—needing another drink so badly I can feel demons on both shoulders.

I head back inside to wait for the second fall-out, grinding to a halt when I see Anna sitting on the bottom stair. Pale face, knees drawn up to her chest—her sundress is spilling all around her like a purple halo.

She rises to her feet when she sees me. "What's going on? I heard the shouting."

"Riddles and lies, and bartender spies." I stop a meter out, thinking how fragile and tired she looks. *She's so empty of moonshine, it's killing me.* "Dante just found out and he's breathing bourbon fumes."

"Nina's a *spy*?" She sits back down in a rush. "What the hell is going on around here? It's like Vi fired a poisoned arrow at this island."

Not Vi…*Vindicta.*

We gaze at each other, trying to cling to something—anything—that will make us work again, before it hits me like burning acid.

I need to let her go.

I need to give her the space to come to terms with my decision.

Despite the danger.

Despite it weaponizing every instinct I have.

"Go to Miami," I say roughly, thrusting my hands into the front pockets of my jeans before I change my mind. The urge to drag her upstairs and lock her up forever is cramping my fingers. "You have one week, and then we're moving on from this."

"Joseph—"

"You'll have a full security detail. I don't give a shit if Vi's dead or dying in a ditch somewhere. Vindicta isn't."

Her face creases in confusion. "What's Vindicta?"

"Go," I roar, losing my temper. "You have exactly ten minutes to pack before I change my mind."

Her green gaze dances across my face, searching for the confirmation that this is what I really want. "What if I can't move past this in a week?"

"That's not even a fucking option." My mouth stretches into a grim smile. "In seven days, I'm coming for you, Anna, whether you still want me or not."

Hurt and anger flare in her eyes. It's this image that lingers as she turns and runs up the stairs, her bare feet sounding like liberty on the white marble.

"Your twister's heading in the wrong direction, Joey," comes a mocking taunt behind me.

Cash is back.

I stand there, motionless, as his cigarette smoke curls around my face and neck.

"Thought you were dead again," I grit out, hearing screams

from the direction of the guest bedrooms as Rick extracts the truth from his bartender.

"Nah." Cash's voice is thick with malice and dirt again. "Not me, little brother. I'm only just getting started."

Chapter Twenty

VIVIANA

Survival is a contract and a dirty knife.

It's an agreement you make with yourself to keep sucking in air and moving forward, and you sign it in blood—slashing lines across your palm and tracing your name through the crimson drips on the paper.

I've signed that contract more than once.

First, when I was a child and thrust into a fate worse than death.

Second, when my world crumbled again, before Papá found me in the ruins.

Third, when I ran from the devil across three continents and straight into a living, breathing nightmare.

I don't know that yet, though.

Right now, I'm still running.

I wait until the door closes and the rope loosens a notch. That's when I slam the back of my skull against Sofía's face. She falls down with a cry and I'm finally free. Lurching forward to grab Santiago's knife from the coffee table, I have it pressed against her throat before she can open her treacherous mouth and scream.

"*Puta*," I hiss again. "You'll pay for this."

"Do what you want to me, but you'll never get off this island alive," she spits back, savoring her taunt as she clutches her bleeding nose. "You're trapped like a rat here, and you know it."

"Watch me. Rats desert sinking ships *and* falling kingdoms."

I decide not to kill her. Her time will come when I have the hours and the means to exact my proper revenge. Instead, I knock her out cold, and then I run from the mansion as fast as my shaking legs will carry me.

I stumble in the dark. I fall down. My muscles ache, and my mouth is filled with silent screams, but I made that agreement with myself so dying isn't an option today.

The sea breeze lifts my dark hair and whips tears from my eyes. I replay the last hour in my head:

Santiago had a daughter who shared my pain and suffering.
Why didn't Papá tell me?
Did I know her?
Was it a lie?

I stick to the beaches as much as I can, slicing my hands open when I slip on the wet rocks. The faces of all the girls I was enslaved with during those terrible years keep flashing before my eyes.

I did my homework before I arrived on this island. I know

the ordinances of it by heart, the same way that I know there are fewer cameras down here than along the main tracks. There are only two ways on and off, and one of them requires swimming in currents that would drown me in minutes. The other is on one of the aircraft down by the hanger on the south side of the island.

No one said this shit was going to be easy.

I take cover in the undergrowth by the hanger for a night and most of the next day, plotting and preparing for my chance.

I watch the same jet depart and return a couple of hours later, my heart skipping to an offbeat when I see Anna's tall, slender frame disembarking behind that seemingly indestructible monster, *El Asesino*. The fact that he's evaded death again is another strike against me. I need to get back to Miami at all costs and plead my apologies to Papá.

I never wanted Anna to get hurt in any of this. I was only ever trying to protect her. That aircraft had to blow—*El Asesino* had to die—so I made sure that she was in Miami when it did. More attempts will be made on her life in the future, but I'll always keep her safe. *I'll never stop keeping her safe.* She showed me something precious in Colombia, and I've sheltered it like a naked flame since then. Whatever happens, I'll never let Vindicta snuff that out.

The pilots disembark last. I watch them drift into the hanger for a group smoke, and then I'm running as fast as I can, up the open steps and into the cabin. Heading straight for the luxury ensuite off the private bedroom, I find a spare razor in one of the cabinets. Freeing the blade from the plastic casing, I set to work on the screws around the air conditioning grate above the basin. Once I've worked it free, I clamber up into the small space, and then I wait.

Five days later, a taxi is dropping me off outside Papá's waterside mansion in Bal Harbour, Miami. It's been a violent and bruising journey to reach this destination. Exhaustion is a dirty outfit, and I'm wearing it from head to toe.

My plan worked. I found myself in New York that same evening. From there, I hitched my way across several states, picking the worst cabs to ride in, which meant I was constantly fending off truck drivers' advances. My lip is still bloody where one of them punched me in the face when I stopped him grabbing my breast. The back of my neck aches where another tried to force me to blow him.

They're both dead and lying in shallow roadside graves—one in North Carolina and the other in the South—but their disgusting intentions still cling to my white Tee. I've been wearing the same clothes for close to a week now, and the thought of a hot shower is more tempting than food.

"Welcome back, señorita."

Igor Bukov, my father's head of security, waves me inside the Mediterranean-influenced property, with its high terracotta stone walls to protect Papá's true identity. Before he bought this place, they held parties here that were attended by politicians, presidents and royalty. Girls were provided as their entertainment, ruined girls, like I used to be—conditioned to provide pleasure and take pain without tears or questions.

Only I wasn't really a girl when I worked this circuit of hell...

I was a child.

I finally escaped, but the parties continued elsewhere. I heard the whispers from my father's men. I wept in private at their boastful roars. These days, they take place in more secluded corners of the world, where the true cost of sex trafficking can never be counted in the darkness.

Curling his lip at my disheveled appearance, Bukov leads me out into a large open courtyard, and then down a wide, terracotta stone hallway and into my father's study. It's a light space that mitigates the worst of his darkness. It smells strongly of sandalwood to combat the stench of illness that follows him around everywhere. Papá loves the smell. He embraces it. He calls it his two-finger salute at a life that's incarcerated him in a useless body.

"Stay here," Bukov orders, his thick accent clotting up his words. "Your father is on his way."

While I wait, I wander along the lines of books he'll never read, aching to touch them and open them. There was a moment in time when I was seventeen or eighteen when I tried to escape my past. I grew. I changed. I studied hard and found myself enrolled at an American college. Then Santiago crushed it, like he's crushed every other sliver of goodness in my life.

"Viviana." The note of steel in my father's voice makes me turn. "*Mi vida*," he adds nastily, making it sound like an insult, not an endearment.

He's confined to a wheelchair now—his body hunched over and broken, with his reptile-like facial scars and thin, patchy wisps of black hair. Despite this, he still has a presence that makes you pay attention. His nurse, Teresa, is his constant companion, but there's nothing saintly about the old *puta*. She's a bleak-faced woman in her fifties with black and white streaked hair. She sees everything and says nothing, like a mean-eyed magpie hoarding dirty secrets.

She's hovering behind him, fussing about with his oxygen

chamber, and ignoring me like she always does. She's in this for the money, but Papá won't be leaving her a dime.

"Papá," I greet, stepping forward, hiding my fear well. I've never failed him before, but like every other member of my family, he's not known for his forgiveness.

"You made it back from his island, I see."

Mierda. Shit. He sounds really angry, in between his frantic gasps for air.

"My cover—"

"Was blown. Yes, we know. We also know that Joseph Grayson survived the plane crash and evaded death in a motel room outside Orlando." He stops to gasp and splutter some more.

I'm sensing the winds of change, but I don't know how strong they are until Benni Morozov strides into the room behind him.

"*¡Hijueputa!*" I curse loudly.

The Bratva *Pakhan* is my third least favorite person in the world. He's an integral part of Vindicta, but I go out of my way to avoid him whenever he's in Miami. Short and thickset, with lifeless iron-gray hair that he wears combed back from his fat, fleshy face, he reminds me of all the men I was forced to give up my innocence to.

"I see the daughter has returned." He flashes me a frozen smile to match his dead-inside eyes.

"What the hell are you doing here?"

"You've disappointed us, Viviana," croaks Papá, driving thorns into my fear. "You should have died on that island at my brother's hand. It is a dishonor that you even made it out of there alive."

"W-what are you talking about?" I stutter, as the winds of change transform into a cyclone of hate. "I escaped. Vindicta

208

survives. Your identity is still safe—"

"Disappointments must be punished accordingly," he caws, as if he hasn't heard me. "That way, if we decide to let you back inside Vindicta one day, you'll be less inclined to fail us again."

My head must be foggy from hunger and fatigue. I can't seem to register what he's saying. In a daze, I watch Morozov stride over to a large oak desk in front of the window and open up a laptop.

"It is all done, Señor Emilio," he calls out, twisting the screen towards us.

From what I can see it's a live, black and white feed from a security camera on a busy street. The plates on the cars and the mailboxes locate it somewhere in the US.

"What's that?" I demand.

"Someone else's punishment, and a little of yours."

My head whips round. "What the hell is going on, Papá?"

He shrugs and wheezes. "Take it like a good girl, *mi vida*, and then maybe I will forgive you. Teresa. Time to go."

I find myself backing away from him with an image of a trapped fly in my head, bouncing off the glass. "I told you, it won't happen—Ow!" I cry out as I collide with the hard and soft bulk of Benni Morozov.

He moves quicker than me—far quicker—wrapping his arm around my neck and forcing me over the desk in seconds, deliberately grinding his stiffening cock against my ass as he wrenches my head sideways to face the laptop screen, my eyes blurring and then focusing on the live feed.

"Get off me!" I scream, but Morozov just laughs.

"Keep biting and scratching at me like a cornered cat, Viviana. It will make it so much more pleasurable."

Those are Miami plates I think wildly, as a car pulls up to

the curb by the camera.

"Power," declares my father from somewhere behind me. "I know it is what you truly desire, *mi vida*. You want it so that no man will ever hurt you again. After figuring that out, it was easy to tailor your punishment accordingly."

At the same time, Morozov starts yanking down my dirty jeans.

"No!" I scream, but he just drives the side of my face further into the cold surface of the desk. "I'll do better, I swear! Anything but this!"

"Would you like to watch, Emilio?" Morozov leers, his strong accent thickening in tandem with his cock.

The cruel sound of my father's cackle destroys all the barriers I've built up over the years to protect what's left of me. "I'll let you have your fun alone, Morozov...Make her bleed. Make her suffer—"

"Like Santiago's daughter suffered?" I cry out, scraping at my memory in desperation. "He told me all about her, Papá. He told me how you sold her into sexual slavery to punish him. That you're just as bad as he is!"

My father cackles again. "That was a sweet, sweet moment, I'll admit."

A fresh horror washes over me as truth becomes lies and lies become truth.

"After you're done with her, tell Smirnov to expect a new whore at his party in Istanbul next week," I hear him say to Morozov.

Vomit surges up into my mouth as a rough finger gets forced inside me, his dirty nail scratching at my insides.

"You could at least be wet for me, *suka*," *bitch*, he hisses, jerking it out again.

There's a harsh, ugly noise above me as he rolls his throat and spits, and then two fingers, only slightly more lubricated, are forced back inside me.

"*¡Hijueputa!*" I scream at him again, fighting and bucking, but a part of my body is already bracing and cowering. *Men like Morozov never stop until they've used you up.*

"Daughters must be punished when they do their Papás wrong," he says with a nasty laugh, followed by the vile sound of his zipper. "I do this to my own daughters from time to time to remind them of their places in the world."

"You bastard! Get off of me! *Get off me!*" But my pleas turn into a wounded groan as he thrusts inside me anyway.

The pain is so familiar, but no less agonizing.

When I was a child, I would float up to the sky to evade it, but I can't stop staring at the laptop screen in front of me. It's locking me into the present. Something awful is about to happen, and I can't look away.

People walking

Grunt.

Cars passing

Grunt.

The thought of my father's betrayal forces vomit up and into my mouth again. I lied for him. I cheated for him. I risked my life for him. *I stared down the devil for him.* We were never in this vengeance together, it seems. It was his to claim, and I was just there to deploy it.

Morozov leans over to lick my cheek from jaw to temple. "I know you're enjoying this as much as me, *suka.*"

I want to shut my eyes, but I'm transfixed by the screen.

That thick, treacly accent that scarred the side of my neck as he raped me over and over again.

No. Not that memory. *Never that memory*.

As awful as this moment is, it will never compare to that.

"Remember, this punishment is for your heart *and* your pussy, Viviana," I hear him gasp as his thrusts increase in pace and violence. It tells me he's close to finishing. All of this will be over soon, but I know he's saving something sick and special for his climax. "Eyes on the laptop, *suka*."

Blinking, I watch in mounting horror as Anna steps onto the sidewalk just beneath the camera's vision. She's wearing denim cutoff shorts and a man's shirt that she's tied in a knot at her waist. Her long blonde hair flows free across her shoulders and she looks like sunshine.

"*Blyat*!" *Whore!*

Morozov stiffens and I feel his revolting cock jerking inside me. At the same time, I see Anna turn and smile at someone in the distance.

"Run, *parcera*," I whisper, but it's too late.

I don't hear the gunshots, but I see her body lurch and shudder as they hit her chest and stomach.

I don't hear her cries, but I hear them echoing around my head.

I don't feel her pain, but I imagine every sharp, blinding stab of it.

And when she hits the ground at a broken angle, I'm lying crumpled and bleeding beside her.

Chapter Twenty-One

ANNA

The day my life changed forever was like walking into a room full of masks.

Some I recognized.

Some I didn't.

But, in time, I would realize that they all had their part to play.

First, came the mask of sadness. I wore this in the privacy of my apartment that morning, like I had on every other morning that week. Six days had passed since Joseph issued his ultimatum, and I was counting down the hours until I was forced to make the most difficult decision of my life.

I was thinking about my parents. I was wondering if losing them was what made me crave my own family so much. My dad skipped town when I was four months old. My mother died in my arms when I was sixteen. With no siblings to share the whole orphan burden thing with, I'd been lonely for most of my life until a tall Texan with dark secrets came to claim me.

The next mask I wore was indifference. This was for the heat of the Miami streets as I left my apartment to run a couple of errands. It was closely followed by frustration when I saw the three men standing by the black armored SUV in front of my block. I'd hoped I'd have a free pass on my last day before returning to the island. *Stupid me.* I may have been a free bird, but I still had a long metal chain attached to me.

Then there was the honest one, the surprised one—the genuinely relieved one—as my husband exited the coffee shop across the street holding two takeaway skinny lattes, because he knows I never drink anything else. I wasn't expecting him until later, but that rush of emotion I felt cemented my decision. I didn't want to be split from my shadow anymore. Whatever difficulties lay ahead, I wanted us to be weathering the shit storms together.

Time would heal him.

Time would change his mind.

Hope is a bird with wings too, but she never has any chains to bind her.

Finally, there are the two masks he wore that day.

The first was the cool and the apathetic. *The usual.* It slid into place the minute he saw me standing there on the sidewalk in my favorite cut-off denim shorts, frayed blue espadrilles and an old shirt of his that I'd knotted at my waist. I saw the curve of his lips, and in that moment—the best moment of all between us so far—I knew that everything was going to be okay. *We* were going to be okay.

Then there was the mask that shattered when the first bullet hit me.

There were four in total, each one ripping another piece of it away, until I saw inside him for the first time. I saw everything—

raw and exposed and bleeding...I saw the amount of pain he tried to hide from me. In a way it hurt me more than my own pain, and as I lay there, dying in his arms, the only thing I wanted was to make it go away.

"Don't you die on me, Anna Grayson. Don't you fucking dare! Do you hear me?"

Why is my body so cold? It's eighty-five degrees in South Beach today.

"Where's that fucking ambulance, Reece?"

I'm slipping.

Sinking.

I remember the first time I saw him.

Red dress.

Understanding.

A shadow can't exist without his moonshine.

Moonshine can't exist without her shadow.

"Eyes on me, baby. Don't look away. Never look away. Tell Cash to go fuck himself. You're my twister, not his!"

We spin for each other, Joseph. Right out of our respective hells and into each other's lives.

"Jesus Christ, I'm losing her. I'm fucking losing her!"

You'll never lose me.

Finders keepers.

I'm yours forever.

Darkness.

Chapter Twenty-Two

JOSEPH

They say we spend our whole lives unintentionally filtering out sounds and voices.

It's called auditory selective attention, and to me, it's the stupidest thing our bodies can do. Words are knowledge, and knowledge is power.

Bitches bitch.

The boastful claim.

And the indiscreet? Well, they're just fucking careless.

After I was rescued from the Little Family Farm of Horrors—after I superimposed myself onto the body of a tin soldier—I made up for my lack of words by listening in on every conversation I came across. It's the only thing that kept me rooted to a world that was trying so hard to push me out.

Not today.

There are no sounds and voices to filter, in or out.

I'm slumped against a wall in an empty hospital hallway

that's the same stale blue color as my disbelief, covered in my wife's blood, and staring at two operating room doors that refuse to open. They're a ten-foot barrier holding all the important questions and answers hostage. They're the mean kid in school who is refusing to share his best fucking toy with me.

It's been eight hours.

Eight hours since she died in my arms.

That beautiful, uncaged heart stopped for a whole minute, but they managed to bring it back to life again in the ambulance. Her vitals were all over the place when she was wheeled into the Emergency Room.

Since then, no one's talking.

No one's reassuring.

All I have is silence, and it's the loudest noise of all. It's the kind of space that gets filled with the voices in your head, the ones shouting about fear and dissent like a red-faced politician on a campaign trail. When he's done kissing babies, he'll let you know all about the nasty, unmentionable shit that's happening to your wife right now.

Those are the sounds and voices I'd tune out if I could.

Cash isn't saying a whole lot today. The dead respect the dying. He's leaning against the wall opposite, flouting hospital policy and lighting up smoke after smoke, the same way I'm aching to do.

I know what he's thinking, though.

He told me I'd kill her eventually. I may not have pulled the trigger, but the man I am, *the man I've become*, damn well shoved her in front of those bullets. What good is a shadow, when he can't block other darkness's out?

A door swings open behind me. It's not the right one, so I don't bother turning around. There are sharp footsteps, and then a familiar voice is calling my name.

"Grayson."

Dante doesn't say anything else. He doesn't need to. Just him being here speaks volumes. He must have boarded a jet the minute he heard the news.

We've never embraced before, but I feel a heavy hand on the back of my head, and then I'm being pitched sideways into his shoulder. It lasts for a second, but it's enough to tell me that this monster I've worked for all these years shares this agony with me. He'll live and die to bring me justice. He's not going to rest until it's hand-delivered and buried in a shallow grave.

Releasing me, he crosses the hallway and starts looking for security cameras.

"Over by the restroom," I say tonelessly, returning my gaze to the closed doors. "The team have already taken care of it."

His cell beeps, the sharp noise echoing in this hallway of nightmares.

"Roman is all over this," he informs me, glancing at it. "He's changed Anna's surname to Grayson, and he's given her a new social security and identity."

"What about us?"

"There's no heat yet. Cops are oblivious." He pockets the cell and slides his hands into his black pants' pockets. "The man who carried out the hit is running for his life, but the decision-makers won't be. It's only a matter of time before they try again. If she survives—"

"*When* she survives," I snarl.

"When she survives," he corrects tersely, "we'll move her as soon as she's able to travel. I've sourced a private hospital a couple of hours away. In the meantime, you can't stay here, Grayson."

He says it like I have a fucking choice.

"I'm not going anywhere."

"Listen—"

"Did you hear what I said?"

He curses under his breath. He knows it's futile to try and talk me out of it. If the situation was reversed and it was Eve on that operating table, he'd be claiming Squatters Rights to this hallway.

His cell beeps again. "Have they told you anything?"

"Not yet."

"Then go take a shower. I'll stay here."

"I'm not moving until someone talks to me, Dante," I grit out. *I'm not washing this blood off until they tell me she's going to be okay. If she dies, I'll wear it forever.*

"Eve's all over the place. She won't stop crying. I'm flying her and the kids to a secure location in Africa. We need to consider the fact that Viviana may have escaped. If so, the island's not secure."

"You should have killed her six weeks ago," I say dully.

"She didn't do this."

"You don't know that."

"Call it a hunch that Eve shares. I trust hers more than I trust mine these days."

"Here." Reaching into my pocket, I thrust a burner cell into his chest. "I kept a link with Rick after you threw him off the island for choosing Morozov's daughter over you. I need you to put your fucking ego to one side and pick up when he calls. It's your turn to make shit right for once, Dante. Nina Costin is a big connection to Morozov. She can help us. Rick swears she's legit, and I'm inclined to trust him."

I can feel the heat of his anger from here.

"Just do it," I say, glaring at him. "For me."

His next words are interrupted by a tired-looking woman in light green scrubs emerging from the operating room. In our line of business, you learn to read the slightest inflection in people, but I can't read anything as she walks toward us. My head is a mess. *Is she walking fast to deliver bad news quickly, or is she walking slow to psyche herself up for it?*

"Hi, are you Anna's husband?" she says, drawing closer.

"Grayson." I close the distance even further, my heart in my mouth.

"Hi, I'm Doctor Carlson. I'm part of the team who's treating your wife today."

I'm staring at her, but all I see is the face of the police social worker who threw a scratchy blanket around my shoulders ten feet from where my dead mother lay.

It's a face full of false promises.

"It's going to be okay, son."

No, it's not.

"We're going to take real good care of you."

Three days later, I was in a home where they beat you black and blue for not saying your bedtime prayers fast enough.

With an icy jolt, I realize she's trying to usher me into a side room.

"No." I stop abruptly. "Do it here."

She frowns and glances at Dante. "Are you family?"

"He's my brother."

She's calling bullshit with her eyes, but I couldn't give a fuck.

"We've stabilized your wife as much as we can, Mr. Grayson. Her injuries are life-threatening, but we've managed to remove all the bullets." She pauses for a breath to consult her notes. "Okay, so she's lost a lot of blood. We've hooked her up with a couple of pints. Right now, she's in a very serious, but stable condition—"

"But she's alive?"

She smiles slightly at the incredulity in my voice. "Yes, she's alive. She's a fighter, Mr. Grayson."

No, she's every fucking phase of the moon, Doctor Carlson.

"Now for the not-so-great news." She rearranges her features into that damn social worker's again, and I steady myself for the bullshit blanket.

"Two of the bullets struck her lower stomach. We've repaired her bowel, but her uterus…there was too much penetrating trauma." She stops to flick her lower lip with her teeth a couple of times. "Did you know your wife was pregnant, Mr. Grayson?"

Fuck.

No.

The air comes rushing out of my lungs.

"We estimated at around five weeks. Very early days."

Estimated

Past tense.

"Is…?"

I can feel Dante moving up behind me in silent solidarity. Today, he's the shadow, not me.

She shakes her head. "I'm so sorry, Mr. Grayson. There was too much damage. She was hemorrhaging too badly. We had to perform a radical surgery to have any chance of saving her life."

"Which…?" *Jesus Christ, I can't get my words out.*

"It means we had to remove her uterus and some nearby tissue." She offers me a sympathetic smile, as if it's somehow going to shorten the drop of the hell hole I've just fallen into. "She's being moved up to the ICU ward now. A nurse will be along shortly to show you where to go."

"What…?"

She guesses at my question before I've finished.

"It means that *if* your wife manages to survive the shock, the trauma and the major surgery, Mr. Grayson, she'll never be able to have children of her own."

Chapter Twenty-Three

JOSEPH

Past

The bar is a dive.

Bad lighting. Broken pool table. Flickering red beer signs and Springsteen on heavy rotation. Circa 1984.

All in all, it's the perfect place to celebrate a tragedy.

I walked in five hours ago, and I'm still sitting in the same corner booth. I'm still staring down the same bottle of Bud. No one's giving me grief about it, though. The clothes I'm wearing keep the owner's mouth shut, the bartenders away, and the clientele respectful.

It's a cheap black suit, but it's all I could afford. I was honorably discharged from the Marines a couple of months ago, and the bills are coming in with red letters on them. White shirt, skinny black tie loosened to my chest, the top button flapping. I bought everything for today because no man in his early twenties has a funeral outfit on stand-by unless he's experienced some real crap in his life already.

Turns out, I have, but I've gotten pretty good at ignoring it.

She left me a note. It's lying on the sticky table next to the Bud, with one word on the envelope:

Joey

Only people who die young call me that.

I recognize the stationary. It's from the set her mom sent her the Christmas before last.

I can't bring myself to open it because I don't want to know her reasons. I don't want to know how badly I failed her. She wore her kindness in a smile, but if you flipped that shit around, the only thing propping it up was desperation.

She was sick, but I thought she was getting better.

She swore to me she was getting better.

The doctors were trying her on some new medication. She hadn't been manic all summer, and she'd started smelling like summer rain and strawberry crush again. Then two weeks ago, she drank a liter of vodka and wrapped the family Ford around another on the rural freeway, doing one-twenty in a seventy. Caleb was strapped into his baby seat in the back, but velocity didn't give a damn about how old he was. Neither did the broken glass that pierced his heart, killing him instantly.

Two weeks later, I'm sitting here all alone again: a twenty-four-year-old tin soldier, wearing nothing but a cheap black suit and a blank expression, when, inside, my grief is carving my heart out with a knife.

I pick the letter up, running my fingers along the sharp edges. Wondering if my son felt anything when the glass stole him away from me.

The ache is relentless.

I swear to you, God. If the devil himself walks in tonight,

I'm selling my soul to bury it.

An hour later, I'm still sitting here when the door opens.

It doesn't take much to change the atmosphere in a place like this. The jobless around here are always looking for an excuse to punch their frustrations out. A newcomer is fair game if they look funny or if they order the wrong beer.

This feels different.

The newcomer is changing the atmosphere alright, but it's not inspiring the drunks to fall off their bar stools and challenge him. If anything, it's making them stare even harder into their whiskey sours.

"Bottle of bourbon," calls out a deep voice. "And it better be fucking aged."

A beat later, Dante Santiago is sliding into the booth opposite me.

He hasn't changed much since I last saw him in Afghanistan eleven months ago, right before he disappeared off the face of the earth. But I read the news. I chase the headlines. I already know that Colombia's Santiago Cartel is under new management.

His hair is longer. His clothes, blacker. His dark eyes burn with a hunger for stuff I haven't had a taste of yet.

I watch his gaze dip to the envelope in my hand as the bartender bangs a bottle of bourbon and two smeared glasses down on the table between us. Without looking up, Dante holds out a crisp, neatly folded hundred-dollar bill.

"Keep the change. I was never here."

"Sure thing."

He pours out two glasses and pushes one into my other hand.

"A man once said to me that hate and grief are like two lovers who fight and fuck their way to inner peace." He quirks his lips. "Personally, I'm more inclined to fight and fuck my way to war."

"What are you doing here, Santiago?" I say roughly.

"I could use a man like you."

"Why? I know nothing about cartel business."

"No." He leans across the table at me. "But you know about hate and grief, and I can twist that shit to make it hurt less." His gaze is stripping my face to the bone. "I could also tell you about the billions you'd make, but I know you don't give a fuck about that…you're the same as me. You need something more. I saw it in Afghanistan, and it's true again now." There's a long pause. "Last month, I lost my daughter, Grayson. This month, you lost your son. What does that tell you?"

I meet his eyes.

I see my own pain reflected there, somewhere in the darkness.

I think about an empty apartment, a cold Monday morning, and a chance to make it all go away. *A tin soldier always gets back up again.*

For the first time today, I pick up a glass and drain it dry. Slamming it back down, I hold out my hand to him.

"Turns out, making a deal with the devil is pretty easy."

He laughs and takes it.

We shake.

"Who needs a soul when it's already compromised?"

Chapter Twenty-Four

ANNA

I can't open my eyes, but all my other senses seem to be working just fine.

I can hear his words.

I can feel his touch on my skin.

I can taste and smell the bitterness of hospitals.

It's pulling me back to the time I fell off my bike, aged ten, and broke my wrist. I remember waiting in the hospital reception with an angry heart and a scowl on my face. I didn't care about the pain. I was just pissed I wouldn't be able to ride my bike again for weeks and weeks.

Reality.

I didn't want mine to be dictated to me.

I don't want to know how badly those bullets hurt me.

I can hear distant voices. They're arguing in the hallway right outside my room.

"Help him, Dante."

"Don't tell me what to do, Roman. It didn't end up so well for the last motherfucker who did that."

The man—Roman—mutters something under his breath. "Vindicta's End Game is to divide us so we're easier to overcome. We lost control of New York to Morozov the moment you and Rick split allegiances. If you were to make a stand with Rick now…"

Santiago curses. "You're being a real pain in my ass today."

"Do this, and then bitch about me later," Roman says smoothly. "If everything goes according to plan, Morozov will be staring down the barrel of your gun by nightfall. It won't be a fatal wound to Vindicta, but it'll be a start. You owe Grayson. You owe the woman lying in that hospital bed behind us."

There's a long pause. "If I do this, you better figure out who's behind Vindicta, and fast. You're the fucking FBI agent around here, Roman."

"What the hell do you think I'm trying to do?" comes the ice-cool response. "But there are trails to Colombia, to Russia… it's like loosening a ball of razor wire. Maybe with Morozov gone, I'll be able to unpick it quicker."

I know a sly challenge when I hear one. Whoever this Roman guy is, he has the measure of Santiago.

There's the sound of a cell ringing.

"It's him," says the man.

Dante curses again. "You know you're just as irritating as your father was."

"You have no idea," comes the chilly riposte.

The voices are fading now.

Does he pick up the call, or not?

I finally wake to darkness.

What an irony after dwelling in the darkness for so long.

Irony.

The word reminds me of a conversation I had with Eve a couple of weeks ago by a pool in paradise and my lips start to tic. There's sound and movement next to my head. Harsh, steady beeping is accompanied by a small figure leaning over to adjust something attached to my neck.

Everything aches.

This is the worst hangover I've ever had.

There's a band of blazing fire across my middle.

"Welcome back, Anna," comes a soft voice with a dancing Irish lilt. It makes me think of emerald bunting and Guinness in the center of Chicago on St Patrick's Day. My mother took me there once, not long before she was diagnosed. "Just take it easy, okay? You've been out for nearly a week."

"Night," I whisper.

"Yes, it's nighttime. Eleven p.m., to be exact,"

"Joseph," I rasp, my fingers fluttering up to my chest. *What's wrong with my voice?*

"You've had a tube down your throat, Anna. That's why you're sounding all croaky."

"Joseph," I rasp again.

"Your husband had to step away. He'll be back shortly."

"I'm here," says a familiar drawl from somewhere near

the foot of the bed. He's a blur. *A shadow.* "Is she awake?" He sounds breathless, like he just ran up ten flights of stairs.

The nurse must have given him a cue, because he's cursing in relief and covering my hand with his warmth.

"Anna, can you hear me?"

He leans over the bed, too—a dirty blond blur now—and my breath hikes sharply. Blood and death are clinging to his skin like jagged spikes.

What have you done, Joseph? Where have you been?

"Anna?" The nurse edges into my blurred vision, and I much prefer her scent. It's soft and round with notes of citrus. "You're on a lot of meds, sweetheart, but we can adjust them accordingly. Can you give me a score of your pain from one to ten?"

"Stomach." My fingers drift there next and encounter cold plastic.

There's a freaking tube in my stomach?

"What…?"

"That's a surgical drain, Anna," she explains patiently. "It helps to remove fluid from your wounds."

A montage of images flit through my mind.

Sidewalk.

Bullets.

Joseph.

Unmasked.

"Pain, Anna," urges Joseph. He knows I can smell his murder because he's retreated back to the foot of the bed.

"Eight…"

Something that feels like a remote control is slipped into my hand. "This is for extra pain relief when required."

I press it a couple of times right away.

"May I have a word, Mr. Grayson?" I hear the nurse say as

she glides toward the door.

I've already slipped back into my original darkness before their conversation begins.

There's a big secret in this room, and no one wants to share it.

It's making me feel like I'm back in Fifth Grade when everyone got invited to Jessie Rutgers' party, except me. Eve was such a kick-ass friend that she turned down her invitation on principal, and then we spent the whole afternoon watching old eighties movies at the local theater and throwing popcorn at Eve's brother who was trying to lick face with his girlfriend for two hours straight.

I remember how it felt though, and despite Eve and I laughing like hyenas and eating way too much junk food that day, there was still a constant ache of hurt and rejection in the pit of my stomach.

I've had the same ache since I woke up five days ago.

In that time, Joseph hasn't left my side. He's barely slept or eaten. He looks like shit, but his version of shit is a hell of a lot hotter than anyone else's. He's my dissolute cowboy in dirty blue jeans and a crumpled navy button-down, and I'm relying on his cool confidence that I'm going to be okay, just as much as I am on the various drips I'm hooked up to.

When I fret about the cops finding and arresting us, he's quick to reassure me that I've been moved to a private hospital in North Carolina, and that extra measures have been put in place to make us untraceable. I have a sneaking suspicion I'm only fixating on it to stop myself thinking about the "big secret".

At first, I was so weak I could barely raise my head from the pillow. The nurses had to haul me out of bed every day in a bid to make me stronger, but with so many wires and tubes coming out of me it was like climbing to the Base Camp of Mount Everest. Five minutes later, all I wanted to do was start the return trip and sleep for the next eight hours.

By the sixth day, I'm making progress. I can actually sit up by myself, and I'm getting cocky about it

"I'm thirsty," I announce, reaching for the water on my nightstand.

Joseph moves quicker, jogging it in his haste and spilling cold water all over the bed.

"Fuck's sake!"

"Maybe you should stick to putting people in a hospital, rather than nursing them out of it," I say dryly, trying on a little black humor for size.

"I don't put people in a hospital, I send them straight to the morgue." He shoots me a look as he mops up the mess. "Health insurance companies fucking love me."

"But not the life insurance ones."

The band of fire across my middle is more like a stripe of dull pain now. Except for the ache in the pit of my stomach…that never goes away.

"Will I ever get out of this hospital?" I hate how fragile I sound.

"You better. This shit's costing me a fortune."

The details of what happened to me are sparse and he's reluctant to share. All I know is that the hit was ordered by the same people Viviana works for, and that one of them, Benni Morozov, is now dead. The significance of this has yet to be explained, but I get the impression that his murder was partly in retaliation for me. He would have died a horrible death because of it, either at the hands of Santiago, Joseph or Rick. Hell, maybe it was a triple hit...

I don't feel bad about it, though. He was a human trafficker—one of the worst. My moral compass never works so well around bastards like them.

"Joseph?"

"Hmmm."

"The operation I had..." His cleaning attempts slow to zero. "No one seems to want to tell me—*ouch*." I wince as I try to sit up again.

"Here, let me help you." The pillows behind my head get rearranged and shoved back behind me. "You had four bullets removed from your chest and stomach, *Luna*. The most I've had at once is three." He leans down to kiss my forehead. "Don't go getting an ego about it."

I force a smile. "I still feel like everyone has an invite to Jessie's party except me again."

He frowns. "What the hell are you talking about?"

"Am I going to have any side-effects, or....?" I trail off, losing courage.

He blows out a breath and pulls up a chair next to the bed. Something in his expression makes me pause. Since his favorite mask shattered on a sidewalk in Miami, it's been harder and harder for him to hide his emotions from me.

He looks guarded. *Reluctant—*

"Anna, you were pregnant."

His words hit me out of nowhere. It feels like someone shot me again.

"W-what?" I whisper.

"You were pregnant, sweetheart." He takes my hand, slipping his fingers through mine, trapping our wedding rings together, like he's anticipating that this news is going to make me pull away again. "Five weeks. I'm sorry. They couldn't save…" He trails off when he sees my face.

Tears fill my eyes for a baby I never even knew existed. Somehow, the level of grief I'm feeling doesn't seem justifiable. *How can you mourn a life that never really lived with you?* But it's there anyway. Worming a hole inside my heart.

"Would you have let me keep it?" I say quietly. Gray-blues narrow as my fingers slip from his hand. "It would have been my decision," I add roughly. "But would you have made it difficult for me? Would you have made me choose all over again?"

He tips his head back and sighs. "I don't waste time and energy on hypothetical situations, Anna. You know me better than that."

"I want to hear you say it."

"I can't give you that answer."

"What if I fall pregnant again in the future?" I say, my voice sounding weak and distant. "I'd rather you just prepared me for it. I'll tell you what, why don't we abstain from sex altogether? That way, they'll be a complete absence of choice."

I'm being emotional and irrational, and a ton of other negative words that end in "nal". This isn't his fault. It's not like he told the hitman to aim for my stomach to kill the one thing threatening our marriage.

"It's not an issue we're going to have to face again," he says slowly.

I glance sideways at him. He's trying hard to conceal it, but there are flashes of pain moving behind his eyes.

"You don't know that," I argue. "Unless you're buying into the whole abstinence thing. Sex makes babies. Lesson over."

"Yes, *I do*." He tries to take my hand again, but I move it

present when she was a kid—the same biological father who happened to be Roman Peters' dead *Pakhan* daddy.

Naturally, Roman's ecstatic at finding out his new brother-in-law is Rick, and he won't stop bitching about it. Dante says Nina's knocked up already, but that's the kind of information I'll be filtering from Anna for the foreseeable. In addition to his newfound fidelity, Rick has completed his metamorphosis from Manhattan coke dealer into New York politician. It's not that surprising, if you think about it. Both jobs require the same back-room morals and fucked-up motives.

Vindicta has gone quiet since Morozov's death, but a dormant enemy should never be underestimated. Dante still hasn't returned his family to the island. He's moved the whole organization to his old compound in Africa. His dead brother razed it to ground years ago, but the rebuilding is going well. The local authorities couldn't give two shits about what's going on as long as Dante keeps the baskets of cash flowing through their offices.

I'm standing by the window in Anna's hospital room, hands in pockets, dying for a drink and a smoke as I watch the sun setting on another wasted day, when I hear her calling out my name.

I turn so fast, my neck aches.

"Anna?"

She's sitting on the edge of the bed in soft gray sweatpants and sweatshirt, her beautiful face tired and pale, but set with determination.

"I want to go back to Colombia. I want to see Gabriela in Leticia."

I had no idea what her first words would be to me after two weeks, but there was a longlist and those never made the cut.

"Why Colombia?"

Her face tightens when she realizes that I might be misconstruing her request.

"It's not for those reasons," she says tightly.

"Why not. It's where we healed the first time."

"You *never* healed for me Joseph," she says angrily. "Not once. As far as I'm concerned, I'm still waiting. I'll *always* be waiting."

All the shit in the last two weeks explodes out of my mouth like bile. "You want to hear my life story, Anna?" I roar, kicking a chair across the room. "It's a real fucking tragedy, so make yourself comfortable. We'll be here all night."

She turns her head away, her dull blonde hair falling across her face. She's lost so much weight in the last two weeks she's disappearing right in front of me.

"Please," she whispers.

I take a couple of breaths as I drag my composure back. "I'll see what I can arrange."

I don't know what prompted this request, but if it gets us out of this stagnate room and situation, I'll shift heaven and earth to make it happen.

I close the distance between us in two short strides. "I'll take you as soon as the doctors—"

"I want to go on my own."

I grit my teeth. "Not a goddamn chance."

"Then I want my own room when we're there."

She knows my answer to that already.

My cell starts beeping in my pocket.

It's Dante.

"Bad timing," I tell him. "I'll call you back."

"On the contrary," he drawls. "It's always a good time

when I have the man who shot your wife in front of me. He calls himself Michail Borodin, and he's a living, breathing execution with your name all over it."

I pause, gazing down at the ruins of the woman Michail Borodin left behind, tasting a bloodlust so sharp only murder will level it.

"You sure it's him?"

"Positive. He's singing already, and I haven't even shown him the color of my knife yet. Says he works for someone called Igor Bukov, and lots of other interesting things."

"Where?" I demand.

"Miami docks. I'll message you the coordinates."

"I'll be there in two hours." Hanging up, I reach out to tuck a strand of hair behind Anna's ear, but she cringes away.

"I have to go."

"Then go," she mutters.

"I'll speak to your doctors on my way out. I'll make the necessary preparations and call Gabriela tonight. We'll leave for Leticia as soon as I have a security detail in place."

"I don't want you to come," she repeats through gritted teeth, but I ignore her parting shot, like I'm ignoring all the other bad and sad between us.

"Don't let her out of your sight," I instruct the men outside her room, and again to those outside the hospital. This place is on complete lockdown, but every single minute I spend away from her is another minute when *I'm* not protecting her.

A two-hour drive takes one hour thirty when you're fueled by a bottle of whiskey, hard vengeance and a dead brother who won't stop haunting you.

I follow Dante's coordinates to a discarded warehouse on the outskirts of the container docks, and park nearby. This place holds a lot of history for our organization. I spilt blood not far from here. Eve sent Dante's brother to his grave. That night set into motion a chain of events that changed all of our lives, one way or another.

Stepping out of the SUV, I'm struck by the sensation that things are coming full circle. I pause, taking in a couple of lungfuls of the salty air, and then I'm dismissing it as the bloated instinct of a drunk and angry man.

I enter the warehouse with a lit cigarette locked between my teeth and a loaded gun in my hand. Michail Borodin has already been strung up and worked over. His naked torso is a patchwork of Dante's favorite pastime: flayed skin, dark bruises, crimson slashes—in truth, there's not much left of him to play with.

Dante's over by a dirty metal table, cleaning his knife with a blood-stained rag.

"You started without me," I say, ripping the smoke from my mouth.

"I stopped as soon as he started talking." A dark smile tilts his lips. "This wasn't my kill to make."

"How considerate of you." I size up the soon-to-be-dead man. "Is it Christmas already? How did you find him?"

"We studied footage of the hit. Roman found a plate and ran it. It was false, so he concentrated on the vehicle. Turns out it was registered to a certain house we know in Bal Harbour."

"You're shitting me."

Eve Santiago's one and only foray into undercover work infiltrating a human trafficking event in that hellhole didn't go as planned.

"I thought the cops shut it down."

"They did. It was bought by an organization soon after. Care to guess the name?"

"Vindicta." I glance at the man who's moaning softly. *I hope he's saying his prayers.*

"We've already raided it. It's empty. Evidence suggests it was recently vacated. Found a load of medical equipment so someone's even sicker than him," he says, jerking his head at Borodin.

"Anything else?"

"The man he works for, Igor Bukov, is head of security for the CEO of Vindicta." Dante throws the knife down and wipes his hands. *He's going to need more than that to remove all the bloodstains.* "Everything was arranged through Igor and Morozov. Now that Morozov is souring the ground six feet under, Roman's turned his attention to another Russian. We find Igor, we find the putrid heart of Vindicta." Dante follows my gaze back to Borodin. "He's had a couple of hours to reflect on his crimes."

"Not enough." I grind my cigarette beneath the heel of my boot.

"Do what you want with him. He's all yours."

He hands me his knife, but I shake my head. I've only got one thing in mind for Borodin tonight.

Walking up to him, I yank his bloody dark hair back and look him dead in the eye. "Do you know who I am?" I murmur, resting the muzzle of my gun under his chin and forcing his head even higher. He whimpers and moans, but he keeps his begging to a minimum. "I'm the husband of the woman you shot like a dog in the street a couple of weeks ago."

Fear flickers in his pained blue stare. I drink it in like it's another bottle of whiskey.

"What did Igor say to you when he heard she'd survived? Was he pissed?"

"P-please."

"Please, what? You want me to be merciful?" I jab the muzzle into his neck even harder, forcing his eyes to the ceiling. "Were you merciful to my wife? Were you merciful when you robbed us of our one and only chance to have a child?" Grief detonates somewhere inside, spilling into every vein. "You killed her moonshine," I rasp, unable to stop it from spilling into my voice, too. "But I fixed her once, and I'll do it again. No matter what she says. I just wanted you to know that before I blow the back of your head off and walk my dirty boots through your remains…you lost, you bastard, because failure is never a goddamn option when it comes to her."

Letting go of his hair, I watch his head fall forward in defeat. A beat later, I'm firing four bullets into his stomach in quick succession to even up the score. I watch him groaning and writhing in agony for a moment, giving him a brief taste of what he did to Anna, before I'm firing my fifth and final bullet into his skull. Hell has a missing inmate, and the sooner he's returned the better.

I'm filled with an uncontrollable rage.

The next thing I know, I'm chucking my gun across the room with a savage roar. The Glock scrapes across the concrete, shooting sparks. It hits the far wall with a crash and the warehouse falls silent. All eyes are on me as I turn and stride toward the door. The tin soldier is slipping from my grasp again, and no asshole wants to catch the tail end of what's front and center on my face.

Dante follows me out, slamming his hand down on the car door as I go to open it up.

"What the hell are you doing?" I say angrily.

"How is she?"

"Waiting for me." I resist the urge to shove him out of the way.

"Five more minutes isn't going to make a difference." He considers me for a moment before sliding his back to the door and folding his arms, blocking my route home to a cold hospital room, and an even colder shoulder, with six-foot-three of his dogged persistence.

My right-hand curls into a fist. I'm considering things in my head that I shouldn't. I'm freewheeling into self-masochism. I'm thinking about the day the rocket hit our convoy in Afghanistan and I pulled him to safety. I'm thinking about a little boy's innocence right before his mother hit the gas on the wrong side of the freeway.

I take a step away from him and run my fingers across my jaw.

"How did you know my wife and son had died that day?"

His face goes very still.

Is that surprise or guilt, Dante? I can't fucking tell in the dark.

"I was keeping tabs on you."

"I left the Marines three months before. Why didn't you make your move then?

"What the fuck are you inferring?" His voice is like stone.

"Did you kill them?"

It's a dark question with even darker roots. I know this man. I know what he's capable of. When he wants something to enrich his business or his bedroom, he obtains it by any means necessary— love and morality be damned. *Just ask his wife.*

"I'm going to remember two decades of history and pretend you didn't ask me that."

"Is it beyond the realms of speculation?" I say, freewheeling some more.

There's a tense pause, and then he's backing away from the SUV and shaking his head. "Get the hell out of here before you say something else you'll regret."

Scoffing, I wrench the car door open. "You should have left me to drink my Bud in that bar alone, Dante. The way I was going, I would've wrapped myself around a truck too."

"And what good would you have been to Anna then?"

"What fucking good am I to her now!"

He slams his fist down onto the car roof. "I walked into that bar, and I fucking saved you, Grayson—"

"You did it to save *yourself*, Dante!" I roar back. "Don't pretend it's any different. You wanted a devoted conscience, and I sold you mine for the price of a bourbon."

My words rain down like embers to a floor of gasoline. I need to cool it before we both go up in flames.

Exhaling sharply, I rest my own fists on the SUV's roof and drop my head—bracing myself for the knife in my stomach again, but it never comes.

Do I really believe he killed my family?

"I'm going back to Colombia. Anna's asked to stay with Gabriela in Leticia for a while. Tell me what you need out there. Send me a fucking email. I know it's a cartel mess after Viviana. I'll take thirty men with me. if I need more, I'll let you know."

He doesn't comment, but I feel him moving closer. "I didn't fucking kill them," he hisses.

No, I did.

I don't even need my dead brother to drill that guilt into me. *I should have paid attention. I should have gotten her more help.*

"Good luck in South America," I hear him say as he starts walking back toward the warehouse. "I hope she finds what she needs out there…I hope you both do."

Chapter Twenty-Six

ANNA

I'd forgotten about the fierce humidity in Leticia. For some reason, I'd stored that memory at the back of mind. It's six a.m. The curtains are flapping gently at the window. My sheets are damp and there's a light sheen of sweat on my face that's cloying and uncomfortable.

I lie there, savoring the first precious heartbeats of a new day before reality stops it dead again. Mornings are the worst. The stiffness in my wounds is unbearable. The slightest movement reminds me of what I've lost, so it's easier to stay motionless, staring up at the white ceiling—which is pretty much all I've done since we arrived here two weeks ago.

I have my own room. In the end, he didn't fight me about it. He just dropped my bags and left when he saw Gabriela fussing over me. I haven't seen him since. He could be back in America or Africa, for all I know. We've traveled past the point of arguing and into a strange new land, one that's neither love nor hate.

It's just…confused.

And mad.

So damn mad.

Some days I don't know who I'm angrier with—him or me. All I know is that there's a tight knot inside my damaged body that's spinning sparks and injustice in every direction.

The room is a naturally warm space, with ochre walls and florid paintings. The wooden floorboards are dotted with rugs, with tight weaves and vibrant colors.

It's cold, too.

His absence is a bitter chill, but I can't forgive, and I won't forget. His words in the hospital made everything crystal clear to me. He doesn't feel a thing about the child we lost, and the fact that I've had my choices mutilated is nothing but a bonus to us.

Each day passes in the same safe mundanity. Gabriela brings my meals up, and for the rest of the time I lie here and listen to the women beneath my window as they tend to the estate's garden. I don't speak Spanish, so I make up their conversations in my head. The nuances in their voices tell me when to add in the sad and funny parts, and everyone always has a happy ending.

Everyone, except me.

Gabriela founded this women's sanctuary a few years ago. They come from all over Colombia for her shelter and protection. Some are older than me, some are younger, but all of them are seeking refuge from sexual violence and exploitation.

There's a soft rap at the door.

"Come in," I croak.

Gabriela enters the room with a tray of fresh fruit. Tall and willowy, with graying hair tied up in a neat bun, she moves like water—holding me captive in her gentle currents as she places the tray down on my nightstand.

"Morning, señora," she says, handing me a glass of juice and a painkiller. "How are we feeling today?"

"Sore." I grimace, swallowing dutifully. I take the bare minimum of these little white pills. I don't feel the same manic urge to sink my problems into a pit of drink and drugs, this time around. Instead, I want to wallow in it, be consumed and defined by it. The jury's out on which is the unhealthiest option.

"The pain will pass, señora," she says wisely, and I know that she's referring to the scars in my heart, not my stomach.

She told me once how she'd been beaten and raped by Santiago's father when she'd worked as his housemaid. She's so much stronger than me because she never allows herself to be defined by it. She wears her scars like a badge of hope for all the women here. If she can survive and thrive, then so can we.

"It's a shame I can't take meds for all of it," I say with a sigh.

She smiles and sits down gracefully on the edge of the bed before glancing at the window. "Oh," she cries, "you have another one."

"Are you sure?"

"See for yourself."

Every morning, someone leaves a painted rock on my windowsill. It's never any bigger than the palm of my hand, and it's always decorated with the most intricate scenes.

Sliding my bare legs out of bed, I stagger toward it, moving at the pace of a crippled snail. Today, my gift is a silver and blue wave design, like calm seas after the wildest night.

"It's beautiful," I say, picking it up and admiring it. "Do you reckon it's bought from a shop?"

She rises from the bed to join me. "No. It's from the estate." She examines the stone carefully. "I recognize it from the front drive."

"Maybe one of the women from the garden made this? I sometimes hear them talking and laughing above the cicadas and bellbirds."

"Ach, don't be kind." She rolls her dark eyes in mock disapproval. "Those girls are always talking and laughing, and never weeding."

"Anything's better than silence."

Her smile fades. "Yes," she agrees. "Anything's better than that."

I catch a flash of her own sadness before she turns away.

"Have you heard from her?"

She shakes her head and moves toward the bed, picking up a discarded blanket from the floor. "Viviana's deception is killing me as much as it's killing you. When I heard what she did to Señor Grayson…" She clutches at her heart and shakes her head again. "I don't even know who that girl is anymore, and I raised her from a small child. This hatred for Señor Santiago…" She sighs wearily. "Like I told Señor Grayson last night, it does not come from my heart. Señor Santiago has been good to me. This place was a gift, and I will always cherish it."

"You saw Joseph?" I say, my heart stuttering.

"He and his men take their meals in the drawing room, away from the girls. He spends the rest of his evenings alone, outside by the pool."

He does?

"I assumed he'd flown back to America."

"Then you assumed wrong," she says, lifting her brows in mild censor at me. "He drags himself away from here every morning to attend to cartel business, but not before leaving strict instructions for your care and security. There are more men guarding this estate than there was in Señor Emilio's time."

She watches in more wordless disapproval as I crawl back into bed.

"You're going to have to rejoin the world, sooner or later," she chides gently

"Later. Always later," I say with a sigh, pulling the loose white sheet up to my chin despite the heat and humidity. I close my eyes, my hand still tightly wrapped around the stone.

"Do you remember what I told you a few months ago about this estate?" I hear her ask, sitting down next to me to stroke my hair.

"That this is where women come to be saved and to heal," I mutter.

"Do you *want* to heal, señora?"

"I don't know," I answer truthfully. "I couldn't stop thinking about this place in the hospital, though. It reminds me of a green field I saw in a book on the Second World War in Europe. During the fighting, it was thick with mud and strewn with razor wire. Nothing grew until the war ended, and then Spring arrived, and everything came back to life."

"You will *always* be welcome here, but you cannot hope to find your Spring within the same four walls," she says firmly. "There are more black clouds in your life, but it's time to force the sunshine through again."

The mattress swells as she rises to her feet. "I will let you have this one last sleep, señora, and then I will be returning later. I would very much like to see you washed and dressed when we take a walk around these unruly and unweeded gardens before dinner. Señor Grayson told me how you were exercising every day in the hospital. There is no reason why we cannot continue that here."

My heart sinks. "Do I have a choice in this?"

"No, you do not."

"You remind me of my mother," I say grumpily.

She laughs. "Then your mother must have been a wonderful woman."

I'm woken much later by a scratchy, scuffling sound.

I glance at the clock on the nightstand. It's two in the afternoon. There's a fresh tray of food laid out next to it. Lunchtime has come and gone. I don't know if it's delayed shock or depression that keeps me chained to this room, but it's a time stealer, too.

The noise starts up again, and I track it all the way to the windowsill.

Oh God, please don't let it be a rat…

Sitting up slowly, I come face to face with the unblinking brown eyes of a boy with scruffy black hair and a smudge of dirt on his cheek. One dirty tan arm is hooked over the sill and the other is out of sight, no doubt wrapped around whatever he's shimmied up to reach my first-floor bedroom window.

We stare at each other in surprise.

"Hi," I whisper.

He finally blinks, and then he's gone again. Just like that.

"Hey!" I call out. "Wait!"

By the time I reach the window, he's nothing but a blur of skinny tan limbs streaking across the grass.

Glancing down, I see that there's a new stone sitting on the sill. This one has a bright golden sun painted in yellows and gold. Some of it is still wet, and it's smudging the tips of my fingers.

I carry the rock over to the nightstand and lay it out to dry. For some reason, I can't stop staring at it. *Who knew such fierce and beautiful colors could transform something so dull and lifeless?*

———————

By the time Gabriela returns, I've had a bath and washed my hair. I'm still separating out my wet, blonde strands with my fingers when she enters the room.

She nods her head in approval at my outfit—a pale blue sundress that seems to have magically appeared in my wardrobe. "Much better, señora. You look like a human being now, instead of a sloth."

"I happen to like sloths," I counter dryly, making her smile widen. "They're the underrated heroes of the animal kingdom."

"It's nice to see your sense of humor returning, along with your sense of fashion."

"Is this one of your dresses?" I say, catching sight of it in the mirror. I've lost so much weight I barely recognize myself.

"No, your husband requested a new wardrobe for you, not long after you arrived." She pauses when she sees my face. "Do not think of a person's distance as a sign of disaffection, señora."

"To be honest, I don't know what to think any more."

She slips her arm though mine as we descend the ornate marble staircase together. "We take this very slowly, señora. Together."

Once again, the double meaning in her words feels like a gentle hug.

"Thank you for having me here."

"It is my pleasure," she purrs, leading me out through a

side door and into the garden. The lawns are lush and green, and slightly overgrown. I much prefer them to the Brazilian-waxed, ultra-neat variety outside Greens Therapy Center.

She leads me along a gravel path that coils around the main building. It's bordered either side by flower beds that are bursting with color.

"Colombia is famous for its flowers," she says, pausing by one. "We have so much diversity, but our favorites are roses, carnations and orchids...like this one—The Cattleya." She points out a bright, purple bloom. "This is our national flower. You will find it growing all over this country. Orchids look delicate, but they're surprisingly resilient, and they adapt to their climates."

"How do you know so much about them?"

"It is easy to be knowledgeable when you love something as much as I love this garden."

I glance at the sloping treetops of the Amazon in the distance that shelter this estate. "I don't trust love," I say quietly. "It keeps picking me up and dumping me in the wilderness with no map or compass."

"There are other ways to have children, señora," she murmurs.

"Not with my husband...He doesn't want them."

She stops and turns. "Has he told you why?"

I laugh bitterly. "Talk is cheap to Señor Grayson."

"Ah." She considers this, before tugging me back into a gentle stroll. "Men's hearts are a strange desert of missed opportunity and peculiar decisions. I know of his reputation, señora. I've seen what can turn a man as hard and dangerous as him. But all fences were built to fall down eventually."

By now, we've reached the former stables and garages which have been converted into apartments for the women. A couple of them are sitting around a small fountain, smoking and talking. When they see me and Gabriela approaching, they smile and wave.

"New arrivals," she whispers. "The Santiago Cartel has recently stopped all distributers with links to prostitution benefiting from the organization. Selling drugs makes more money than selling sex. Many women are finally tasting freedom again; I wish Viviana could have witnessed this," she adds with a sigh. "She was the one who insisted on this."

At least she did something right before she tried to kill us all.

"How many women do you have here right now?"

"Around fifty, I believe."

"And children?" I ask, remembering my staring contest with the boy earlier. I slow our pace to a crawl. This is the furthest I've walked since my operation and my stomach is starting to ache.

"Not many. Usually, if they fall pregnant, cartel pimps often force them to have unsafe abortions." She catches sight of my face, and promptly turns us around. "I think this is enough exercise for one day, señora. You have my permission to be a sloth for the rest of the evening."

"Sounds perfect," I say, with a weak grin.

I go to give the women another wave when a flash of a face catches my attention in one of the top windows.

I stop dead, searching frantically for another glimpse.

"Is something wrong, señora?" enquires Gabriela.

"No—I…" I shake my head at my stupidity. "I must be more exhausted than I thought."

And delusional.

There's no way in hell that Viviana Santiago could be back in Leticia, too.

Chapter Twenty-Seven

JOSEPH

I pinch the bridge of my nose in irritation. This meeting is quickly descending into farce. With news of our strict embargo on the use of all Vindicta vessels to export our product around the world, Vindicta's shipping rivals' have hiked up their prices. This, in turn, has set tempers blazing amongst the newly resurrected *Los Cinco Grandes*. They seem to have conveniently forgotten that the Santiago Cartel is the fucking scorpion king around here. Our word is law. We control their processing plants now, and every single one of these petulant bastards works for us.

"Where is the compensation for this, Señor Grayson," Luis Ossa Junior moans loudly. "Señor Santiago is crazy if he thinks we'll nail our dicks to the table for these amounts. We've lost huge revenue with the closure of our whorehouses. I refuse to pay double for the same shipping service. Lower the percentages you expect from us, and maybe we'll consider it."

Business was never my strong suit. I'm an enforcer not a negotiator, but I need to learn fast in order to put my long-term plan into action.

Pulling out my knife, I lay it on the table in front of me to a deep and heavy hush. Leaning forward, I rest my forearms either side of it. "Care to repeat the question again, Ossa?" I tell him in perfect Spanish. "Maybe without the demand this time."

The short man glares at me, inflated two feet above his chair by his own sense of importance. Without Santiago by my side, they're testing my boundaries. They want to see if *El Asesino* is on vacation or in permanent hibernation. Unfortunately for them, I'm present and correct, and I'm about to show them how much. I may not be a Santiago by blood, but I've been an integral part of every manifestation of this fucking cartel for close to two decades, and I'm not about to stop now.

An hour later, I'm walking out of the bar in the center of Medellín leaving two severed fingers behind and the complete submission of every man in the room. The next time Luis Ossa Junior wants to wave his middle fingers at me in a salute of dissent, he'll have to do it with his thumbs instead.

———————

It's a six-hour flight back to Leticia. I don't normally leave the estate for this long, but business dictated my time today. I've restored order with the other cartels, the deadlock has been crushed, and our product is flowing through all the usual channels again.

I message Dante as soon as we're in the air.

Ossa under control.

It's brief. Succinct. We haven't spoken in longer than bursts of single sentences since Miami. I get the impression he's keeping his distance for the same reasons I am with Anna. Space is a room where everyone breathes a little easier and thinks a little clearer. It's also a room with a door, and I'm holding fast to that thought.

Early evening is dusting the Amazon in pink and gold. As soon as my Jeep hits Emilio Santiago's old driveway, I'm glancing up at her bedroom window. The curtains are closed. *Again.* My patience is wearing thin, but my marriage isn't an issue that can be forced with a knife and a threat.

My cell starts ringing as my driver stops the vehicle by the front steps.

Withheld number.

"Grayson."

"It's Roman," comes a cool voice. "Have you got a moment?"

"Yes, what is it?" Exiting the vehicle, I head straight for the usual place, tucking a cigarette between my lips and barely breaking stride as I light that fucker up. As I do, I notice that my hands are still red from the meeting.

"Viviana Santiago," he says heavily.

A low groan escapes the back of my throat as I rip the smoke from my mouth. "Tell me that bitch's body has been found floating face-down."

He blows out a breath. "Just hear me out before you start growling at me. I received a tip off that Petrov's old party circuit was under new management in Florida. I took it seriously, and I brought it to Santiago. We had a plan to go in and neutralize the whole damn place yesterday. Only thing is, when we raided, we weren't the first in line."

My footsteps slow. "What do you mean?"

'Everyone was dead, except for the girls."

"So? There's another vigilante anti-trafficking organization following our lead. Maybe we should get together and exchange fucking Christmas cards."

"Not an organization, Grayson...*Someone*."

My footsteps stop altogether. I don't like where this is going.

"What did the girls say happened?"

"That one of their own got hold of a gun and went psycho."

"Good for her," I say lightly. "What's it got to do with Viviana?"

"They all gave her description."

"Are you *shitting* me?" I say angrily. "Don't be so fucking naive. Half the girls in there were probably from South America."

"I showed one a photograph." There's a long pause. "It was a clear identification, Grayson."

Fuck.

I flick the cigarette away in disgust. *So, the bitch made it off the island, after all.* "This doesn't make up for what she did, Peters. For all we know, those men were enemies of Vindicta, and she was sent in to clean them up."

"Not when the same girl said she wasn't there by choice. She'd been beaten up pretty bad, apparently."

"Smoke and mirrors. Those kinds of bruises wash off in water."

"I have a theory." *Oh Jesus. Here we go.* "Viviana's fallen out of favor after Santiago called her out. They got pissed and sold her into the trafficking circuit as punishment."

"Don't try and make me feel sorry for her, Peters," I scoff. "She crashed my fucking plane, remember? For all we know she was the one who planned the hit on Anna, despite what Dante says."

"Like I said it's just a theory…but if she's scared, where's the first place she's going to run to?"

"Colombia," I murmur, turning cold.

Roman lets out another sigh. "All I'm asking is for you *not* to kill her on sight. I know what you and Dante are like with payback. You shoot first, regret later."

"I won't have any regrets shooting her, Roman," I warn.

"Before you do, consider that she might be one of the only people who knows who's really behind Vindicta."

There's another pause. "Does Santiago know about this?"

"Not yet, but he will soon. How's Anna?"

"Broken."

With that, I hang up.

I reach the outdoor pool with murder on my mind and on my hands. Crouching down next to the water to dip them into the icy coolness, I freeze when the same kind of ice hits my spine.

Slowly lifting a wet hand to my waist, I spin around with my gun outstretched.

There's a small boy standing behind me. He sees the gun and cries out in fear, dropping whatever was in his hand. It lands on the terrace stones with a loud clatter.

I quickly hide my gun with a curse as he turns to run. "Wait," I thunder, tossing my cigarette to the ground. He freezes on the spot like I'm a cop with a grudge. "You speak English, kid?"

There's a pause, and then a slow nod. He can't be more than nine or ten, and he's more bones than meat.

"You got a name?"

He nods again slowly.

"You going to share it with me?"

He blinks and stares.

"The mute type, huh?" My lips twitch. "I know a little about that." I watch him bend down to pick something up from the ground. "What's that?"

With a frown, he holds it out to me. It's a flat stone, about two inches in length, with some kind of purple flower painted on it.

"That's pretty neat." I angle my head for a closer look. "You do that?"

He nods again and his serious expression loosens up a little. I glance about for his mom, but there doesn't seem to be anyone else here.

He motions me over to the long glass table, where another lifetime ago Dante went head-to-head with his brother over a girl called Eve. I find myself doing what he says, sliding my gun back into the waistband of my jeans as I walk. He lifts a dirty satchel from the ground and places it on the table, and then he starts to unpack the contents, which amount to dozens of silver tubes of paint. I watch him as he works, noting the care he takes with each item. When everything is out, he rearranges them into neat rows, and then delves into the pocket of his black shorts. Producing a new rock, he holds it out to me.

"You want me to paint it?" I take a seat at the table next to him. He nods, and a rare grin threatens to burst free from my face. "Jesus, kid…These hands are made for something else. Not arts and crafts."

He's not taking "no" for an answer. The next thing I know, a slim paintbrush is being thrust in my face.

Fucking hell, this is ridiculous. I just chopped two fingers off a man in Medellín, and now some kid wants me to play Sesame Street games with him?

He's still watching and waiting for me to take the paint

brush. When I shake my head firmly, he gestures at the side of the house, almost pleading with his eyes. My chest constricts when I realize he's pointing at Anna's room.

"You want me to paint a rock for *her*?"

He nods again, beaming at me for the first time—a full wattage smacker.

"Kid, I think it's going to take more than a rock to fix us." I sigh, reaching for the packet of cigarettes in my shirt pocket.

He shrugs and starts to squeeze tiny amounts of paint onto a plastic palate, and then he's looking at me expectantly again.

"You want me to tell you what to paint?"

He nods furiously.

Blowing out a jagged line of smoke, I tip my head back and my gaze lands on the only thing that matters.

"The moon," I say thickly. "Paint her the moon."

He smiles another full beamer at me, and sets to work.

While he decorates his rock, I sit a little way off, smoking and watching him. His black T-shirt is way too big for his body. The collar keeps slipping off his skinny shoulder every time he leans over the table. His black hair and skin are streaked with paint and dirt, and something else I don't want to think too closely about: *Neglect*. Still, there must be some kind of education kicking around in there if he's fluent in Spanish and English.

I make a note to ask Gabriela about him next time I see her. If his mom needs more money, I'm not exactly short.

It's peaceful out here tonight, like it is on every other night. The pool lights are flickering into life as dusk gives way to darkness. I come here to be closer to the only woman I see, but who can't see me anymore.

This is where I fought for her.

This is where I'm losing her.

The rawness of that fact makes me drag so hard on my cigarette I choke on it.

After a time, I feel a gentle tug on my shirt sleeve and the rock is presented to me. There, in swirls of silver and white paint, is the boldest, strongest, most complete moon I've ever seen.

"You did good," I say roughly, offering up my hand for a high five. He smacks it back, and then places the rock carefully on the table in front of me.

Funny kid.

Gathering up his tubes of paint, he stuffs them into his satchel. Tossing me one final smile, he throws the strap over his shoulder and disappears off toward the main house.

"Hey!" I shout after him, rising to my feet. "What the hell am I supposed to do with this?"

But he's already been swallowed by the shadows, and I already have my answer.

———

Later that night, I don't walk past her room like I always do. Instead, I pause outside the door, making decisions in my head that I know I'm going to regret.

She's fast asleep and breathing deeply—a slender blade beneath a white sheet, with her long blonde hair spilling all around her. She's bathed today. I can smell citrus and lavender in the air, and my cock's pretty happy about it, too. There's a dress lying discarded at the foot of her bed, which I find even more encouraging.

Are you coming back to life, my Luna*?*
Are all your pretty pieces mending?

I place the rock on her nightstand, resisting the compulsion to rest my mouth against her forehead. I want to rouse her, to love her, to wrap my arms around her. There's a possessive growl sitting at the back of my throat, urging me to take what's mine, but I know I can't force this.

Even so, I can't bring myself to spend another damn night in a cold, empty bed without her, so I head for the easy chair in the corner.

I'll be gone before she wakes.

She'll never know I was here.

Before I can think of a third justification, I'm fast asleep myself.

Chapter Twenty-Eight

I wake to the heavy creak of his boot on the floorboards.

This is the seventh night he's crept into my room after midnight, only to disappear again before six a.m., leaving me with ghosts and memories.

I pretend to be asleep. I slow my breathing and I stay extra still as he places another painted rock on my nightstand. They're different from the ones the little boy brings me. His are always the same. I'll have seven, counting this one, and they'll all be as bright and whole as the last.

That's not me, though. That'll never be me again, because I'm busted and incomplete and I truly am broken now. *And I know he never fucks broken.*

A single tear escapes my eye as he settles into the chair with a deep groan. I never tell him to leave…I think I want him here. I want to fall asleep with his rich scent filling the air between us, because underneath all the anger and the hurt and confusion, I miss him.

I miss him.

Sometimes so much that every breath I take is like a razor blade digging deeper into my chest.

I don't realize I'm moving until I hit the edge of the mattress, leaving a gaping space and an invitation behind me.

What follows is a long moment when I forget to breathe so he knows I'm awake. There's more creaking of floorboards. I hear the soft clink of his gun hitting the nightstand and then the mattress is caving in beside me.

He doesn't touch me. He doesn't dare bridge that gap yet. Instead, a single spider-web thread forms between us—so fine and fragile it could snap at any moment.

I fall asleep to an image of that thread wrapped tightly around my finger.

When I wake to bright sunshine again, he and the thread are gone.

Chapter Twenty-Nine

ANNA

"I think I know who's been leaving me the rocks on my windowsill."

"Oh?" Gabriela tugs me to a halt and cocks her head with interest.

These walks before dinner have become the highlight of my day. I've started gardening with some of the girls during the afternoon, too. None of the heavy stuff, it's still only two months since the operation, but I'm deriving a weird satisfaction from yanking up weeds. In a way, it's contributing to my Spring. I'm not a muddy, ruined battlefield in Normandy anymore. The war is over, Winter is passing, but I'm not quite ready to start growing again, yet.

"There's this little boy—"

"Edier, of course!" she cries, patting her chest. "I'd forgotten how talented he is at drawing. It must be him."

"Edier?" I ask, frowning.

Any joy at solving the mystery drops from her face. "He arrived with his mother, Salome, a few months ago," she confides. "She was married to a man high up in the Hurtados Cartel, before he was arrested in one of the raids by the Special Operations Command."

"What happened to her?" I ask, sensing an incoming tragedy.

"She died soon after. Her husband treated her very badly for years. Sometimes a free bird cannot cope with her newfound liberty."

Like me. I would have killed myself with drink and drugs, if Joseph hadn't saved me.

"She took her own life. Edier found her, and he's refused to say another word since. I can't bring myself to send such a traumatized child away to an orphanage in Bogotá. Instead, I make sure that he's fed, and that he has a bedroom in one of the apartments. He's a devil to catch and wash, though," she confides with a sigh. "And he refuses to change his clothes. I just hope that the space and security here will be enough to mend his broken heart."

"He's so young to have had such awful things happen to him."

Gabriela nods in agreement. "I worry about the effects of his mother's death. A boy's childhood paints a picture of the man he becomes."

I think of Joseph.

I think of a farmhouse in Texas.

"Gabriela," I say, pulling her up again. "Do you have a cell or a laptop I can use?"

"But you have your own," she replies, looking confused. "Señor Grayson left them in your room the day you arrived. I put them in the top drawer of your dresser."

"Do you have the internet, too?"

She nods, again puzzled by my sudden agitation.

"Do you mind if I cut our walk short tonight? There's something I need to check."

"Of course, I'll get one of the girls to bring the internet code up to you."

"Thank you." I slip my arms from hers and give her a kiss on her smooth cheek. She looks tired again tonight. Worry lines are etched into the skin around her eyes. There's something wrong, but she refuses to say what. Every time I ask, she bats away my concern with a delicate eye roll and a gentle slap on my arm.

The next hour is an extreme test of my patience. I can't run yet, so the journey back to my room is a ten-minute hobble of grit and frustration. Then, I have to find an adaptor for my iPad and wait for the damn thing to charge…

With shaking fingers, I type in the name of the small town that Joseph took me to in Texas. Cheap real estate listings flash up, along with some kind of planning application, the outrage over the closure of a local school…until *finally*, I find what I'm looking for.

A shiver blasts up and down my spine when I see the photograph. It's the same place where he fucked me on the hood of his black Dodge as if the world was going to end. *It's where he told me he was coming to die.*

With my heart burning, I read about a boy with gray-blue eyes whose entire family was murdered by a father with undiagnosed Schizophrenia. I read about how the father tried to shoot him, as well, but that he'd missed and ended up killing himself. I read about how no one found him for a whole night and day, and when they'd finally arrived, he was sitting like a frozen statue on the front steps, next to the dead body of his mother.

I read about how he'd refused to speak afterward, his hurt and confusion wider than an ocean. And when I finish, I can't see the iPad screen anymore through a veil of my tears.

Oh God, Joseph. How are you still living and breathing with so many ghosts chained to your soul?

I understand now. I understand his wall of silence. The clues have been there all along, he just couldn't tell me about it himself. He hasn't recovered that part of his voice yet, because those knife-like sentences are still stuck in a nightmare.

Scraping the tears from my eyes, I type in his wife's name.

More heartbreak.

More pain.

I see a boy who'd died at barely a year old.

Caleb.

I see a laugh in action, with baby teeth and arms outstretched.

I see what our child might have looked like had they survived.

I need to find Joseph.

I glance at the clock. It's ten p.m. *Didn't Gabriela say he spent his evenings by the pool?*

Rising from the bed, I wash my face before heading downstairs. The house is quiet tonight, the atmosphere tense and expectant, but when I reach the pool area, only the moon and stars are waiting for me.

Frustrated, I kick my sandals off and sit down on the edge to wait for him, slipping my feet into the cool water. The rippling surface reflects a distorted sky. He always demands we own our badness, when in truth his father has always owned his. He's never had a chance to know anything different. It's what's pushed him deeper into places where people like Santiago dwell.

Before I can stop myself, I'm sliding, feet-first, into the

water. My black dress billows up around my waist, and then we're sinking like a stone. When I reach the bottom, I scull my hands to keep me in the depths until my lungs are raw and burning. There's a scream rising up inside me for two broken people who never set out to be law breakers and murderers. A man and a woman who found love in a dangerous place, and how I'm such a fucking idiot for letting it all slip through my fingers.

There's a violent force in the water behind me. My eyes spring open as an arm wraps around my waist and drags me upward. We break the surface together, coughing and spluttering, and wiping droplets from our eyes.

"What the fuck do you think you're doing?" he roars, pushing me against the side of the pool, crowding me out with the size of his body and the strength of his anger. "Next time you want to commit suicide, do it in a more public place. That way, I can save you quicker."

I love how he can still love, despite all the hate in his world.

I just *love him.*

"You always save me," I whisper, wrapping my arms around his neck and pressing my lips to his. His mouth is a frozen fortress, and then it's a welcome home sign as he drives his tongue between my teeth to explore every inch of my mouth.

"I thought I'd lost you." He groans into the kiss, reluctant to break away fully.

"You can't lose the moon," I say, wrapping my legs around his waist, too. "She's always there."

"You turned blue for a while."

"I'm not so blue anymore."

He kisses me again, more violently this time, tearing at my lip with his teeth.

"I'm so fucking sorry, Anna. You deserve—"

"I take it all," I say shakily. "The guns, the bullets, the scars, if it means I can have you."

"You'll always have me."

We rise from the water, still locked together. He carries me up the pool's steps and toward the house, with me wrapped around his body and dripping. Just before we go inside, I see a flash of white over his shoulder and I swear I see a little boy grinning at me.

He lays me down on the bed and peels the wet clothes from my body. When I try to hide my scars, he pins my wrists to the mattress, before kissing every single one of them.

"Don't," he murmurs. "They made you live. I'm going to worship every single one of them until the day we die."

"We?" I say, frowning up at him. "I don't think death offers a two for one deal, Joseph."

I catch a brief smile before his head disappears inside his wet T-shirt. "You can't get away from me that easily."

When he drops his jeans, he's hard already. Thick and long, bobbing in front of me like temptation and terror.

"What if I can't do this?" I say, panicking suddenly. "I know the doctors said it should be fine, but what if—?"

"Hush." He leans over to mute my fears with another kiss. "I just want to lie with you, Anna. To feel your skin against mine, heartbeat to heartbeat. Everything else will fall into place in time."

Lying down next to me, he pulls me into his arms. With his breath heating up the nape of my neck, his hand skims downward and flattens against my largest scar.

"I thought you didn't care about the baby," I whisper. "I thought I was trapped in a town called grief all on my own."

I can feel him shaking his head against my hair. "No."

"I followed the clues you left for me. I followed them all through your past. I cried for you, and then I cried even harder when I thought I'd lost us."

His palm convulses for a brief moment against my stomach. "That's *never* going to happen. You're mine, Anna Grayson. Mine forever."

"I think it's okay to be broken." I pull his hand up to my heart and hold it prisoner. "It's okay to have jagged edges. That way, they can stick to someone else easier. It's how you make two people whole again."

We lie in perfect, peaceful silence for a moment.

"I saw behind your mask when I was on that sidewalk… I always want to see behind it, Joseph. Not just when I'm dying."

He disappears for a moment to take something from the pocket of his jeans. When he lies back down, he offers me his clenched fist.

"Take it," he says roughly. "This is my mask. It belongs to you now."

When I unfurl his fingers, I find a toy tin soldier resting in the palm of his hand. He's chipped and damaged, and he's seen more battles than I'll ever know about, but I love him more in that moment than I ever have.

With a groan, he yanks me astride him and buries his face in the side of my neck, assaulting me with his rich heady scent. Curling my arms around his shoulders, with the tin soldier still locked in my hand, I feel a pulse reawaken between my legs.

"Joseph, will you do something for me?"

"Anything."

"Give me your hand."

Trailing the backs of his fingers down between the soft valley of my breasts, I take it lower still, through the wasteland of my scars, before rising up on my knees to encourage him to go further. Taking his cue, he continues the journey alone, sliding down through soft hair to palm my pussy and throbbing clit.

"Tell me to stop."

"I can't do that," I rasp, pressing my forehead to his.

"Is this the part where you admit you have willpower issues?"

Catching my response with his mouth, he starts to circle my clit slowly, and I let out a shuddering gasp.

"I feel you," I say, crying out from the sheer relief of it. "Oh my God. *I feel you.*"

"We'll always feel each other, *Luna*," he growls, tipping me onto my back and lowering his mouth to my pussy. "You said that once yourself, and now I'm finally starting to believe it."

Chapter Thirty

ANNA

"Gabriela says his name is Edier," I say, laying out my painted rock collection on the white sheet to show him. "His mother died a few months ago, and now he's all alone. She doesn't have the heart to send him away."

Joseph's sitting up in bed, with the rest of the sheet tucked around his hips, smoking a cigarette with heavy-lidded eyes. My dissolute cowboy is a golden god this morning.

He exhales over his shoulder. "He's a cool kid."

I smile. "Yes, he is. Super talented too. Look at this one." I hold up a rock with bright multi-colored swirls and black wheels. "It looks like a *chiva* party bus I saw in Cartagena once. And that one looks like…" I trail off, as I glance from one rock to another. I've always been crap at puzzles, but when it clicks, I see everything.

On shaky legs, I stand and walk to the closet, grabbing the first dress I see. It's the pale blue sundress that I wore the first time I left this room.

"What the hell are you doing?" he rumbles.

"Reverse floor show." I flash him a tight smile as I slip the dress over my head and start rooting around for clean underwear. "I've forgotten to tell Gabriela something," I lie smoothly. "I won't be long."

Walking back over to him, I give him a long, lingering kiss. He treated me like glass last night. He shattered me, and then he fixed me. His mouth and his hands were the ultimate healers.

"Quit smoking," I tell him, pulling away. "I want you around for as long as possible."

His resultant grin slithers with wicked intent. "Come on my face like you did last night, and you have a deal."

"I'll let you come on mine, if you promise to cut down on the whiskey, too."

He barks out a rough laugh. "Dirty girl."

"Later," I promise, with another smile. *I can't let him suspect anything...*

"Don't be long." He relinquishes me with a frown.

"Delayed gratification is a wonderful thing."

My heart is hammering so hard as I leave the house and follow the path that leads all the way to the women's apartment block. It's the kind of chest carnage that leaves me gasping and dizzy, and worrying about cardiac arrests.

If I'm right about this, though, they'll be far more important things to worry about soon.

It's quiet today. There are no girls chatting and smoking by the main entrance. Everyone is either at breakfast or tending to the gardens.

Letting myself in the front door, I climb the narrow staircase to the top floor, counting window positions in my head as I stop for breath-breaks every few steps. There are four apartments, but I know where I'm headed. Once there, I rap sharply on the painted wood, but I'm not expecting an answer. I wait for ten seconds, and then I barge in anyway.

A tiny entranceway leads into a small living-space that's sparse and functional. One scuffed brown couch, One table. Two chairs. There are no pictures on the wall, or belongings of any kind scattered across the floor or surfaces. She may be hiding herself well, but I know the kick of that spicy perfume anywhere...

It's a brand called treachery and deceit.

"I know you're here, Vi." I spin a slow circle with my arms out, to show her I'm unarmed. By rights, I should be scared, but a cold, hard anger has overtaken that emotion. Moreover, if she wanted me dead, she's had ample opportunity over the last few days to stick another knife in my back. "I know you're hiding in a dark corner somewhere, like the dirty coward you are. You can see I don't have a gun, so why don't you finish off what you started?"

After a long pause, a door creaks open to my left. There's slow movement in my periphery.

"I would never shoot you, *parcera*."

I turn, expecting to find confidence in brown cowboy boots. Instead, I'm greeted with a shrunken, thinner version of desperation in blue jeans and a loose-fitted T-shirt that reaches to her knees. She's cut her black hair into a jagged, uneven bob that stabs at her skinny shoulders, and her dark eyes are dull and guilt-ridden. She looks more like a beaten dog that's slunk back into the room for more punishment, and that's exactly what I'm going to give her.

"You fucking bitch," I hiss, and walking up to her, I slap her hard across the face—the sound echoing in the small room like a whip crack.

Her head stays flung to one side from the force of my blow, strands of greasy dark hair still strewn across her face like rotten seaweed. For some reason, her resignation angers me even more.

"I hate you!" I scream, losing it completely, pummeling her with my fists before shoving her away from me like she's toxic. "The hell you've put me through! Give me one good reason why I shouldn't go straight to Joseph and tell him all about you. It's a miracle that we're both still alive, but our baby isn't, Vi." My voice breaks with emotion. "You killed my one and only chance to be a mother!"

"Do it," she chokes, finally righting herself. "Go tell him now. It's what I deserve."

"Gabriela knew, didn't she?" I say, solving another puzzle in my head. "That's why she's been looking so pale and worried this week. The betrayal was eating her up inside."

"*Parcera...*"

"Stop calling me that!" I scream again. "I'm not your fucking partner, Vi. I was never your fucking partner. Partners stand equal, and you were walking all over me from the start. You were scamming me the minute I stepped off that plane in Colombia. There was no deal to save Manuel's bar, because you'd already sold it to Vindicta. Joseph told me all about it. Did you pay Fernandez's men to rape you, too, or is that the sort of shit you get off on?" I shake my head at her in disgust.

"No," she whispers, clutching her cheek. "Anna, please—"

"You let them into this estate a couple of months ago, didn't you? You let them kidnap me, and then it was *you* who put that roulette gun in my hand, not Fernandez. You were so sure I'd fucking turn on him, instead of you." I laugh scornfully. "Bet the old man never saw that coming."

She starts crying, but I don't have any patience left for a single one of her tears.

"How did you guess?"

"I saw you a week ago in *that* window," I say, jabbing my finger at it. "I thought I was going crazy, but then I looked harder at the paintings on the rocks...I thought they were just pretty pictures, but they weren't. They were snapshots from our past. The *chiva* bus, the ocean by Santa Perdito. Why did you do it, Vi?" I demand. "Is this just another one of your sick and twisted mind games?"

"I did it, so you'd remember something good about me," she says hoarsely. "I did it so I could stack those memories up, and maybe, one day, they'd reach high enough for forgiveness."

I laugh bitterly at this. "Are you delusional? You shot my husband, you crashed his plane, you tried to kill him *again* in that motel room...trust me, Vi, there aren't enough painted rocks in the world that could achieve those dizzying heights."

"Please don't blame Edier for any of this," she begs, sweeping a hand across her eyes. "He was just doing what I asked him to."

"I would *never* blame him," I say angrily. "I know exactly how much of a scheming cow you are."

"At least let me explain—"

"Why the hell would I let you do anything?"

"Let her talk, Anna." Gabriela appears in the open doorway of the apartment, looking old and crushed. "Words can't mend what she's done, but an explanation might bring you some peace in all of this."

"How could you allow her to come here?" I yell back, feeling the sting of a double betrayal. "After everything she's done!"

Her kind face disintegrates. I was right. This deception is tearing her apart. "Because I swore an oath to the orphanage that I'd raise her as my own, no matter what," she says, pleading with her eyes for a sliver of understanding. "I owed it to her to listen to her story."

"She's a damn snake. She'll just keep biting you, over and over."

"Anna…" Vi takes a step toward and then rapidly retreats when she sees the look on my face. "I know you don't believe me, but I never meant to hurt you. It was *he* who warped me, twisted me…*he* who made me hate a man through lies and deceit. *He* who insisted that it was Santiago who had sold me at four years old—"

"Sold you where?" I demand.

Her face crumples under the terrible weight of pain and misery.

I recognize that face, I think with a jolt. It's the same one I saw staring back at me in the mirror every day after Joseph rescued me.

"Holy shit," I breathe, sitting down hard on the edge of the couch as a memory comes rushing in like a violent tide. "That's why you reacted the way you did when I told you the name of the man who'd abused me. It was him, wasn't it? The trafficker, Sevastien Petrov."

She nods, fighting tears again. "I was stolen from my mother's arms at four-years-old, along with my cousin, Isabella. I didn't even know who she was back then. I didn't even know we were related. By the time I escaped, four years later, I didn't even remember my birth name." She flashes me a razor-blade smile that cuts me to the core. "They only ever called us 'girl' to dehumanize us. We didn't deserve anything else. We were just pretty little toys to be played with and abused. Thirty 'girls' who they ruined beyond repair."

Nausea swells in my stomach. *How can one man have perpetuated such abuse? From Eve to me and Viviana...*

"You escaped and ended up in the orphanage?"

She nods, sitting down on one of the chairs at the table as the truth forms a fragile truce between us. "By chance, I found myself trafficked back in Colombia. The man I was supposed to be 'entertaining' that night fell asleep. His guards had gone for a smoke...I took the opportunity, and I ran. I was picked up on the street the next day. The only name I responded to was 'girl', so they had no choice but to institutionalize me. A month later, Gabriela was helping at the orphanage. She didn't know I was Emilio Santiago's daughter, but I reminded her so much of Isabella she agreed to adopt me. It was a chance fate that saved me from another hell."

"And this is how you repay her?"

Gabriela steps forward. "What she said is true, señora. I couldn't believe it when I saw her with my own eyes. They are so alike."

"How did you know Viviana was your real name?" I ask skeptically.

"Gabriela received an anonymous letter when I was ten. It also said that my true parentage would come to light when I was older. 'Viviana' was a name that sounded so familiar to me, so we figured it must be true. It was only *after* that I found out it was *he* who sent the letter."

"'*After*' what?" I say, pouncing on the word. "And who the hell is 'he'?"

Her eyes drop to her floor.

"Tell me, Viviana… Is this the same guy behind Vindicta? Behind all of it?"

She nods slowly, and I see the hate flaring in her eyes.

"He summoned me not long after Manuel was killed. I'd just enrolled at a college in the US, but I was a mess again after losing Manuel. He looked like a monster from a nightmare, and he was spouting all these monstrous things at me. He told me that it was Dante Santiago who had killed Manuel in cold blood—a boy who'd loved me like a sister from the minute Gabriela bought me home—and not the lie that had been fed to us. He told me that it was Santiago who had sold me and his own daughter into Sevastien Petrov's trafficking ring when we were four. And the hurt, *parcera*…" She shuts her eyes tight as if she's frightened of what they'd betray. "The *rage* he made me feel for Santiago. I wanted to rip him apart with my bare hands. I was prepared to do anything to make it happen. Now I know it was a lie."

This time, I don't shout at her for calling me "partner". In a way we always will be. We're both survivors from the same hell.

"Vi, Dante didn't kill Manuel," I tell her. "Your father did. Eve was there. She watched him shoot Manuel in our old apartment."

There's a sob from Gabriela at hearing the brutal way her son died.

Viviana's mouth drops open in horror. "No…no it can't be. That means that *everything* he told me was a lie. He swore—"

"Santiago would *never* have sold you and Isabella to that bastard. Santiago is the Devil, make no mistake about it, but he was searching for his daughter for *years*. It consumed him. It pushed him into the darkness. He's the one who eventually destroyed Sevastien and his whole pedophile ring in his quest for answers. What happened to Isabella haunts him like a ghost."

I watch her sink to her knees, her hand pressed to her mouth to muffle her screams. With each new revelation, I'm tearing down the bars to a cell of lies that's trapped her inside for so long. It's the same cell that's made her do unspeakable things to people.

Lie, steal, *murder*...

"Who is the monster, Viviana?" I ask quietly. "Who's really behind Vindicta and why does he hate Dante so much?"

All of a sudden, there's a loud crash downstairs. We're still scrabbling to our feet when Joseph comes storming into the small apartment, breathing fire and fury. He sees only one person in the room, and it's not me this time. He has her up against the wall by her throat in seconds.

"Where the fuck is he?" he roars, jabbing the muzzle under her chin so hard, her skin caves into shadow. "I swear to God, you'll pay for what you've done."

"Joseph, stop!" I cry, trying to tug him away, but he pushes me back to the couch.

"Get out of here, Anna. You too, Gabriela, that's if you don't want to see your adopted daughter's execution."

I grab Gabriela's trembling hand. Neither of us are going anywhere.

"I-I don't know where—" Viviana looks terrified. *What the hell has happened to her in the last few weeks?* There's no fight anymore. No life...

Joseph drops the muzzle of his gun to her shoulder. "Lie to me one more time, you fucking bitch, and we're evening up the score." He clicks the safety off. "*One*...."

"I swear, I don't know what you're talking about!" she screams. "He threw me out of the organization weeks ago."

"*Two*..."

"He said I'd failed him when Santiago found out about my betrayal."

"*Three…*"

Her body seems to shrink against the wall. "As my punishment, he let Morozov rape me while I was forced to watch Anna being gunned down."

Her confession brings a beat of shocked silence to the room as we struggle to comprehend the horror of it.

Her pleading eyes find mine. "I swear I didn't have anything to do with what happened to you, *parcera*…I *swear*."

"I believe you," I whisper back, and I do. Whatever bad things she's done in the last year, this doesn't count as one of them.

Eve was right. Our friendship was never part of the deception, but it happened anyway. It caught her unawares, and for a second, she wavered between hate and hope.

"What did Morozov do to you after that?" Joseph asks roughly, his gun dropping from her shoulder.

She shrinks even further into the wall. "He trafficked me to another part of Florida."

There's a pause. "So, it *was* you who killed everyone at that party?"

"Yes," she croaks. "I came straight here after. I had nowhere else to go."

He finally drops his hand from around her neck, too. "If you're lying to me…" He lets the threat settle for a moment. "I need you to tell me shit right now. He's gone AWOL, and we need to fucking find him."

"Who's gone AWOL?"

"I just had a call from Eve." He takes a step back from Vi, but he never takes his eyes off her. "Dante went to meet Roman in New York last night, but he never showed. His SUV was pulled from the Hudson this morning."

Viviana's eyes widen in shock.

"Oh my God," I breathe. "Do you think Vindicta's responsible?"

"Yes," he says grimly, lifting his gun to Vi's head again. "Now talk, before this apartment gets a crimson makeover."

"I'll tell you everything," she says shakily. "I know where they might have taken him, as well."

Chapter Thirty-One

DANTE

The past has a way of catching up with you.

You can be sneaky as fuck about it, evading her for as long as possible, but she'll always be the cool kid in the school hallways of life, sticking her leg out and laughing as you hit the ground.

I'm a man who lives without regret, save one.

I love, fuck, kill, destroy. Rinse and repeat. But since she entered my life recently, my one regret—*that I hadn't been able to save my first daughter Isabella*—has been steadily morphing into something bigger.

For the past few months, I've felt her creeping up on me again.

She's hiding in the shadows.

She's the itchy trigger finger to my gun.

She's the high walls that I'm struggling to knock down.

And now the past and her are about to collide…

And they're planning to put a fucking bomb under me.

The truck hits the SUV, side-on, doing double the limits. The impact causes our vehicle to slice through the barriers like paper and flip us upside down as we hit the water. We're moving so fast, the roof fleeces the dark surface like a skimming stone, before we're rolling and sinking.

"Move!" I yell to my driver, thinking quickly. "Shoot the fucking windows out."

Mine disintegrates on the bullet's impact, and icy-cool air and water come rushing in. I'm out easily after that, kicking myself to the surface—guided by a voice that sounds a lot like Eve's. She's always in my head when I need her light the most.

My driver emerges soon after that and we reach the safety of the bank in a couple of strokes.

"What the fuck?" he moans, and then the breeze of a bullet slices my cheek, and the back of his head is exploding all over my shirt.

Shit.

That's when I know it wasn't a regular traffic accident.

"Get on your knees, Santiago," snarls a voice, with that all-too-familiar, thick Russian, brogue that makes me want to kill things. "Hands above your head."

"Igor Bukov, I presume?" I drawl, doing as he says, but taking my sweet time about it. I open my mouth to make another smart remark, when the fucker smashes the butt of his gun against the side of my head and I'm back in dark waters again.

When I wake, I'm staring up at the bars of a cage, with no knife and no gun. The lights are low, but I can make out my immediate surroundings. It's a six-by-six, made of silver steel with a concrete base, there's no fucking way out of it, and there's nothing else in here except soaking wet clothes, blind rage and a nagging sense of disbelief.

The cage is in some kind of basement, with black shadows lurking in every corner. There's a wall of TV screens a couple of meters in front of me.

Rising to my feet, ignoring the hard knot of pain on the side of my head, I rest my wrists against the bars of my new home and cluck impatiently at the darkness.

"So, you're an inventive fuck, Bukov, I'll give you that."

There's a wheezy laugh from the shadows to my left. "You must have known you'd always end up in a cage, Dante. At least this one doesn't require the standard one hour of outside time a day."

I feel like I'm back in that crashed SUV and sinking fast. Underneath the gasps and the splutters, there's the bones of a voice that I recognize. It's rising up from my past—from the kind of childhood I will never subject my own children to.

There's a low humming noise and one of the shadows starts gliding toward me. As the darkness slowly peels away his disguise, my sinking SUV hits the bottom of the Hudson with a resounding thud.

It can't be.
Eve.
Fucking.
Killed.

Him.

"Hello, brother," Emilio rattles, his grin snaking over what's left of his mangled face. "I've been expecting you."

He's sitting hunched over in a silver wheelchair—a shrunken pile of shit and vengeance—spewing hate at me from the one eyeball that still remains in his skull.

"You don't look as well as I remembered, Emilio," I say dryly, clawing back some of my composure. *How the fuck is this happening?* "Perhaps you should have stayed dead in Miami."

"Perhaps you should have checked whether I was dead or not." His words dissolve into a fit of frantic coughing and gasping, giving me a shard of hope that he'll be dead for good in the next few minutes anyway.

"As you can hear, I'm dying again, brother," he rasps in disgust. "But I'm planning to take you down to hell with me."

"Not today," I answer coolly. "I have a plane to catch."

"Oh, but you have to play along. Otherwise, you don't get to learn the fun secret."

"That you're the cunt behind Vindicta and all the other shit that's been happening over the past few months?"

He shakes his head slowly. "I think you figured that out for yourself. No, I have a much better secret than that. But first, we need some entertainment…Igor, if you please."

The wall of TV screens flickers into life. There are twelve in total. Eleven are playing live security feeds from different rooms in my newly rebuilt compound in Africa. The twelfth one is still flickering and unset.

In mounting anger, I watch Eve and Thalia moving about the kitchen, while Sofía and Ella are playing on the floor in the nursery…

My home. My heart. My everything.

"You *motherfucker.*" The only thing running through my veins now is ice.

"Wait," he cackles. "The family isn't complete." The twelfth screen finally flickers into life. "We couldn't miss Viviana out now, could we?"

It's no cozy family home viewing for her.

Instead, I watch in mounting revulsion as she's forced over a desk by Benni Morozov. I turn away when he starts to rape her, the Russian's vicious grunts driving nails into my ears.

Thank fuck Rick gave him the murder he deserved.

"You've got the family tree all mixed up, Emilio. You really are a twisted man for letting Morozov do that to your own daughter."

He wheezes out his biggest laugh yet, coughing and barking his way to a mechanical humor orgasm. "So now we get to the good part."

"I swear to God, if your men lay one finger on Eve or my kids—"

"You'll what?" he taunts. "Kill me?" He wheezes off into more hysteria as my fists clench around the bars. "Let me tell you a story of two girls, Dante. Two dark eyed, dark haired girls. One was my daughter, born to a useless whore, and the other was yours, born to another whore who you murdered with your own hand." My fists clench harder around the cold steel. "They were so perfect and pretty you'd think they were sisters, and they fitted Sevastien's specifications perfectly. Both our father and I agreed."

"I don't want to hear about your sick fantasies, Emilio," I growl, but his grin only widens until his whole face is a leering mass of scar tissue.

"They were enjoyed, until one became unruly. She had

the audacity to bite the faces of the men she was born to serve. There was a devil running through her veins that couldn't be suppressed."

"Too bad she didn't kill them, too."

"She managed to escape in Colombia," he rattles on. "She was picked up on the street and sent to an orphanage. Gabriela Gonzales found her there, by chance. I knew the moment she'd been located, of course, but Sevastien's tastes were more European by then, and my business interests lay with our cartel. I also had a feeling she'd prove useful one day, and how right I was."

He inches his wheelchair forward another meter, but not quite far enough for me to reach through the bars and snap his scrawny neck in half.

"You kept her alive as a weapon of hate for future use."

"Exactly, but she had no idea *who* I was until your whore of a wife shot me. That's when I made my move. All I had to do was whisper a few lies into her ear and point her in your direction." His grin fades. "Play the tape of Viviana over," he orders.

"Which limb would you like me to remove first, Emilio?" I say idly. "As my brother, I think it's only fair you get to choose."

"Oh, Dante," he cackles. "I'm just about to remove your heart."

"Then get the fuck on with it!" I roar, punching the bars, absorbing the explosion of pain to keep my focus away from the filth happening on screen to Viviana.

He leans forward in his wheelchair until the sour-milk stench of approaching death washes over me. "Sevastien came to see me in the hospital a few months after the events in Miami. He told me the most fascinating thing: they never give the children names in the trafficking circuit. All are simply referred to as 'girl'. Real names offer them hope, you see—a link back to their families. It makes them harder to *break*."

I couldn't hate this man more if I tried.

"After four years, no one could tell the difference between Isabella and Viviana anymore, and by then, they were so conditioned they only answered to 'girl'."

The ground starts to shift beneath me. It's loose stone and moving pieces.

"Viviana was always the feistier of the pair…the one most likely to run away. Assumption played her part, until one of his men saw her again in a nightclub in Los Angeles.

He recognized her right away, but he needed proof so he swabbed her glass." Emilio leans forward even further until I can count every damn scar on his face. "Isabella lives, Dante. Your daughter didn't die."

Your daughter didn't die.

"This is bullshit," I say hoarsely, starting to slide with the avalanche. "Andrei Petrov found her bones in a cellar in Amsterdam…"

"Every forensic form can be modified, if the price is right."

I stumble away from the bars and he crows in amusement. "I told you it was one hell of a secret, Dante."

Meanwhile in the background, *my fucking daughter* is still getting raped.

The avalanche gains momentum. I feel myself crashing to my knees, but I don't feel the pain as his words continue to wash over me.

"It's the ultimate revenge, brother—instructing the one thing that drove you so deep into your darkness in the first place to destroy you."

"You bastard," I grit out, still blocking out Morozov's grunts.

He's right. I'm finally in hell.

Hell.

"I sent her to the island to die at your hand, knowing you'd found out about her treachery. Imagine my disappointment when she managed to escape...did you let her go on purpose? I think you did."

"You. Know. Nothing."

Even breathing hurts.

"You didn't kill her six weeks ago because you knew, deep down, who she really was. You felt it as her father. *You knew!*"

I'm sliding out of control now.

I searched the world for her.

I tore myself in two for the truth.

"I think it's time we said hello to Eve, don't you?" I hear him say.

No.

Not more agony.

"Instruct the teams to move in. Shoot to kill."

Blind rage lifts me from the floor. Sprinting at the bars of my cage, I try to prise them apart with my bare hands. "Get away from her!" I roar at the security footage.

But nothing's happening. The feed isn't changing.

There's no screaming.

No storming of my compound.

That's when I see it...the tiny tic at the corner of each screen. It's recorded footage and they're all scenes on a loop from a previous time.

I owe you Joseph Grayson.

I drop to the floor again and brace myself.

A beat later, a massive explosion is ripping through the building.

Chapter Thirty-Two

DANTE

I never pictured in my head what my reunion with Isabella would look like.

Before I was given the false evidence that she'd died at the age of twelve, I'd never dared to assume that one day that light would re-enter my life.

God knows, I didn't deserve it...

Then, there she was—my past and my one regret finally converging—with the dust settling and the remains of the building now under Joseph's control.

As my brother is dragged out and stored up for his final, bloody reckoning by my hand later, I see her walking toward me. I see myself in her face, her eyes, her movements, like I did subconsciously that first time we'd met in Leticia, all those months ago.

She slots a key into the lock of my cage and turns it, and I reflect on the symbolism of the moment with a grim smile. I've been locked in a different cage since the time she was stolen from Gabriela's arms at the age of four. Now, here she is, finally setting me free.

She goes to speak, but I beat her to it with something I've been wanting to do for twenty-three years.

Within two strides, she's finally in my arms.

I hold her as she cries her years of suffering into my shoulder.

I hold her as her feet give way from her pain.

I'll be holding her in my arms like this for the rest of my fucking life.

Above her head, I see the tall figure of Joseph watching us from the distance. I give him a nod, and he gives me one back.

A thousand words unspoken.

A thousand more understood.

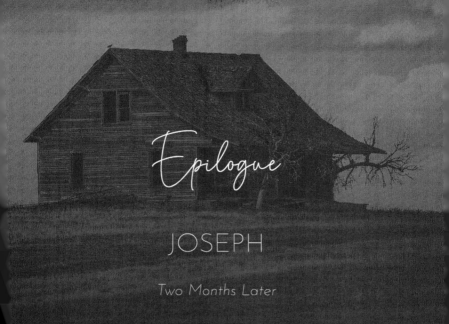

Epilogue

JOSEPH

Two Months Later

We drench the foundations in enough gasoline to light the old farmhouse up like a Fourth of July firework. Within seconds of striking the match, the flames are roaring twenty-feet high—licking the Texas night with more heat. There's a blood moon grinning down on us.

We retreat quickly after that, and now we're enjoying the show from the end of the driveway. Anna and Edier are dancing against the violent backdrop, throwing crazy shapes in the red and orange glow, as I rest against the black Dodge, arms crossed, and watch my past go up in smoke.

I left the tin soldier on the top step of the front porch.

I left him where he belongs.

"Come and join us!" Anna twirls in a circle, her black dress flaring out from her hips and showing me glimpses of heaven. Her hands are all tangled up with Edier's as the young boy laughs in delight. We adopted him as soon as we returned to Colombia.

He started speaking a day after that. I took control of the Santiago Cartel, and we live with Gabriela in Leticia, where Anna helps run the sanctuary.

We finally have our house in the jungle.

We finally have the child I've always longed for, but never allowed myself to have.

We did it our way.

"Joseph?" she prompts, pausing her dancing for my reply.

I smile and shake my head at her.

I'll dance when I'm good and ready, Luna.

Turning back to the blazing farmhouse, I see silhouettes forming in the flames. There's me and Cash sitting on messy hay bales in the entrance to the main barn, playing cards and swapping shit, like we used to do all summer long.

As I watch, he turns and lifts a hand to me.

"So long, Shadow," I hear him yell.

"So long, Sun," I murmur, and I know that's the last time I'll ever see him.

Anna slips her slender arms around my waist. "Are you okay?"

"Better now." I draw her in close, feeling her soft body molding to mine. "And if Edier wasn't here, I'd be lifting you up on this Dodge and making us fucking fantastic."

"Don't you mean fantastic fucking?" She laughs and swats my straying hands away. "Later," she adds with a whisper, with that dirty spark in her eye that means my night's only just getting started.

She's a natural mother, filling our home with laughter, and I check my business at the door every night. I'm not a perfect man. I'm not even a good man, but with Anna I'm right where I want to be.

Dante and Eve returned to the island, the same time we returned to Colombia. Our roads finally diverged, but it's still the same bloody asphalt on both sides. Isabella returned with them for a time, and now she's re-enrolling at UCLA in the Fall. Turns out, forgiveness isn't such a bad word in the Santiago household anymore.

The grave on his island is now a monument to all those who have suffered from the sick perversion that is human trafficking. It's not so much a Tomb of the Unknown Soldier, as a sign for Dante, Roman, Rick and I to keep those motherfuckers out of business. I'm meeting with them in New York next week to discuss a new Romanian upswing in that direction.

"Hey, Edier," I shout, and my son turns and waves at me, the fire on the horizon streaking his black hair with red and gold. "You wanting burger or fries?"

"Burger *and* fries," he cries, diving into the backseat. Ever the food diplomat.

"Fries," says Anna, blowing me a sexy-as-fuck kiss as she slides into the front seat to wait for me.

I take one last look at a place I don't run from anymore, and a place where I'm never coming back to die, and then I'm swinging into the driver seat and slamming the door.

"You good?" she asks softly.

"I'm good." I drop the Dodge into drive and hit the gas. "Now, let's get the fuck out of here before someone calls the cops."

The End

Acknowledgments

To my husband and my two beautiful girls. I'm running out of adjectives again… Let's just say that I love how you bring me cups of tea and hugs when I'm writing. I love that I've inspired you to write yourselves. As Anna would say, I just…*love you.*

Cora, my author guru. I would be hopelessly lost and clueless without you. Without your love and guidance, Dante would still be sat at 2546000 on the Amazon charts. Thank you from the bottom of my green tea.

Sammy, Kathi, Sally and Julia. Thank you for cheering me on from the sidelines. You've been there from the beginning, and you're more priceless than gold.

Nyddi… Thank you for your excellent, last minute proof-reading skills. I'm so sorry that I've totally wrecked the ending of the Santiago Trilogy for you before you've even read it!

To my wonderful PA, Siobhan. Thank you for hopping aboard the Santiago show and for keeping my life in order. And to my amazing Street Team for promoting me every day! — Joy, Jayne, Ashley, Piia, Chelle, Janie, Isidora, Sheri, Sarah, Tracey, Sierra, Sandra and Laura…

To all the book bloggers and bookstagrammers who are still

taking a chance on a sort-of rookie. Thank you. Thank you. *Thank you.*

To Claire & Wendy at Bare Naked Words PR. Thank you for being so wonderful and supportive in every aspect of my life. #fuckcancer

To Maria at Steamy Designs. Thank you for taking on all my demands, not disowning me, and for weaving your magic.

And finally, to the readers. You make every invasive scan, test and operation worth it. I'll be writing these stories for you until they prise my laptop away from my lifeless fingers. Thank you for making all my dreams come true.

Catherine

About The Author

Catherine Wiltcher is an international bestselling author of twelve dark romance novels, including the Santiago Trilogy. A stage 4 cancer thriver and a self-confessed alpha addict, she writes flawed characters who always fall hard and deep for one another.

She lives in the UK with her husband and two young daughters. If she ever found herself stranded on a desert island, she'd like a large pink gin to keep her company... Cillian Murphy wouldn't be a bad shout either.

Sign up to her newsletter for book updates and exclusives!
www.catherinewiltcher.com/newsletter

SINFULLY SEXY ROMANCE

The Santiago Trilogy
Hearts of Darkness
Hearts Divine
Hearts on Fire

Grayson Duet
Shadow Man
Reckless Woman

Standalones
Devils & Dust
Black Skies Riviera
Hot Nights in Morocco
Unwrapping the Billionaire

Anthologies
Men of Valor
Stalk-*ers*
Possessed By Passion

Printed in Great Britain
by Amazon